The Red Stags
of
Munster

Rod Hunt
©Copyright 2001

Published in the United States by Çaira Press
Postal Box 103, Big Lake, MN 55309 USA
Tel 763 263 2237

Library of Congress Control Number: 2001 129085

ISBN 0-9712693-0-0 (paperback)

SAN: 2 5 4 - 1 5 0 5

© Rod Hunt 2001

Printed in the Unites States of America

Acknowledgment

No one could have been more patient or understanding than my wife, Norma Kolbinger. In addition to everything else she has given me in our life, her gift of Ronald Pearsall's book, **Myths and Legends of Ireland**, brought the mystical Ethné to light.

I would like to thank my brother, F. Keith Hunt, for his many hours of editing and helpful criticism and also thank Brenda Hill for her longanimity in the face of typesetting changes. Both have earned a rest from me.

There is a lady, 50% Welsh and 50% Irish, but 100% genius in the field of genealogy. Her name is Angela Perkins and she lives in Kinsale, County Cork. I could never have expanded the main characters, Bawn and Nonthus, or the dozens of little-known personalities who surround the feature players without Angela and the book could never have been writtten.

I must also thank the wonderful family of the late Richard Hale, also of Kinsale, for the hours he was able to spend with me in the formation of the story. Bless and keep you, Hilary, and the two great sons, Liam and Ben.

To the fantastic land and people of Ireland, I owe an eternal debt of gratitude for showing Norma and myself the true life as it surely is meant to be.

iv

THE RED STAGS OF MUNSTER
LIST OF CHARACTERS

Donal McDonell McLairadh MacCarthy Mor of Kerry
Chief of all MacCarthy septs; Bawn, the Earl Clancar.

Donal MacCarthy Mor of Kerry
Called 'Nonthus,' bastard son to Clancar and heir to his
Celtic title.

An Drimuin
MacCarthy Mor, chief of all MacCarthys, father to Clancar,
grandfather to Donal Nonthus.

Éilis MacCarthy Cremin of the Cork MacCarthys
First wife to Clancar, mother of Nonthus.

Pat Spleen
Scottish bonnacht. Forever friend and companion to Donal
'Nonthus' MacCarthy Mor, from bedchamber to battlefield.

Nicholas Browne
Master of Molahiffe, an English planter, son of the Queen's
surveyor Valentine Browne and husband to Shiela.

Ellen MacCarthy Mor
Legitimate daughter to Clancar, wife to Florence MacCarthy
Reagh.

Florence MacCarthy Reagh
Tánaiste of the Cork MacCarthy Reagh sept, husband to Ellen.

Ethné
Legendary foster daughter of Angus and Mananan who
perchance sitteth on the left shoulder of Nonthus.

Randall Hurly of Rincurran
A very small person and a huge hero; the keeper of the Fieries
Hoard; the Daanan gold.

Katherine O'Sullivan Beare
Owen O'Sullivan's youngest daughter and wife to Donal
Nonthus.

Sheila O'Sullivan Beare
>Owen's eldest daugher, jilted by Florence MacCarthy Reagh and later wife to Nicholas Browne.

David Barry, chief of the Clan Barryroe
>Lord Barry Mor, Viscount Buttevant, Owen O'Sullivan's nephew-in-law and cousin to Florence.

CRUCIAL CHARACTERS

Queen Elizabeth
>Tudor Queen of all Britain and Ireland, cousin to Donal 'Bawn' MacCarthy Mor, and the Monarch who bestows his hated title of Earl Clancar.

Queen Mary
>Daughter of Catherine of Aragon and Henry VIII who takes Clancar as lover but loses him to Ireland and his clan.

Ainé Daly
>MacCarthy clan poet, a drunk, mistress to Clancar, mother to Frank and Cormac.

Lady Blowden Ap Huw
>A Welsh lady of forgotten morals.

Jezebel Lee
>A yummy yum yum whose moral decay benefits all who know her, but especially Nonthus.

James Fitzjohn Fitzgerald
>The14th Earl of Desmond and a strange one, at that.

Honoria Fitzgerald
>James' daughter, Second wife of Clancar. mother of Ellen and Tadgh.

Gerald Fitzjames Fitzgerald
>The 15th Earl of Desmond, "Mad Gerald."

James Fitzthomas Fitzgerald
>The 16th Earl of Desmond, nephew to Gerald. Called the Straw or Sugaun Earl.

Thomas Butler Ormand
 'Black Tom', Queen Elizabeth's "Irish Husband".

Thady Mor MacCarthy Phale
 Early master of Molahiffe by wife Maude's inheritance from clan Fitzmaurice.

Sean MacCarthy Phale
 Thady and Maude's son, and a brilliant bowman who could charm the birds from every tree in Munster, given the opportunity.

Liam McWilliam Burke of Connach
 A thoroughly horrid man, but a magnificent warrior both for and against Nonthus.

Hugh O'Neill of Ulster
 Chief of the Ui Nial, Earl of Tirowen, head of the Irish Catholic Army.

George Carewe
 Murderer, sometimes Lord President of Munster, and Elizabeth's full-time intelligence agent in Cork, Kinsman to the Fitzgeralds.

Warham St. Leger of Kerricurrihy
 Sometimes President of Munster, and a hard man.

Robert Deveraux, Earl of Essex
 Elizabeth's General in Ireland, who allegedly plots with Hugh O'Neill against her.

IMPORTANT CHARACTERS

Tadgh MacCarthy Mor
 Legitimate son of Clancar, heir to the Earldom and pawn to Florence. Dies in France whilst in evil hands.

Walter Tibbet
 An Drimuin's trusted aide and not so trusty watcher of his daughter, Mhurien.

Donal O'Sullivan Mor of Kerry
> Brother-in-Law to Florence, chief of all the O'Sullivans, the subject race of MacCarthy Mors, Keeper of the MacCarthy Mor White Rod of Office.

Owen O'Sullivan Beare
> Earl of Beare and Bantry, chief of the Cork O'Sullivans.

Julia O'Sullivan Bantry, nee Barry
> Owen's wife and aunt to to David Barry.

Donal "Cam" O'Sullivan Beare
> Owen's nephew and usurper of his power and title.

Frank MacCarthy
> Illegitimate son to Clancar and Ainé Daly. Has mental challenges.

Cormac MacCarthy
> Illegitimate son to Clancar and Ainé Daly. He is only some what better off than his brother, Frank.

Frank Cremin
> Father to Éilis, Clancar's first wife, who is mother to Nonthus.

Thomas Butler Cahir
> Cousin and enemy to Earl Ormande.

Don Juan D'Aguila
> Spanish commander at Kinsale.

Diarmuid Moyle MacCarthy Reagh
> Beloved brother to Florence.

Hugh O'Donnel
> Earl Triconnel and an impatient commander at the Battle of Kinsale.

The Red Stags
of Munster

Table of Contents

Prologue

Over the rolled and folded edges of the Slieve Mish Mountains and along the rough passage threading through the bogs beside the Maine River come three heavy goods carts. It is now 1180 AD. They are pulled by sweating bullocks and are managed by two large bearded men on horseback and three very small men ariding. Sitting in the front cart is a small, young girl with a tiny plump man who holds the reins. As they make their way through the swirling wind and rain towards a distant castle, the carts groan and the bearded men grumble as is natural in such a time.

When the mystical party arrives at its destination, the heavy drawbridge descends as if on its own and an eerie light illuminates the sombre arena. Now inside the deserted courtyard, they quickly dismount and begin to unload the wagons. There are heavy chests to be taken down, and these are moved amid the exhortations of the smaller men. They continuously berate the larger men to make speed, whilst the young girl encourages them. Pushing and heaving, the group makes its way into the interior chambers of the castle, through the great hall where their shadows loom in monstrous images on the walls and rough hangings. Slowly, nay, ponderously, the procession gains the mural staircase and grinds its way up to the ramparts.

Now the chests are swung upward to a place where a long, shallow, grave-like trench has been prepared. The two men look nervously at one another and a bit of worthy apprehension sets in.

"You picked a filthy night for hard work, Finney. What you suppose is next?" asks one.

"Leave the wee lads alone a minute. They have to say their words," says Finney in reply.

Those two make their stealthy way to one end of the lower battlements while the leaders, the small girl Ethné, and her companion Randall Hurly, supervise the final laying of the trove. Murmuring strange-sounding, ancient incantation on hands and knees, they smooth the sand and dirt, then effortlessly replace the weighty flagstones.

"Tell them to hurry it up, Finney. I'm drenched and I've a fierce thirst overcoming me."

"Tell them yourself. I'm not talking to that lot!"

Then Finney turns and looks up to where they were wailing

1

away, and the light, the glow and all the little sparkly bits are swallowed in the rain and mist. In the swirls of gusty winds, the little folk have disappeared completely.

"They're gone! For the love of Mary they are vaporized just as sure as we are standing here! Where in hell's name could they be?" shouts Finney.

"I expected this, damn their eyes! Look! The moon is now full out!"

"I'm leaving and I'm saying nothing to nobody! How did we get into this in the first place?'

"As I recall it was by the taking of drink at Rosie O'Kelliher's and we were bargained into doing some heavy lifting for another jar or two by that little fella who called himself Randall Hurly."

"Ah, well, then that explains everything. Let's get out of here before they come back for us!"

Those two make away at full gallop which was slow by any measure, the horses being of poor quality and better suited to pulling their master's plows than being ridden by desperate men who have only just that night stolen them. After one mile and two furlongs they are outpaced by the nightly activities of a badger strolling down the boreen.

"Tell me, Finney. Does the velocity aboard these things seem a bit slack to you?"

"Forever slow, it is. And he's shakin' me beans and grinding them up on his backbone in the process!"

"Let's get off these buggers and hoof it."

"Fair enough. Where are we, if you don't mind me asking?"

"I haven't a single hint, Finney, me boy, but it's away from where we were by some."

2

Chapter One

A Lord is Born

I ndan na nGall gealtar linn
Gaoidhil d'ionnarba a hErinn;
Goildo shraoineadh tar sal soin
i ndan na nGaoideal gealtair.

In poetry for the English we promise that
the Gael shall be banished from Ireland;
in poetry for the Gaels we promise that the
English shall be routed across the sea.

𝕿hen on Hallow E'en night in 1529, three hundred forty nine years later and 16 rook kilometers away, a wild and roaring wind starts above Carrantuohill in the Macgillycuddy Reeks in the land of Kerry. Shrieking down the narrow glens on the tail of wailing banshees, it strikes thunderously at the massive gates of Castle Lough looming over Lough Leane. The sentries on the outer bailey walls huddle in their heavy cloaks, reluctantly scanning the darkness, awaiting the distant dawn and relief from the cold.

Below, inside the great hall and beside a dying turf fire, sits an Drimuin, chief of the clan MacCarthy, master of the surrounding castles and ploughlands and King of Munster. With him are his daughter, the beautiful 15 year old hormone-laden Mhurien, and his senachel, Walter Tibbet, a grizzled and battle-hardened veteran of 20 years service.

"God save me from women, Walter. Especially women in labour and more especially, my wife in labour! I'll lay a £ to a penny this one will be a runt too!"

"I'll take that wager, Chief Donal. You shall have a fine son, I know it!"

"One lives in hope. I need an heir and a strong one. What with three errant daughters and one dead boy the sept needs a Tanaiste."

Mhurien sits staring at Walter, her long and elegant legs stretched out in front of her.

3

"And that one sitting there."

"What about her, Donal. She looks absolutely fine to me."

"She would to you Walter. But between her and her sisters, Elaine and Sabbah, I get no rest at all."

"Father, I would never do anything to cause you anguish."

"I think you already have."

Walter is now pre-occupied with the toe of his boot and the shape of his left hand, not to mention his suddenly doubtful future.

"If you mean Walter here, he's hardly made a sign of recognition to me."

"I don't mean Walter especially. You're always disappearing behind doors and barns and sheds and trees!"

"You disappear behind barns and sheds, Mhurien?" asks jealous Walter.

"Oh, Walter. They're only boys. There is nothing I wish to learn from them!"

"That's what I mean, daughter. There is hardly anything they can teach you. Now, run along to your sisters and behave yourself."

A loud yowl comes from the upstairs birthing room and is responded to by the keening of an Drimuin's huge wolfhounds, roused from their fireside sleep and rending unquiet the lakeside fortress.

"Sweet Jesu! What a household. Not a moment's peace in twenty years."

An Drimuin snatches his silver mead cup and flings it at the unruly pack and they scatter amid more howls and the skittering of paws slipping on the flagstone floors as they try to momentarily escape. Their heads reappear soon enough from behind the wall of the mammoth archway.

"From the sound of it, mother is near to giving birth."

"How would you know that?"

"Father, I'm fifteen. I know about such things. I know a great many things, don't I, Walter?"

Walter's shoulders droop perceptibly and his eyes are now riveted on the composition and texture of the stones of the floor. Nothing else in this whole wide world matters at the moment. To himself he says, "Lord, get me out of this situation and I'll leave the lovely bitch alone forever! Amen."

Walter's urgent need is met by the divine intervention of an Drimuin's sudden attention to his fully developed daughter.

"Go to your sisters, Elaine and Sabbah, this minute!"

"Must I go, father. They are with mother."

"Just go some place, Mhurien, I don't care where."

"You don't care where I go, father? That is very hurtful!"

"My God! I didn't mean it that way. I mean, go some-place to await the birth other than here! That is all I meant, dear girl."

"That's much nicer, father"

Mhurien rises languoruously and smiles sweetly at her father who, is now hunched in his chair with his head turned back toward the hounds. She winks at Walter and brushes her hip against his hand as it rests trembling on the side of the armrest. As he looks up, she thrusts her magnificent breasts to new heights and leaves the room.

Up the twenty-seven steps toward the master bedroom goes the wayward hoyden and stops she not. She hesitates at the door, but upon glancing in and seeing the actuality, makes room for the maid to carry a large steaming pitcher inside where great commotions take place and vital bustling goes forward. Her shifty glimpse takes in her mother, Siva, in obvious discouraging pain and any number of nursemaids backing away from the mid-wife who is scolding and fussing. Within this panoramic vision is two-score Maude Phale, a withered, brow-beaten shrike and hag, whose very nature denotes her miserly existence as the wife of the sub-chief, Thady Phale.

"I told the old goat I was too old for another one of these!" groans Siva.

"Ah, yer fine, my dear. You're splendid fine," says mid-wife Maude.

The observation brings forth ponderous grunting, furious groaning and rapid breaths of stale air.

"Sure and you can say that sitting there on your back-side!"

"Would you just concentrate on what you must do?"

"Come out of there you great monster!" shouts Siva.

"That's it then, work away my lady, work away!"

5

Plummeting 46° southwest in the maternity swirl regains admission to the great hall and the presence of a hyper an Drimuin and the reprieved Walter in unchanged positions. Walter is now trying to figure out how to keep the conversation on Siva and not Mhurien.

"Damn this waiting! Why can't women ever be on time with anything?"

"Steady, my Lord. She's a strong woman in every way."

"You needn't remind me. I sometimes worry about what her strong-mindedness has done to our daughters."

"It cannot harm them, my Lord. They all seem most wonderous to me."

"Well, thanks be to God for their health, but Siva is always going on about the strangest things. Now she wants a female senachel at our Pallis castle."

"That is strange, all right. Could it have merely been her pregnancy speaking for her?"

"No, old friend. She was determined to have a company of female warriors ready to battle the women of Ormond."

"She what? A company of....?"

Thumpita, thumpita, thumpita, thumpita in increasing cadence and descending diatonic scale, the determined and toothsome maid Fiona bursts forth through the heavy wind-curtain.

"Sir...a son, sir! You have a son. A fine lusty boy and her ladyship is well!"

The great head of the 6'8" an Drimuin shakes in disbelief. Gradually the tension in his huge frame is released and evaporates into a fog from which he certainly hears the hysterical skirl of pipes and a bauran begins beating a cheering tatoo. He lifts his eyes heavenward.

"Thank you, Fiona, and praise God! A son! You must proclaim him Tanaiste, Walter. Do it now! Donal McDonell McLairadh MacCarthy!"

Pushing himself forward out of his chair he rises, his chest thrown out in new pride.

"I shall see my wife, Walter. And my new son. My son Donal."

Then an Drimuin stops and turns. He takes Walter by the sleeve of his safron leinte.

6

"Tell me truly now. Was the moon out when the lad was born? It might prove a lucky omen on this cursed night if the moon shed her light on my son's birthing."

"There be no moon tonight, sir. The storm is too hard. But, as he was born a flash of forked lightning lit up the sky. I swear I heard the banshee women singing in the wind just as clear."

'Do you think forked lightning and fey women singing a good omen at a birth?'

"Them who know say those banshees can be lucky if they like the look of the child born on one of their special nights."

"Lucky? Those heralds of death and misfortune! Please God this lad holds on to his life and is not an imbecile who falls into the fires. Let us go see what sort of son this hellish night has produced for Siva and me."

Young Fiona is still at the archway and dancing four to the bar in excitement. Her huge smile quiets the wind and an Drimuin is swept up the steps in a joyous realization that he stands half a chance of having the heir he has prayed for.

He is smacked at the door to the master bedchamber by the voice of his wife who is giving loud orders to a quaking nurse and Maude Phale as if she has just returned from a strenuous day's hunting and the servants are at bay. Spotting her massive husband's frame in the archway she lets rip with her greeting.

"I've got you your son, you see, an Drimuin? What do you think of this issue, my Lord MacCarthy?"

Like a thunderhead, he gathers himself over his wife and newborn child; he examines both with an up and down look the length of ten seconds.

"You have done well, my wife. Thank you!"

"His hair is as gold as the sun. Look! His skin is unwrinkled and as smooth as cream."

"A changeling! I knew it! I knew it! It had to happen on such a night!"

"Don't be such a superstitious old cretin, Donal!"

"You are probably right. A pigeon to a pheasant, he'll inherit the MacCarthy pride and cunning. His eyes show intelligence and he is a hardy child. Why shouldn't he be a great leader of our race, changeling or not?"

"That's more sensible, dear heart. He will be a great chief, I'm certain of that."

"The way he lays there guzzling your milk he may well turn out to be the biggest sot that ever lived!"

"He's healthy and he has teeth, I can tell you that. Now, all of you leave so I can have a bath!"

The birthing entourage is slowly taking its leave, babbling and bubbling compliments and coy comments on the dimension and shape of the baby's wrinkled tally-whacker.

Never one to retreat on order, the mid-wife Maude Phale hovers over the birthing bed like an angry vulture.

"He'll be fey, alright. What's more it is well known those born on Hallow E'en have some fateful flaw."

The still powerful Siva reaches up her right hand and clamps it over the startled Maude Phale's tooth-free mouth.

"Be quiet, you slanderous shrew!"

"A drunk! That's what he'll be; a drunk or a gambler or a feckless destroyer of his people. That's what the runes will say, you can be sure!"

Some husbands know what to do and an Drimuin in that moment of that night does. He looms his way back to the bed and takes Maude's arm.

"We'd thank you to keep your unwanted opinion to yourself, Maude Phale MacCarthy. You offend us mightily and that rat-trap of a Molahiffe Castle could find itself in an even more desperate state than you can imagine. I will forgive your bad grace if you stand godmother to our son here."

"I cannot refuse, my Lord Donal."

"That is correct, Maude. You cannot refuse, nor can you refuse a proper birth gift. See to it that my son gets a good hansel' or I'll rock Molahiffe on its foundations and bury you and cousin Thady beneath the rubble."

To other Irish chiefs, the ridding of the English who have taken their land might have become an obsession. To an Drimuin, they have become irksome and fatuous; a boring bunch of idiots whose fate he is certain he alone knows. Not on your Brendan's voyage, he is soon enough to find out.

He is one day riding with his captain of the Castle Lough guard, the grizzled, hard drinking, hard headed Charlie Cremins who himself became an English victim when his lands in Carbery were taken. Along with six of an Drimuin's finest Scottish bonnachts and ten kernes, the two are setting out to do harm to their protagonists, the neighboring clan Fitzgerald, by capturing a few hundred of his mountain cattle from their Desmond country and making the smelly creatures their own. Charlie, a block of Irish oak, either through stupidity or vanity, disdains body armour and carries his battle axe unsheathed, on his lap in the saddle.

Hmmm, hmmm and hmmm. Viewing him thus as he rides with that battle axe coming closer and closer to bodily damage one would have to say his nature was in truth, one of stupidy, not vanity.

"Do you ever get the feeling you are being watched, Charlie?"

"What do you mean, 'watched?' Like someone is looking after you or like someone is looking at you?"

"Like you're being watched. Like somebody was in the trees or something just watching you go by?"

"I was once having that feeling with a lady in Bristol, Chief."

"I guess that will have to do. Anyhow, I don't like the feeling I've got."

"What feeling is that, my Lord?"

"That I'm being watched, you twit! Like James Fitzgerald is waiting for us. Like he's waiting to trap us."

"What matters that? Should he be so daft as to be out here at near dark he will be dealt with."

"Not if he and his henchmen are in the ditches on the Rathkeale road."

"He wouldn't dare...."

Just then the furse and gorse and ancient weeds erupt alongside their path and 31 raging heather-humpers come charging at them with the Florentine banner being carried by the leader as though it was an outing in some Medicean square. Amidst the cursing and swearing and the sudden clash of sword and steel comes the roar of an Drimuin.

"Suffering Mother of Christ. Here they are! Charge them! Turn them aside!"

Which is what they do. Charlie and the troops are battling hard to split the Fitzgerald forces and push them up

9

against the hillside, and so on they get to the business of finishing off the attackers. Charlie is by now getting into the spirit of the thing and humming in grunts, swinging his battle axe high above his head as he lops off the Florentine flagstaff and grievously wounds the flag-bearer in the process. The yipes and yelps of the battle dogs and the snorts and cries of the horses and horsemen subside in due time, but some pitiful moaning amongst the young persists.

"For Christ's sake, will you stop your whinging. Can't you ever learn to be a bit more stoic?" shouts an Drimuin.

The simpering stops as Charlie rides to his side.

"Well, Charlie. So much for our surprise raid. Those lads will have old James pissing in his trews to get at us now. Check our wounded. Best we move back toward Castle Lough and home."

Charlie grunts again, a bit out of breath. An Drimuin's horse is edgy, keyed from the encounter and very excited about the activities he's just been involved in and wanting more.

"Christ's teeth, you'd think that Desmond bunch would be busy enough defending against those Ormond raiders all the time coming through here!" he says as he moves off to attend to his men. In a few moments he is back to where an Drimuin has quieted his horse and is calmly wiping the blood from his sword on his mantled arm.

"Young McPherson is cut badly, my Lord. His sword hand is fair hanging by the skin I'd have to say."

"Cut it off, then. Put a thong around the stump and wrap it in fern or a bit of the moss. Let his cousin hold him on his horse and you lead McPherson's horse with yours," said an Drimuin. "He'll be right as rain in the morning!" he added with the spark of enthusiasm still burning from his recent skirmish.

"Yes, sire," says Charlie, looking an Drimuin up and down to make sure his Chief is fully fit.

Charlie returns to his men and a murmur swells as the men sense they are through there and out of danger.

"If you are finished we can leave. Let's get on with it."

The troop gathers itself together and they start toward the south.

"So another raid and still no decent cattle to eat," says one of the kernes.

"You're damn lucky Charlie was on our side. Christ's crutches, did you see the man swing that fooking axe?"

"Slathered them, didn't he? Swish, slash, thunk and blonk, he give it to them, he did," says a third.

"Shut up you!" roars Charlie and they tramp away in silence and end their day in the castle courtyard on the south-eastern side of Lough Leane.

An Drimuin stays with Charlie as he wiggles and waggles his way through the horses with the stableboys, poking and prodding and patting and making certain none of his charges were slashed or stabbed in their bellies.

"If it isn't the damned Fitzgerald Desmonds, it's the pompous Butlers of Ormond who continuously challenge me. It is getting a bit depressing."

"They do test their luck against you, sire. You're fairly pinched between the two countries and them Butlers is cozy with King Henry," said Charlie.

"That's it exactly. How can I be king of Ireland when I can't keep those raving maniacs out of my back garden?"

"Worse to come, my Lord. We're only just getting started. When that whore-mongering king floods Ireland with his Scots, all hell will break loose."

"The rage that James Fitzgerald must have...he will hate the king even more."

"Given that it is all bound to happen, those Ormonds will find out soon enough their loyalty to the Crown is poorly placed and of little worth."

"I doubt it. The Butlers will always find a way to profit!"

"It's good that someone can."

"Watch your sarcastic tongue, Charlie. You could lose it!"

"I live by your good humour, my Lord. May I instead ask about your good wife and new son?"

"She is suffering as only Siva can suffer after childbirth. One would think she is the only one to have ever borne a child."

"Seeing the size and the weight of the young man, I can understand her possible discomfort. Small wonder the Crown is anxious to find a way to rid the land of you."

"I must confess I do feel awkward in that land of midgets."

11

"It really is most strange, my Lord. The English are such a puzzle."

"Puzzle-pated, they are, though I'm sure they must feel the same about us. As the Romans have said, there is no solving the mystique of island people."

"But we are island people, too, my Lord."

"We are an enigma, Charlie...perhaps the greatest and the last."

Chapter Two

Bawn and the Tuatha De Dannan

*MacCarthy Mor were willing enough to
be ruled, but wanteth force and credit to rule.*
Sir Henry Sidney.

Soon enough there comes the time when Castle Lough
has a visitor from Molahiffe Castle. as was hoped for but not so
much expected. Into the great hall where sit an Drimuin, Siva,
Mhurien, Elaine, Sabbah and the little squirter, Donal, comes
loping forever Walter. In his tow is Sean, the incorporated son
of Thady and Maude Phale in all his hawkish, good natured and
impoverished glory. For the occasion he is wearing his battered
leather jerkin and the ancient tweed trews which serve both
himself and his father as best clothes. He carries with him a
cracked buckskin pouch which catches everyone's attention
with the exception of that of Mhurien whose focus is on loca-
tion, where you can bet.

"What brings you here to so rudely interrupt our dinner?"

"God save your lordship. I bring the young tanaiste a
christening gift."

"What sort of gift would that be, Sean?"

"My mother begs you to accept her own dowry, which
she has only just managed to keep in these hard times. She is
now left penniless, for this treasure is all she owned in this
world, as I can suppose you already know."

"Get over it, Sean. What other lies does she wish you to
tell?"

"She has bid me to say how she is shamed and humiliated by your excessive demands upon her good nature..."

"Dear Lord, this is a bold lad from such a pit as
Molahiffe!"

Given this bit of an interval from direct examination,
Sean's bright green eyes meet the roguish stare of Mhurien and
a sweet reminiscent grin spreads over his cheerful freckled face.

He is summoning recollections one, two, three of the pleasant interludes spent behind various outbuildings at numerous clan celebrations with the chief's yearning daughter.

The look doesn't escape yer man Walter.

"Leave your gift and get out of here before I cut that shameful tongue from your unkempt head, Sean Phale. And, take your evil eye off my Lord's daughter."

Still in the staring mode, young Sean turns not his head nor body, but there starts a gurgle and a gargle as his suddenly deepened voice replies.

"So that is how it goes, cousin Walter? Keep her and welcome to her. I cannot compete with your wealth and perfect style."

"You must not be discouraged, Sean. It may be only a phase I'm wandering through," states the undulating Mhurien.

"Why is it you are still standing there making such unusual noises with your mouth? You were told to leave, young Phale, so be off with you. And leave my daughter alone or more than your tongue will be cut off!" says an Drimuin.

As the poor and twice deprived Sean slides to the door, an Drimuin shoves the pouch across the littered table to where Walter still stands. Walter snaps out of his momentary funk with the practical reminder that there may finally be some money about. The first coin out of the bag is stabbed by his dirk rather more vigorously than seems necessary.

"It's gold, alright and in fine purity. It must be worth a Fitzmaurice ransom. A plausible start for your young son."

"This indeed is the Phale back rent with interest, Walter my lad, and there is far more where this came from or Maude would not have handed it over so readily."

From the other end of the table, somewhere in the deep recesses of Siva's bright bosom comes the sound of said son at work on his dinner. Slurp, slurp, he says and his mother comes to voice.

"You know, dear, he really is a most fetching child. Fair as an angel he is and most alert with a sweet temper. Let a black fiend take that old harridan Maude for predicting evil for him."

"She's a witch and a swift one, that curmudgeon Maude. She should be burned along with that stinking excuse for a castle, Molahiffe."

"But she's still the best mid-wife in the parish, husband."

"There will be no need for her again now we have our son and with a proper birth gift to us."

"I'm pleased to hear you say that, as it is certainly true. T'was our last good and rewarding effort in the feathers that did it...and with so many Donals in your family I think we must call him by another name. I will call him Bawn, for he is fair and favoured, and will be most gifted."

The fair head so described suddenly pops from its dining parlour, screws up his cherub face and emits an earth shattering, ear splitting yowl. Lady Mhurien's early maternity senses spring alert to detect a need on the baby's part.

"Oh, poor lanabh. He wants more to drink."

"If you were in my seat, young lady, you'd soon enough realize that's all he's done since the day he was born. I'm near ravished!"

Enough has now been said and forward moves the family of an Drimuin, who is great in these parts. We skip, nay, we tumble, stumbling over the next few years in much the same condition as inhibits the progress.

Bubbly, boisterous little Bawn's avaricious childhood bowled forward too, at a rage, and in his fourth year he made a discovery. Into the castle stables, carefully tended, swept and kept by the quartermaster Eugene McSwinney, went Bawn to see to his daily mischief. McSwinney, capricious and louder than the humming of a human brain, gathered the stable lads about our oversized junior master with the pure intention of debobbling the tyke. It is drink being taken.

"Here, then, little chief. Have a sip of this. Once you've tried it you'll desire it for life. It's woman and bairn to them as loves it."

"What is it, Eugene?"

"It is called by the famous name of iuschabau, the water of life. Go ahead and have a slurp," says Eugene with an evil smile in his voice.

Young Donal McDonnell McLairadh MacCarthy, eager to comply, takes not a sip but a belt at the jug. Eugene is waiting for the penny to drop and is ready to erupt with joy and laughter.

"Ohhhh my! I like this very much, Eugene. It is so

15

smooth and tasty! May I have some more?"

Eugene, thinking the little chap must have been drinking badger's urine all his life to think the poteen smooth, recovers nicely from back on his heels and leans over Bawn to make his new point.

"Not today. I think you'd now drink all of the little we get!"

"When, then, will you have more?"

"That will be when you cross my palm with brass, my man."

"I have no coyne left. You won it all from me yesterday when you taught me the games of cards."

"So we did, Master Bawn, so we did."

Eugene scratches his mop, then his crotch, better enabling him to get a proper purchase on a hard fought thought. His swindling eyes light up.

"But, if you promise to bring that old anlase from the armoury tomorrow, I'll let you have my share today. What say you to that bargain?"

"Your share for an old squirrely dagger? Done and done, say I?"

In a flash the jug has gone to Bawn's sweet, childishly beautiful lips and down flies the flood of fluid. He gives his best effort to imitate a proper mouth smack and hands the empty back to Eugene who takes it in heft. Unnecessarily bolstered by the charge of electrical alcohol, Bawn has a run at verbalizing the creative sensation emanating from somewhere near his filthy socks.

"Soon I shall drink as much and more than the best man in my father's kingdom! I will be the best horseman, the best swordsman, and the best drinker in all of Munster!"

"Christ's Cross, the little toad drank the whole fookin' thing in one opening! What have we got here?"

Bawn lets out a swooning last whoop as the iuschabau hits his white and crinkled cranium. He rises into the air like a chubby swan and flops face first into the golden straw.

Willie Waterbug, the smallest of the stable functionaries and a fierce enemy and challenger to dung, stands over him, fork in hand and observes.

"I think what we got here is a dead drunk boy of four."

16

Eugene, still thinking at maximum velocity says, "I think you could just be right, Willie." The lads all put their hands together and lift him from his bier of slurry and place him gently into the sweet, straw-filled, softness of the nags' ample manger.

"I'd say he'll be fairly dry in a hour or so," spins Eugene.

"Dry, maybe Eugene, but dreadful sick he'll be."

"Then he'll learn something from all this."

"Oh, Eugene, I doubt that. As you told him, 'once you've tried it you'll desire it for life,'" says Willie Waterbug.

"If he does, he won't last long. It's the killer of dukes and earls, same as for all of us mere Irish."

That night, after Walter has found Bawn in the manger and suspected his condition, returned him to his nurse to be put abed, an Drimuin and Siva are drifting about in their own chamber bed. Mother, first to speak, calls attention to the situation, which is not far from the father's mind in the first place.

"We must take Bawn in hand. He was drunk as a pig on cider when Walter plucked him from the manger today. Another act like that and I'm near to pushing him out into the bullrushes."

"I'll put a maid on him. That will curb his wandering and mingling with the crowd about the horses. He's restless and active, that's all," says an Drimuin.

"You call what he does being active? Just this week he loosed 500 cattle from the enclosure and led one of the boars through my garden!"

"I'll have a talk with him in the morning, dear Siva."

"Well, while you're talking to him find out why he stole the poor servant boy's best and only jacket, freed your hawks and used an unrepeatable word to the Bishop of Cashel!"

"When I caught him stealing the jacket he said the boy loved him and would give him anything. He is quite charming, you know, being only four and all."

"Charming, you great oaf! He is incorrigible! Something must be done or all our help will leave. Just last week he pushed his nanny into the cistern and peed on her as she tried to climb out!"

"That's it then. I'll be packing him off to Molahiffe this week. That wizened old witch of a Maude was right. We have

17

a changeling here and since she recognized it, she can deal with it."

In a circular mode, Siva considers that she has contrived a conundrum and wishes she had not revealed Bawn's conduct so brusquely and so uncompromisingly. Like a dervish her mind whirls away from an Drimuin. Her thoughts then move back toward him, no, wait, now she thinks the other way as she turns toward the obstinate fire glowing in the corner. Wait! She is spinning her adequateness back to him. An Drimuin, amidst the thrashing of his wife and competing with equal whirls and twirls and with far greater bulk with which to work, has turned the huge bed into a puddle of feathers and linen.

"The Saviour's sandals, woman, are you now going to whimper to keep the sunny little tramp?"

"No, but are you certain and set on Molahiffe for him then?"

"I am. Now give me some covers and go to sleep!"

She relinquishes two meters by rolling back toward him.

"He really is a loving boy. I think you have another purpose in mind when you send him to that creaky keep of the Phale's."

Siva of the auburn coloured covered head is now alert and eyeing an Drimuin cynically. She has arranged herself by propping her ampleness up on her elbow and strong left arm. She peers at him in prolonged moments. He is not unaware of this symbol of her perspicacity and his defensive response comes quickly into play.

"How well you know me, dear wife. It is time I told you the story of the Fieries Hoard. You've heard me mention it many times, have you not?"

"It has to do with Molahiffe Castle?"

"It does and I'll be as brief as three centuries allows."

"Time is small on a cold winter night, husband. Say on!"

"Very good, Siva, a start at least. When the Tuatha De Daanan poured out of the Isles of the North and into the Duns of mortal men, they brought a wonderful chest of jewels and gold with them. It was said that however much of the gold was spent, the chest would never be emptied."

Siva's great eyes twinkle like a child's. "A fairy's chest?"

Warmed by Siva's response, an Drimuin takes a pleased

breath and says, "That's exactly what it was. Eventually the days of the Daanan people ended and the land was over-run by barbarians. Through the centuries, though, some of the Old Ones survived. In the bodies of men of certain Irish tribes ran the blood of the tuatha. One such tribe was Hurly whose men, as you know well enough yourself, were once lords of the whole southern shore and later lords by force of the lands of Maccus and Prehagne around the great area of the Kinsale Head."

Siva stirs at this and asks, "The Hurlys of Cork are decendants of these God-like people?"

"Unbelievable as it seems, viewing their present appalling status and behaviour, the same."

"Dear God, an Drimuin, what caused them to fall so far?"

An Drimuin is not offended by the new map Siva has drawn and quickly straightens out the bend in the conversational trail. He carries on himself as though the navigator has died.

"I'm going to get to that shortly if you will bear with me, dear. For centuries the Hurlys were the secret keepers of the magic treasure chest, and as long as they kept the chest it would remain bottomless. If it passed into other hands, it would be as any other cask of gold."

"And this, or these, are the chests that are lost?"

"So it is and the man who finds it has the spending of it until it empties, but even the finder must reserve part of the contents for the Old Ones or the curse will follow him forever."

Intuitively, Siva reacts enthusiastically. "The curse of the Daanan gold! Now I am beginning to see! But, how can anyone know where to find the golden hoard? It is hundreds of years gone."

"There is a trail, known only by me and exceedingly vague it is at that."

"A trail known only by you, husband. Tell me about it."

"As I know the story, in the 12th Century the Lady Niamh Hurly was abducted by the O'Mahoney clan whose castle of Don Daniel stood on the Glasslyn River. He demanded gold for the lady's safe return. All her distraught husband had of wealth was in the magic chest. He dispatched his cousin Randall Mic Rhua Hurly, with the gold and neither were ever seen again."

"And what of Lady Nimah. Has nothing ever been heard even in tales of her?"

"Oh, yes. We do know that."

"What is the story then?"

"I only know that since the gold never reached O'Mahoney, he forced Lady Nimah to divorce Hurly and marry him. O'Mahoney said Randall Hurly stole the gold and did a runner. When the MacCarthys of Cashel over-ran the O'Mahoney country, Thady Og MacCarthy decimated the O'Mahoney clan and siezed Don Daniel."

Siva is excited and senses some answers coming soon. She puts a finger to an Drimuin's massive chest and pushes.

"What about the gold, you terrible prevaricating MacCarthy you?"

"I haven't seen you so excited since our wedding night!"

"Let you not be misled, my dear. I'm after the money, not your rapidly depreciating physique!"

"You are a cruel and heartless woman, Siva. None-the-less, I press on. There was, of course, a dungeon of Don Daniel and in the dungeon lay a skeleton clutching the treasure. Engraved upon one of the casks were the words, 'This is the gold of the Daanan people'."

"So it was first found by the ancestors of our very own subject clan, and it could be in the possession of that miserly bunch under Thady MacCarthy Phale!"

"That is absolutely possible, for as the story goes, the ancestor tore a chest from the boney arms of its guardian and forced it open. The contents were said to be worth a Pope's ransom and more. Whether it was the sight of the wealth that overcame him or whether the curse took effect will never be known, but he instantly fell dead on the dungeon's cold stone floor."

Siva crosses herself before asking, "What happened next?"

"That will do you no good, Siva, but I will finish off your agony and curiosity by saying that Thady Mac Thady, his son, took up the chest but never dared spend it. He took it west to Fieries and settled near Fitzmaurice's Dun."

"And those were the builders and owners of Molahiffe Castle and demense. The Fitzmaurices who lost their everything to Thady Mac Thady."

"Yes. Where our dear Thady and Maude live with their son, Sean, and the same place we are sending our son, Bawn, tomorrow."

In the dim light of the nearly dead turf coals, Siva flops on her back, again taking more than her share of the bedclothes with her as she pensively says while staring through the darkness at the vaulted ceiling, "Still, it could be just a story, dearest husband."

"Certainly it could be just a story, but I think not. I think it is all true and that I will find the hoard somewhere within the baily of Molahiffe."

"A proper bedtime story, all the same. Very satisfying, I'd have to say," states the wife of the chief.

"There is still a difference between satisfying and being contented, dear!"

"Not tonight, an Drimuin. We've a hard enough day tomorrow. So. Goodnight, dear!"

"One lives in hope, my darling! Goodnight and pleasant dreams."

Chapter Three

Bawn at Molahiffe Castle

*"Then, there was injected the virulent poison
of religious division. The failure of the
Geraldine League led the various magnates
to seek forgiveness of Henry VIII. This was
given at the price of their renouncing the pope."*
T.J. Barrington

On such a bright, warm day better things should be
happening to a powerful chief than to be delivering his son to
be fostered at a run-down, damp and dirty old fortified castle; it
being with a leaky, windstruck, noisome keep in the middle of a
wood of poisonous yews. But such is Castle Molahiffe, built
upon the ancient earthworks and parts of two other such disas-
ters, all connected by runnels and tunnels and holes running
sideways. There is naught good to be said for the structure, and
the only redeeming feature of the landscape is that on the rare
clear day one is blessed with a view of the Slieve Mish mountains and the incredible green of the River Maine Valley.

There is something else in the clever and calculating
mind of an Drimuin and scant attention is being paid to Bawn,
who dashes about from side to side to hither and yon on his fat
little pony whilst his father rides steadily in the company of
Walter the Worried. He is instead thinking of how much more
pleasant his life will be once he has discovered the Fieries
Hoard. He thinks, too, of how much or how little he can escape
with giving to the Old Ones should he find it soon enough to
enjoy the treasury which would then remain. A new roof on his
keep, a splendid arrangement of brood mares for his stable of
stud horse, a larger grating over the murder-hole and new boots
and beer all around, envisages he with a smile while the little
fellow runs wild and torments those other than his father. All
that is going to be said between himself and Walter has been
said in the first two hours of the journey and it had gone stub-
bornly silent as they arrived at the castle's gate which stands

23

open to reveal further steadfast shabbiness amidst its squalor.

Having been warned of the arrival of the chief of the Clan MacCarthy in advance by the swift and silent observations along their way of his son Sean, old Thady Phale is casually scraping the dung from his leggings as an Drimuin and his party ride into his courtyard and his life. Sean stands waiting with the usual adornment of his ever present bow and quiver.

Bowing but ten centimeters from the waist, Thady offers his hospitality.

"Welcome, Lord Donal. You have brought your sweet son for our fostering! We are much honoured by your trust in this house of Phale."

"I have indeed brought my son to you for fostering, Thady Phale, but he is more than a handful as you will discover."

Thinking then to soften the blow with distorted logic, he adds, "Were it not in the oldest and best of traditions to so quest this fostering, I'd not bother you, but such is the way of the clan."

"I'm sure we can manage to find the best in him, my Lord. Isn't that true, Sean?"

Sly Sean looks at the child, but then directs his acquiescence toward ever present Walter. "Oh, to be sure, father. If he compares to his eldest sister Mhurien, there are wonderous good things to find inside young Bawn."

With the attention of all now centered upon his road dirt face, Bawn takes command of the meeting.

"What is that big thing hanging on your back, Sean?"

"This is the bow I made from yonder yew tree. It is the best in Munster, little friend."

"I want it," states the disagreeable little toad.

An Drimuin takes a swipe at the obliquus bugger's head with his tasseled whip, but misses by an eyelash as Bawn tacks to one side.

"Shut up, you! Now then, Thady, I want nothing half-learned. You will put him on his purgation. He is to obey, study his Latin and English and act human for a change when you are done with him or I will have your scrawny behind up for a target with Sean to do the archery."

"How long do we have to reveal this miracle of which

you speak?"

"As long as it takes. Isn't that right, Bawn? You'll stay here until you've mastered it all."

Bawn, for the first time, recognizes that he himself is the real target and he wants no part of the arrangement. He turns his pony toward the gate and gives it a fierce boot on both sides of the poor creature's flanks with his heels.

"I'm going home!"

"Get back here immediately!"

Contumacious Bawn is not slow to notice the true meaning in the voice of his father and for the first time obeys without hesitation. He turns the pony back to the group and presents a deceitful smile to cover his own distressful manner.

"He is an independent little man, isn't he, my Lord?"

"He is a diabolical monster, that's what he is, and he drinks too much for a six year old."

"I can honestly say that I would never have believed it. Rest assured, he will get no drink here."

"He also seems smitten with gambling, but he has no mind for such dalliance. Makes a botch of every game of chance he attempts to learn."

At this news, Sean's green eyes brighten and he joins in the commentary.

"Oh really, my Lord? He loves the games, does he? Fancies a bit of rogue gambling now and again?"

"Yes, he does, but take notice of this, Sean Phale. Regardless of what I've said, don't try to outsmart him or you'll end up even worse off than you presently are, even bearing in mind what sqaulor I see here."

The Phales, both father and son, look to each other and sweep into the mode of shocked innocence.

"We'd never do a thing like that, would we Sean?" asks pappa.

"Oh, no, never would we do a thing such as that!" spouts sonny.

An Drimuin looks at the two of them and shakes his thorny head. He picks Bawn up in his arms, holds him a moments distance and tousles his pretty and fair scalp. The boy is fighting to escape the embarrassment and is soon released, freeing him to run to the nearest outbuilding and hide.

25

"As I said, don't try to outsmart him. You never could."
He re-mounts his horse and shouts a goodbye to Bawn who has
taken up the pursuit of a rat.

"I must now leave. He is yours for the time being and
I'll be by again when he's finished here."

Out of the building shoots Bawn and he leaps onto his
pony in preparation to leaving with his father. Sean catches the
mane of the animal and stops boy and pony. Bawn slashes at
Sean's head with his wee whip but makes no contact whatso-
ever.

An Drimuin has turned at the sound of the commotion
and sees the drama being performed by a dancing pony with a
boy on his back and being held by a very strong man whose
long bow is still in place. Content that he is finally out of the
situation, he smiles to himself and turns his horse back toward
the gate.

"...and good luck. I'll be back to search for the hoard,
Thady!"

"Very well, my Lord, but there is no treasure here."

"We shall see, Thady. We shall certainly see!"

An Drimuin completes the turn and rides jauntily
through the gate while his son is giving good value in his efforts
to escape or at the very least, to yet get in a proper lick on Sean's
nut.

That scenario having ended, the moment an Drimuin and
Walter are on the drawbridge and at the gallop homeward, the
double Phales dislodge Bawn from the pony and take both into
the impoverished stable. Sounds similar to the smacking of
smooth skin emanate from the darker recesses and undeniable
sobs of a spoilt brat fling themselves into the universe.

After a year of such conductive discipline it comes to the
wandering mind of Sean that there may be some danger in two
phases from the terrible trainee's father.

"Has it perhaps occasionally occurred to you, father, that
there may be severe repercussions should his father learn of
Bawn's character shaping process? He does absorb a considerable amount of teaching pressure."

"Not to worry, son. We were instructed to do nothing
half way and that he was to learn thoroughly all we have to
offer him. His father would never object. No, sir. He would

not."

"What if the boy were to complain, should his father ever come back to visit him or personally enquire via Walter?"

"He wouldn't believe him for a minute. Neither one would. Count on it."

"I am free, then, to whack the little bastard at will?"

"Do you not recall what an Drimuin vouchsafed? We are to mold the student and give him everything we have to offer. That nothing was to be done by half."

"So by that he meant we were to mold him as one would clay?"

"That would be correct, according to my thinking. He, like clay, needs to be pounded into shape. He must be handled and turned and turned and pounded again or he will never resemble that which we have been told to develop."

"What a splendid thing education is, father! So we have done thus far."

"And, Sean, if we are to develop him he must be kept after. You must take him into the barnyard and continue his lessons with bow and arrow today."

"Where is he then, father?"

"At my last sighting he was playing with his pet rat, Earl of Desmond, in the kitchen. He was dunking him into the slop pail again and again."

"So he is beginning to respond after all. He is teaching his rat by our methods. Edification is wonderful, is it not, father, and emulation of our practices sets a high standard, indeed!"

"Indeed. I hadn't quite thought of it that way, but you're onto something I'm sure. Carry on, then. Great stuff altogether!"

Bawn is found and invited to accompany Sean and gain knowledge of the art of archery. The youngster follows him from the kitchen carrying his swamped rat, near drowned, is he, by the tail and skipping merrily in the tracks of his young mentor.

"Hear me now, young master. Drop the rat and take this bow. Let us see where your practice has taken you."

Bawn nods eagerly at Sean's distinctions and waps home four of five into the soft target of a cow-pie set against the fence post.

"That's very good. Very good, to be sure. In time you shall improve."

"What I want to do is use a bow like yours."

"You will, Bawn, when you are a little older, a little bigger and stronger."

"I'll never get any bigger or stronger on the food your mother feeds me. What was that we had today?"

"That was swan."

"Swan! That was swan? It tasted like rotted fish!"

"Calm down, Bawn. You are frightening off the goats."

"I don't believe I like swan. When did it die?"

"Firstly, all swan tastes of fish. Secondly, my father killed it this morning by the Maine River, I think."

"You think! I think he found it a week ago at least!"

"There are those who say that finding a dead swan is very good luck. It saves the time of hanging them to age."

"That's disgusting!"

"Disgusting or not, that is the way of things at Molahiffe Castle. My father is a conservative man by nature and dislikes waste. However, that has nothing to do with learning in a positive fashion. Pay heed to this, Bawn."

He drops to the ground, rolls onto his back. He then springs acrobatically to his feet and looses an arrow into the centre of a target 100 yards distant.

"I call that my jump shot."

"You've got doggie shit all over your raggety tunic."

"A small price to pay for perfection. Probably been there for days," says our Sean, thus ending yet another episode in the tutoring of Bawn.

Deep inside the castle keep, there exists a room of small size and little defensive significance but one designated by Thady at the direction of an Drimuin, i.e., Donal MacCarthy Mor, chief of all MacCarthy in the land save MacCarthy Reagh, to be a place of study. A new and enhancing feature is added with the regular visit and tutelage by Friar Lawrence Meade, a fat and food-stained old Franciscan. His charge is the giving of language and politics, and fat and food-stained or not, nothing escapes him. He is witty and possesses a needle-sharp mind, a cheerful mouthy disposition and is a man of many stories. He

28

and his accompanying nephew, Johnny Meade, help push the gloom away. The chess game in progress is broken by the sheer boredom of youth against the odds and the Friar offers yet another tale from his mental bag.

"Did I tell you about the time Christopher Columbus asked for me to accompany him on his journey to the Americas?"

"No! Did he really? Did you go?"

The Friar, sensing a break-through with Bawn and Johnny, quickly presses forward.

"No, sadly I couldn't go because I caught the ague just before sailing time. I was in the Vatican just then, doing a bit of close contact praying with the Pope."

Bawn, again losing interest in short term upon hearing the Friar didn't go anywhere, asks, "So, who was Christopher Columbus and where are the Americas? Would they be down the river?"

The Friar recognizes ignorance of geography in its most base form, leans his head into his hands over the table and thinks to himself, "Lord God! Of all the dopey rich kids, I have to get this one!"

The Friar decides upon another tact.

"More to your liking, then. Did I tell you two the story of how I came to be a Friar without appointment?"

"Yes, to me you did, several times, but tell it to Bawn, please," says Johnny with a further jab into adult ego.

"Very well, I shall! It happened while our King Henry VIII was married to Catherine of Aragon, a Spanish Princess who had once been betrothed to King Henry's eldest brother, Prince Arthur of Wales. Prince Arthur died and Henry wanted desperately to have a male heir for the custom of rule from male progeny, but he should have know better, in my opinion, than to have married her if that was his purpose."

Hoping to speed along the story, nephew Johnny puts in his shilling. "But he did marry her, didn't he?"

"Yes, he did, but as in the Book of Leviticus it says, 'If a man shall take his brother's wife it is an unclean thing,' and in Deuteronomy it contrarily but clearly predicts, 'When brethren dwell together and one of them dieth without children, the brother shall take her and raise up seed for his brother.'"

29

"So then what?"

"It appears that Leviticus was the better prophet. Six daughters were born but no male heir for twenty years and by then Catherine was too old to bear yet another child. Only the girl, Mary, survived."

A yawning Bawn senses a finish, and asks, "So that ended it?"

"Not on your life," says the Friar. "Henry was not to be beaten and he went back to Leviticus after all that time and discovered yet another helpful verse. It said, 'If a man shall take his brother's wife he hath uncovered his brother's nakedness; they shall be childless.' Henry was fast after other ladies in his pursuit to produce a son, within or without the papal blessing."

Still trying for a conclusion, Bawn asks, "So, if that wasn't the end, what was?"

"Things were hotting up. Henry had been pursuing Anne Bullen, the sister of one of his former mistresses, Mary. Anne was a lovely lady, comely, raven-haired, light complexioned and unattainable, holding out on King Henry for the full title of Queen."

"That would have to be when you lost your job, right?" asks the helpful, storywise Johnny.

"Most emphatically. When the King's hose smouldered and Anne finally extinquished them in the natural manner, he told the Parliament the people were abused by the Sancta Romana Chiesa and they should give the King the power to investigate and reform the abuses. He'd be his own Pope!"

"The bastard! Did they go for the story?"

"They did, young sirs, they did. Though not as harsh as it has been in England, we have been dispossessed. I took to the road and you must take to your beds. It's getting very late."

And late it was, for near all was ended for that year, and in the next, great events portend.

Chapter Four

Bawn is Snatched From Molahiffe

Molahiffe Castle was actually three castles
joined by imposing walls and mysterious tunnels ...
King, History of Kerry

An Drimuin on the march with his trusted senachel, Walter and Fast Frawley, an ox-stupid lout of 22 who acts younger with no choice in the matter. Arriving at the Castle Molahiffe, there is but a single purpose on the mind of at least one. He wants to look for some gold and he will make that straight with Thady. Without welcome or escort, they ride diectly into the courtyard of the ruinous castle and the head of the Phale MacCarthy sept rushes out with his son Sean to more or less greet their Chief. An Drimuin pushes forward and drops his reins.

"The time has finally come, Thady, to collect the gold that certainly lies hidden here."

"My Lord, could you possibly think that Maude and I would live like this if there was any gold in this castle or anywhere around it?"

"I do. What baffles me is that you would choose to do so. I say you are afraid of the ancient curse. No one loses such a treasure. You know where it is, damn you, and you shall tell us where!"

"If I had known of it anywhere within miles I would have been on it like a hawk. Maude would see to that!"

An Drimuin's lengthy arm reaches out toward the keeper of Molahiffe and the huge hand attaches itself to the scruffy area at the juncture of shoulder and neck.

"Thady, you may not be much on the outside, but inside I know you to be a horrific and hopeless prevaricator. I'll undertake to say your mind and mouth are absolutely unacquainted with any element of truth."

"I beg my Lord to reconsider such a slanderous state-
31

ment."

"Beg away, there, Thady. We have much more important things to do than stand here like a group of curates arguing about something you say doesn't exist and with me knowing it does."

"Why, my Lord, do you belittle me and scurriously attack my integrity and yet trust me with your son? I am at a loss to know why I am so put upon, especially seeing as how Maude so generously gave up all our coyne to welcome luscious little Bawn into the world of Munster. And, I, if I may be so bold, I beg to request your thoughts upon such things."

"You may request nothing and I warn you to guard how you speak to your chief! Now then, let's get on with it. We have work to do here."

An Drimuin pushes past Thady and his son Sean. They make their way to the door of the cellars off the keep, and begin their plunge.

The two other wise men, Walter and Fast Frawley, are marching in single file behind their intrepid leader with much bumping and banging of their pick and shovel. Behind them comes Thady and the four make their way toward the sub-basement of the sub-basement of the basement where connections were once made to the many tunnels linking this castle with the two others in the Fieries complex. Lighted by candles and lantern, their shadows grow long, moving from pillar to arch to wall to ceiling in symphonic syncopation with their crackling steps over crumbling rock. After considerable trudging and the mysterious checking of points by the lost an Drimuin, unfamiliar to everyone on this earth, they arrive someplace.

"This is it, lads. This is the spot I've studied about and searched for."

"What is it we are to do now, sir?" asks the trembling Fast Frawley.

"What you are to do is start the digging, you twit! Walter is to take the shovel and you are to take the pickaxe and start right there in the northeast corner and work your way along that wall."

"Right now, sir?" asks Frawley.

"Whenever you are ready, Frawley. Sooner rather than

later, if you please."

"Right, sir. Whack along the wall there and Walter will come along with the shovel and move the debris?"

"That's right, Fast Frawley. You whack the earth with your pickaxe and Walter follows up with the shovel work," replies an Drimuin while looking at Walter and indicating there may be more than just a trace of stupidity in the area. Walter raises his eyes heavenward, half in agreement with what an Drimuin has said and half for the reason of questioning the quest in the first place.

"So be it, my Lord. If you have no further need for my services I shall return to the surface to attend to your son's further learning," says Thady.

"That would be wise, Thady. We'll just get on with our business. Leave your lantern but take a candle."

"Thank you, my Lord. You are a generous man," says Thady and he takes his leave.

The earth is crisp with the ages of dryness in the deepest bowels of the castle. Whonk, whack, wham goes the pickaxe. Scritch, scratch, screek goes the shovel scooping and thunk, thunk thunk goes the earth landing in the pile as the twosome remain industrious as long as an Drimuin watches. Fast Frawley takes a quick break to ask his master a question.

"How deep shall we dig, sir?"

"To bedrock or treasure, whichever comes first."

"I pray it be the treasure, sir, as bed-rock looks to be deeply away."

"Carry on, then."

"What will you be doing, sir?" asks Frawley.

"Why, I shall be over there in the corner."

"What is it you will be doing in the corner, sir?" further asks Frawley while scratching his bald poll in mystification.

"I will keep a look-out for any raiders, Fast Frawley. 'Tis you who will be doing the important work!"

Fast Frawley goes to nodding his head enthusiastically at the news of his importance and newly recognized skill, two things he himself has always doubted. He gives a final nod in an Drimuin's direction and lets go with a series of daring over-head manuevours with his pickaxe and blasts it home into the dirt in front of him.

"That's it. Right, sir!"

Just then a loud cracking noise, followed by some ominous groans of a heavy nature are coming from the wall. One can see there is a notable change in base of this fortification as Frawley's enthusiasm is beginning to show results. The very foundation of the ancient structure complains strongly at the assault, and sounds similar to the crumpling of a beseiged fortress bailey as its under-pinning weakens.

"Holy Mother of God! What have you done?"

"It appears we have started to help the keep to fall down upon us!" says Walter.

Frawley doesn't even give it a glance, so immersed is he in his flayling activity with the pickaxe.

"In the name of the Holy Father, will you stop what you're doing, Frawley? The whole place will be collapsing on us. Stop it!" says an Drimuin.

"I was just getting into the feel for the job to be done," responds the flea-brained burrower.

"Let us take ourselves out of here before we cannot!" exclaims an Drimuin.

The three are quickly into motion and their fear straightens the maze of passageways back to the natural light of things. There they are glad to see the attention of the Phales is upon Bawn, giving scant notice to the dusty and dirty threesome emerging with more than slight embarrassment. An Drimuin's son is involved in some military drill involving a horse which he seems to be very good at handling.

"You are well suited to that horse, young Bawn. Now, with that lance, bring the tip down slowly as you ride toward the target," speaks Thady.

"He is a skinny nag and he can hardly walk with myself and the battle gear all at the same time!"the lad responds. "Bring me that big black bastard over beside that pile of rocks."

"That pile of rocks is our castle!" says Sean.

Thady glances sideways and indirectly at the dusty figures of an Drimuin, Walter, and Fast Frawley, and now quickly doubts the chief's previous near jovial mood.

"You heard the sweet lad, Sean. Bring over that big black bastard beside the pile of rocks," says Thady.

Sean looks not at an Drimuin, but at Walter and reads

murder.

"I will just nip over there and get the big black bastard, then."

Hacking and still coughing a bit, the three dust themselves off and appear to disregard the training session at hand which now ceases in mid-air as an Drimuin calls to his son.

"Get your things, Bawn. We are leaving here."

Bawn, sensing his father may not be upset with him, though he is undeniably upset at something, nevertheless looks around uncomfortably for a place to disappear for the moment. Unsuccessful, he slides off the lee side of his scraggly mount and stands behind that nag's inadequate flank for shelter. Thady is trying to be serious and unknowing, but has a hard time of it. He must do something before he bursts out laughing at his chief and gets himself killed or worse.

"What happened, my Lord? You look as though you were buried alive!"

It isn't as if an Drimuin cannot hear Thady's question. He is better satisfied to ignore him.

"Come out from behind that horse, do you hear me?" says an Drimuin to Bawn. "I said you are to get your things!"

Sean must speak as his father is petrified at being so purposefully ignored. His story is not a pleasant one.

"That would be difficult, my Lord. He has no things," he says.

Thady takes courage that an Drimuin is surely paying attention to his son and not to him.

"Sean is right. The money, the clothes, the new skein...even his pet rat, Earl of Desmond, are gone."

"Gone where? I've sent him many things."

"...which he promptly lost to the lads in the stables," reports Sean. "He is fair mad for betting on games. He never seems to have much luck."

"Drinks a fair bit, too, does your Bawn. What he didn't gamble away he used to buy poteen, I'd have to say," adds Thady.

Bawn is still determined to escape and starts to make a move toward the keep while the others are jawing away. Fast Frawley is still a bit foggy as to why he is there and not down digging for gold, but takes it all in good strides as he watches

Bawn edging around the suffering horse. He now whistles lightly through his teeth as if coaxing the lad on. Sean sees the play developing and works toward involving the boy into the conversation, instead of bearing the heavy burden with his father. He is abundantly aware that he and poppa Thady are about to be erupted upon by the effusive chief.

"That's the truth, isn't it, young master?" he asks in the direction of the stupid horse.

Bawn's left foot pauses in tentative step as he is stopped by Sean's question.

"Everything was stolen, father. Everything you sent to me was stolen."

An Drimuin is not nearly as surprised as he is putting on, but he does theatre with grand gestures and strong voice qualities. He roars a reply.

"Gambling? Thievery? That's it, Walter. We are taking the boy home. Bring our horses!"

Sean is alert to the escape for himself and Thady and he leans forward toward the broken down stable door, behind which are three very good horses whose home is assuredly not there. As an Drimuin and the others make ready to leave, Thady speaks up.

"I take it from the looks of you that you were unlucky in your efforts to find the golden hoard."

"We did not, no. The foundations of the keep have settled somewhat, however. What a poorly built castle you have, Thady."

"It suits our modest needs." He is anxious to end the adagio on a positive chord. "We did as best we could for the little tyke since he arrived," he adds with a thinker's footnote.

"I'd have to say from the looks and sound of things you did nothing to fulfill your charge as foster to my son."

With Thady leading two of the three horses himself and the third being handled by Eugene McSwinney, the get-away scene is set. Thady is not about to cause the departure to abort, but he does wish to put in a few good words about himself and the son of his chief.

"He shows great promise in all fields. He will be a great commander if he can stay sober and on his horse."

"And, he would be very good with the short sword and

the skein as well if he yet had one," adds Sean.

"Get up on my horse, Bawn. We will have a little talk along the way."

Bawn looks to the right, looks to the left, does the hokey-pokey and shakes it all about, but nowhere is there anything that even faintly resembles a helpful Hegira. Dismayed, he sighs loudly and resignedly.

"Don't whine at me, you little renegade. It's you got yourself into this and properly viewed, you should appreciate it is your old father who again gets you out. Now, get your un-dernourished rump up here or I'll toss you across the back!"

Which is what Bawn promptly does with no flourish or fanfare.

Walter, in his turn, takes his time to adjust the rope on his horse's head before he, too, mounts. Sean is watching him carefully, awaiting the broadside he is sure to receive.

Rumble, rumble and a soft roar emanates from Walter's diaphragm and escapes his curled lips now pointed in Sean's direction. With his mouth close to Sean's face he whispers, "Harken ye," he says, "I don't think you two would be safe around Castle Lough. You especially, Sean. There would be no one there who'd now welcome you."

"I wasn't really planning a visit in the near future."

"Good. I think that is especially wise as pertains to Lady Mhurien, too."

"I'm sure that's so, Walter Tibbet, with her in season since she was nine years old and you sniffing around her behind."

"You insolent little pup! I should smash your head now!" snarls the aroused Walter.

"Best you have your try while in your master's view. I will skewer you with a steel tipped hazel from this yew tree bow if you get within 100 meters of me on this property again. With or without his protection, Walter, and that is a promise."

"You will get what's coming to you, Sean!"

"But I already have, Walter, many times before you and many times since. And, too bad about the gold not being here."

An Drimuin, with Bawn now securely held in front of him on his great horse, is anxious to get on with the journey home. He is clearly becoming impatient with the whispered and furious conversation between the two. Thady himself is trying to find a reason to leave, and each member of the party seems to be delayed in their busy-ness. Ever the possessor of the observant eye, an Drimuin senses his daughter is the subject of the testosterone driven animations and ground shuffling agitations of Sean and Walter. He is not going to stand for much more.

"If you two are through dancing, we shall get on with our journey."

Walter slowly withdraws his face from that of Sean, keen is he to ram a dirk into the youngster's gut, but turns instead at the sound of his master's voice. He throws the rope over the horse's head, swings a leg over its back and is still staring at his adversary as he turns the animal toward an Drimuin and the gate. Only then does his voice become audible to the ears of those in his present company.

"Don't forget what I've said, Sean Phale MacCarthy. Remember my words!"

Sean casually flicks his hand to his forelock.

"Oh, I shall forget what you said before you leave the causeway. As a matter of fact, I cannot remember a word of what you said and I'll spend not a whit of my time trying to remember it."

"Come along. It will be dark before we gain the bailey of our own castle if we dally longer. It's not important to me to stay!"

The three men and the over-sized young boy meet at the drawbridge and start across to the embankment on the other side of the lane running past castle Molahiffe. As they ride off, Fast Frawley is attempting to suss out what everything is all about. Confused by what has happened despite his sweat, and without one iota of comprehension, he asks explanation from Walter who is fuming away under his breastplate.

"What is happening to us, Walter? Why did we leave? Did I do wrong things, Walter?"

"No, Fast Frawley, you did nothing wrong. It's the scut of a son of Thady Phale MacCarthy who did something wrong. He'll get what's coming to him!"

"But when you were whispering to him I heard him say he already had gotten what was coming to him. What did he mean?"

Walter is by now tiring of the references to his crossing with Sean.

"Just shut up, Frawley. For your own sake, just shut up!"

Forlornly, Fast Frawley screws up his tattered face into yet another contortion created by lack of knowledge on the puzzling subject of love. His shoulders droop and even his horse seems to understand that neither of them will ever know anything about anything.

In the background, still within the castle courtyard, Thady and Sean await their unwanted visitors' disappearance. Thady claps his son on the back and starts to laugh. Sean has never seen or heard his father laugh, either inside their hovels or outside in their miserable courtyard. He is not stunned, but knows he should be both glad and proud.

"I crave your pardon, father. What makes you laugh?"

"I've never been so glad to see the back of anyone before!"

"And, I have never seen a Lord so filthy!"

So relieved are they and so pleased with their own and each other's rare successful performances, they both break out in laughter anew. They are near collapse from the unaccustomed mirth and they are gasping for breath.

"They found no hoard down there, son!"

"Nor will they ever!"

"Nothing has ever earned a tankard of porter more than that!"

"Do we have porter, father?"

"No, but it is a grand thought! We shall have to make do with some of that filthy French wine in the cellars!"

"There is plenty of that, father. Shall I tell mother to join us?"

"Good Lord God, no! Why ruin everything?"

A silent Bawn sits in front of an Drimuin on his cantering horse. Ahead rides the still angry Walter Tibbet and behind, forever the rear guard, is Fast Frawley, struggling with his blank mind. Unaccustomed to not being the final say, Bawn boldly turns his fair head and finds his father's angry face with his coaxing eyes. He is of the opinion that his innocent mood will prevail and that an Drimiun will be swayed soon enough and

39

forgive him of all his sins and transgressions. An Drimuin glances down, but smiles not and is grim in his demeanor. The failure to find his gold and learning that his son is now a nine year old near-derelict who will someday himself be King of Munster, does not leave him filled with joy.

Bawn purses his lips and prepares to speak, adding a smile for effect along the way.

"Stay quiet, you. I have something to say to you and you had best listen closely," states an Drimuin.

"I always listen to you, father."

"You have never once listened, but you will listen now. You will be leaving for Askeaton Castle as soon as I can see James Fitzgerald."

"But, father, is he not your enemy?"

"At present he is less the enemy than you and that is precisely why you are going there. Where Thady Phale has failed to tame you and to train you, I assure you, Lord James will not spare proper discipline."

At six or sixty, everyone knows that the everlasting brood of Fitzgeralds are of a slow-dragging past century, claiming descendency from the legions of Florence and about as Italian as the Anglo-Irish could get.

"Could it be they are mad?" swiftly thinks the threatened Bawn. "Yes," he concludes, they could. And, has he not insultingly named his rat for Lord James? Yes, he has.

"But, father....," starts Bawn.

"Just be quiet, you whining puppy. If you so much as make one stupid or improper move while you are there, I will see to it that you are turned over to Mighty Moriarity in the Boggeragh Mountains. And, there you will stay at his camp until I come for you! Is that clear?"

Gulping great gasps of horse scented air at the thought of the legendary Gallgoidel cast-off Moriarity, Bawn is stunned once more to dead silence and apprehension.

"Did you hear me, Bawn?"

"Yes, father. I heard you."

A moment of pause as an Drimuin makes the moment of confession come to fruition.

"I mean it, my son. I love you, but you must learn to be a chief. You are the last hope of the MacCarthy Mor. There will

40

be no more children to follow you in this sept."

"I will not fail our clan, father."

"See that you don't!"

Chapter Five

Bawn is Fostered by the Fitzgeralds at Askeaton Castle

The Desmonds, throughout most of their history, were quite ungovernable
                    P. J.Barrington

ℜiding together the three, an Drimuin, Bawn, and the puissant Walter Tibbet, moved slowly northward along the River Deel. To their conglomerate eye comes Askeaton Castle in its looming glory. There stands a massive castle, squarely set on its rock plateau, hunching threateningly like a snarling cur. On one side, in the penumbra of its extended shadow, is the blackness of the Kylmore Wood.   On the other side is the bright gold of the Galtees Mountains, shining in the brilliant sunlight. In the icy frostedness of the valley and with the sun glow bouncing iridescently, the vision of power cannot be denied.

"Oh, Mary, Mother of Jesus! Is that where I am to stay?"

"It is, and stop your forever cursing in the name of our Father, for Christ's sake!"

The trio stops and they look across the fields at the battlement and the outer bailey.

"I'm not going to like this place. It's like some ugly crypt!"

"You are not yet inside, master Bawn. Take a taste before you spit it out," offers the wily Walter. In his own mind he is thinking that perhaps the lad is right. It does, in all that lays before them, look threateningly and desperately dead.

"There are many things to learn and many things to avoid learning here, Bawn. These are the masters of duplicity and deceit who wear the English Mask while espousing their hatred for the same. It is an opportunity you may never have again. It merely gives off a false tone of personal integrity."

"If they are so confused, why are you letting them teach me? What was wrong with Friar Lawrence? And, I'll probably never see Johnny Meade again and I like him very much."

"You will learn to think as they think without becoming the kind they are, Bawn. It's really quite simple."

"Not for me, father. I'm but nine and badly initiated by Maude and Thady, not mentioning Sean and that cheating Eugene McSwinney. And, you know how much I shall miss Johnny. Walter knows about such things, don't you Walter?"

"I cannot say for certain, but I have to think that Johnny Meade and you will be meeting up again before long," Walter told him.

"Let us move on. We've talked enough," says an Drimuin sourly.

Two grumpy guards approach them as they ride forward and little is said between them. Inside the main gate of Askeaton, the three arrivals see the tilt yard, the smithies, the armourer's workshops and the stables. There are the well-tended gardens full of herbs and flowers, and between the gardens there are fish ponds, vegetable plots and orchards where fruit will flourish in the summer.

Ushered inside, the main hall is a noble sight, hung as it is with the Geraldine Ape tapestry and other gym-crack from the days of the claimed Florentine ancestry.

At a large table sits James Fitzgerald dressed in the latest Italian fashion of brocade and silk, and at the far end are his tormented sons Gerald, who is seven, John at ten, and James, just half past eight. This assortment of medieval relics are heirs to the vast estates and power of the Desmond lands, and on the face of it are astonishing copies of their father in manner and in dress.

Gerald, two years younger than Bawn, is hyper and detectably bonkers. John is haughty at ten and strongly silent with his sharp chin up, while James is furtive and possesses darting eyes with which he glances everywhere, up and down, sideways and back. James is , - well, James is James.

This is a difficult pack for Bawn to sort and deal, but he keeps his eyes on Gerald in particular, fascinated with the mystery of the madness he is already beginning to exhibit at age seven. An Drimuin acknowledges Earl James' greeting and wants nothing more than to ditch the son and get out and on the way home again. The sinking thought occurs to him that this is all he has done while in Bawn's presence. He is constantly trying to get away from him. He speaks to start the show.

"Taking my son for training at your castle will greatly enhance his skills and learning, though he is already far advanced for his age."

"We shall surely care for him as a son. It will do wonders for both our houses to have Bawn with us for as long as you see fit." replies Earl James.

"It is that business I came to discuss, Lord James."

"Continue, please. This is most intriguing."

"He is a bit different, my son Bawn is."

"Oh yes. I've heard about him. He's quite lively, isn't it?"

"Lively? Well, yes, he is. I've had him in training at Molahiffe, but you know how Thady and Maude can be. Not a hint of reasoning."

"So I have heard. We are more formal here."

"Yes, Lord James. For the good of your sept and mine, I think it prudent for you to accept him into fostering and cultural, ah, cultural development."

"Fear not. We shall do all we can to make a proper warrior of him, won't we, my sons?"

The three young men now straighten their legs and smile wickedly. John's sharp jaw moves in speech.

"I think, my Lord McCarthy, that I can speak for the three of us. Let me say that we shall follow your wishes. We will not spare him either!"

"In fairness that is all anyone can ask for my son and heir. I bid you goodbye," says an Drimuin and he and Walter are escorted from the hall by Earl James and the three sons while Bawn is left standing alone in the middle of the dead centre of things.

Very soon, Walter reappears and comes forward to stand in front of the new resident dissenter. He bends sharply to Bawn and whispers, "This is your new home. May you survive their lunacy and return to us a better man, Bawn."

Bawn hunches his good-sized shoulders and turns his head to whisper back. "I shall survive, Walter. But, will they?"

"I fear they will....the Norman part, at least."

Now Walter is gone and Bawn is taken to meet the wife.

She is Mora. Then he meets the daughter, Honoria, who is tall and pretty and isn't as balmy as one would expect and is his own age and only a little more. Lady Mora speaks.

"Perhaps you have not been made fully aware of the importance of our sept, despite your mother being a member of it."

"I know very little, my Lady."

"Then I shall help you," says she.

Harrumph, Haw and Ahem before she gets to the chorus.

"We Geraldine Fitzgeralds are the descendents of the mercenaries of Florence who had fought with Duke William in the Battle of Hastings. One of their men had married Nesta, descended from the Princes of Gwent and Dyfed. I myself am an O'Carroll Mulrooney. Is that clear?"

Bawn's good senses may not amount to a hill of cabbage, but this time he goes to the heart of the matter, hard to the wall.

"Yes, my Lady. Were your ancestors really moon worshippers?"

Our Mora is set back upon her ample haunches at the audacity of such an unheard of thing as moon-worshippers. In her family, indeed!

Then she finds the lost track and slips her wagon back into the well-worn ruts.

"Oh, no, my dear boy. Not really."

Some past scubba generates a flicker of dim light in her now glazed eyes as she suddenly recollects a picture of the sun's midnight reflection upon the River Deel.

"Still, there is a good deal to be said for bright moonlight."

A generous pause as she recalls certain ceremonies below the standing stones of Glandore in the soft straw of summer when she was single and lonely. Oh, my goodness, this will never do! The lantern slides closed and the moon retreats, perhaps forever.

"What a silly boy you are."

Finger adjustments are made to the tight collar she wears acting as the bodily covering for a mindful of treasured, but near Protestant, protected memories.

"Do you have any other questions, my dear?"

"Yes, my Lady. None of your family has smiled since I've

been here. Are you all unhappy that I am here, for if that is so I shall find my way home."

"Oh, no! It isn't that at all. We are particularly delighted that you are here with us. We are, it would appear to some, uncommonly reserved, being very aware of our noble background."

Bawn has opened his mouth to reply, thinks better of what he was going to go with and taps his teeth with the fingernails of his hand instead. Then puts in his tempered remark which states what he means with better control of the volume.

"Begging your pardon, my Lady. I could not be so noble myself. It looks as though it hurts considerably."

Lord James feels the need to step into the breech before his Lady is gussied-up with mental configurations akin to those of his own family. He turns from Mora and Bawn and gestures to his sons sitting somewhat dumb-founded at the table.

"I think our young guest is tired and would like some rest. Show him to his quarters, please. Tomorrow will be a busy day."

James, John and Gerald are now not quite as certain of themselves as they were moments before when their intention was to make him as uncomfortable as possible and perhaps a bit more. They are eyeing him with a good deal of quashed eagerness to do bodily harm and exert the extreme anguish of mental superiority. Their steps from behind the table to the centre of the hall where the young fella stands are less a march than a hesitating ballet. Who is this uncouth intruder? How can we harm him without getting harmed ourselves. They realize he has innocently, but perhaps not innocently at that, bested their mother who has belted young ones for unvarnished impudence in the past. This MacCarthy is either very quick or very bold. Worse yet, he could be both. Worst of all is that he is quick as well as bold while being as stupid as they had been told. Real danger exists before them and John makes the judgement that they must answer to their father with less temerity than he himself is exhibiting.

"We shall be very happy to show our new friend to his quarters. If he will be required for any services before the dinner hour he will be there, won't you, Bawn?"

"Yes, I suppose I will."

That night before the log fire in the great hall the table is set with many foods which are still unheard of at Molahiffe. There is all manner of things as he readily sees. What he fails to see is the grace and genteel manners of a proper family dining together, as they would be doing at home. Surely his mother, Siva, would be aghast at these other Fitzgeralds' lack of grooming.

Even at age nine, he notices the sleeves of the velvet jackets are plated with grease from dragging through the gravies and best bets are that there are runny noses involved in the course of many a day and night. Hmmm, Hmmm at that. No finger bowls. There are no signs of the latest fashion called the dining fork. The servant girls' aprons wipe the sweat from their hands, arms, brows, bosoms and probably their rotund behinds behind the swinging doors of the kitchen. And there is no indication of any training about how to throw bones to the dogs who roam beneath and beside the table on the great stone slabs of the reed covered floor. The cooks are swearing at the helpers and a baby is crying as though scalded, which was the truth; she was. A bottle is broken and someone is momentarily catapaulted out the doors, but quickly recovers and blasts his way back into the kitchen in pursuit of the purveyor of injustice who sent him sprawling and caterwauling into the dining area in the first instance. Head down, Bawn is about to eat his soup when the beef is smacked down upon the table and his dish disappears as a round loaf of bread takes its place. Carry on, carry on; the food pours out and the gnarled remains are swept away down some dark corridor. It is immediately obvious that if anyone slips approaching the table he will be too late to eat.

Is this part of the English Mask he must learn? He thinks not. Does the squalor of Molahiffe make more sense than this? Perhaps a lesson here somewhere, but what can it be?

Dinner is done.

Into the hall two lute players silently appear with a little girl of no age who smiles nicely at Bawn, but pays not the slightest heed to the others. Pluck and strum, pluck and strum; there they start and so sings the fragile golden girl with voice of purest water with cress flavours.

Quietly, oh, so quietly does she sing, yet clear and fancy pretty. Their eyes meet, Bawn's and hers, and bashful though he is not, his peering ceases as he drops his head to look at the desecrated table. When he once again gains courage and does so lift his face toward her, she is gone and the song has been sung. Perhaps the mead; perhaps the travel; perhaps the now rising moon. Where can she be; the lute youths still plucking? Stirred to speak, he looks around the table at the final gorging before him and sees now that he has caught Earl James between knife and tankard.

"My Lord, if I may so ask, who is the little girl who sings?"

"What girl is that, Bawn?"

"The young girl who sang Róisín Dubh just a moment ago, my Lord."

"I saw no girl and heard no one sing, young man. Have you often these spells of fancy?"

"No, my Lord. I thought I saw...I thought I heard a girl from the corner singing with the players."

"Father, that would have been Ethné."

"And who is Ethné, pray tell, Gerald?"

"She is some girl I see here at times."

"Well, son, I have never seen her and if there was hearing of singing to be done one would have to think I would do it."

"I'm pleased you heard singing, Bawn. I often hear singing," Mora says.

Honoria, ever present and never heard, sits in outnumbered silence.

"That is different, my Lady, I'm sure, than what Bawn thought he heard," offers Mora's husband.

The lute players seize this opportunity to disappear themselves, well aware of the moods of Lady Mora and her unseeing spouse, Lord James. There is nothing more left in the musical corner than the last whisp of blue light from the skies outside.

"We shall begin the morning excercises in the courtyard," announces Earl James. "I would suggest you be ready when John summons you."

"Oh, father! Why is it always me who does the summoning?"

"Because you are the eldest and because I said so, John. Now, off to bed, all of you. Be quick about it."

All must do as told.

In the early light of morn Bawn finds his chamber dull and lifeless. He dresses quickly, but knowing not what to do, falls back upon his pallet and quiets his mood. Is there a light knock upon the chamber door? Yes, and it is followed by the entry of a shy serving girl with water in a basin and a basket of bread, a pitcher of milk and a pot of stirabout.

Scrub and rub and he is done cleaning last night's eyes and mouth, the latter foul from rancid beef. He falls to the stirabout to break his fast and pours down the rich milk, sopping great lumps of buttery bread along the way. Sitting as he is, his legs are soon moving happily in time to his chewing and he hums last night's song. His mind wanders over the beautiful face of the singing angel.

Bang, bang, a different knock. John bursts in unbid.

"It is time," says he, doing his summoning as though to the gibbet.

Down below goes Bawn, to the group assembled along the bailey wall and father James is swishing and slashing at his morning foes. The other boys are yawning but watching. Honoria is standing, no, leaning, against the wall in the shadows of the early rays of brightness. John is playing bored and put-upon, showing he knows his earlier lessons from the master.

In the tilting yard one notices a changed demeanor in Lord James. He has undergone a gentlemanly transformation and smiles brightly at Bawn.

"Good morning, Bawn. I trust you slept well, for you will need your strength. Take this," the Earl says, tossing him a sword. "It is a rapier, the French sword and a gentleman's weapon. See how light and fast it can be in trained hands."

Bawn extends his greeting and looks at the slender weapon.

"It seems meager arms, my Lord"

A rapid flourish and the air falls dead at Earl James' feet.

"The purpose is to keep the point in front of you at all times. This is not a commoner's sword. This is the sword of the elite."

Another whipping display and he looks to Bawn.

"But, what will I do with it in mortal combat?" the lad

50

asks.

"Oh! Dear me! He wants to know about mortal combat. Shall we test him in mortal combat, brothers?" asks John sarcastically.

Earl James glares at John but goes on with the lesson.

"That is why you must keep the point in front," says Lord James.

"But, if I had a broadsword, I'd smash through to you."

"You would be dead at four feet, my boy."

"My body armour would save me and I'd fair slash you up."

"My skein, as you will note in my left hand, would be in your arm-pit."

"My fusil would have killed you long ago."

"Your fusil is bound to misfire. I'd pick both your eyes out of your helmet!" says James, warming to his oratory.

"I'd still want the fusil, my Lord."

"They are but a passing fancy. A good swordsman and a good horse will win the day."

Seeing all the attention Bawn is getting and how little is devoted to him, John grows angry and settles his account.

"He'll never understand! He's but a kerne."

Lord James hears nothing, so intent is he.

"Follow me, Bawn. This is thrust; this is parry."

He puts Bawn through the drill for a time and then rests one hand on his hip and his rapier tip on his boot top. To the others he says, "He's very agile for a gangling boy...and he is fast as forked lightning."

Young James speaks as if Bawn is gone. "He's a clumsy oaf without proper dancer's grace."

The right hand of Honoria's stops drumming on her lips and she steps forward from the shade.

"Perhaps I could cure that fault, father."

"Little sister could give grace to this lout? I doubt it much!" says John.

"May I try, father?"

Lord James looks to his daughter and then back to Bawn. He is thinking something other than dancing and swordsmanship.

"Perhaps later, my dear. We shall see."

51

Lord James leans forward in concentration, then relaxes and asks Honoria, "Have the O'Mahoneys arrived as yet?"

"They are to be here this evening, father."

"Then best you go to make yourself ready for our guests. That is meant for you, too, lads. Get on with it. You stay here, Bawn."

The excused break into a trot in anticipation of the coming festivities and all thought of lessons are gone.

"You are invited, of course, to attend the party, Bawn," states Earl James.

"Thank you, my Lord. It is most kind of you."

"I don't suppose you have ever attended a castle party before, have you?"

"I have been at Molahiffe, sir. There are no joys at that place."

"So I have been given to understand. Anyhow, you are invited to ours."

"Will there be dancing and drinks?"

James gets a grin going on his face. "Yes, there will be an abundance of both."

"That does sound a proper party, then," says Bawn.

"Quite so, young man. Quite so."

Chapter Six

Bawn's Education and Betrothal at Age Ten

"The Desmonds, like other magnates, had
complex marital habits, James no less so..."
Daniel McCarthy Glas

𝔄midst the flushing of false compliments the guests are
arriving and the party is starting. The light chatter is freely
spoken by Mora while horses and their owners are greeted by
James at the gate. Inside swirl many young blades and the
ladies from adjoining estates, dying on the dance floor in their
efforts to be Irish. Bawn has slipped badly from his good
behaviour and is casting about for a favourable eye within his
alcohol impaired vision. Aha, thinks he, or the like. In the
gloaming he repeatedly sees Fiona, with huge dark and mischie-
vous eyes that any drunken boy can tell show uncommon
intelligence. Fiona is winsome for being but ten and from all
appearances amidst the din of drink and music, a quiet charmer
susceptible to the impure intentions of the pretender to the title
of MacCarthy Mor.

The Fitzgeralds are either unaware or uninterested that
the boy is intoxicated and swimming the breaststroke through
the crowd to get to his victim. He thinks she will be a victim, at
any rate, but thus far his rate of conquest is near non-existent,
what with inopportune immaturity to start with and drunken-
ness to obliterate possibilities since he was seven. Their encounter earlier in the evening leads her to summarize her feelings
about doing the Munster two-step with him anymore, forever.

"No, Bawn, I don't care to dance with you anymore. You
step upon my feet and that hurts."

"I shall try to do better, Fiona. I shall be as gallant as
King Arthur and ask another chance."

"King Arthur is it? Not with those manners and that
sloppy dog following you everywhere!"

What she has said is true. There is a huge and sloppy dog left over from yesterday's dinner that has adopted Bawn and persists in accompanying him into even the most boring of situations. Bawn semi-turns to locate his faithful friend and sees that he has started making preparations to lift his right hind leg in the direction of the squatting out-of-work monastarian, Friar Padraic Tolan of the Strade Friary in Mayo, who has little better to do than cage drink and bone from his stable of sympathetic castle owners.

"Excuse me, but I must quickly rein in my great horse, Satenta."

"I think you are digustingly drunk. I am going to my room."

"Do you hear that, Satenta. She is going to her room!"

He is near to falling down as he makes the quick turn back from getting the dog away from the priest, but not before the beast has completed his mission against the leg of the bodhran player whose social and economic status does not permit even the slightest kick at the cur.

Bawn watches as Fiona leaves the hall. Satenta howls after her causing great embarrassment to the lovely girl and hastening her departure.

The party continues and the games are on, the conduct and purpose of which are oblivious to Bawn, who continues to regret Fiona's lack of understanding. Earl James and Mora now call the guests together in the centre of the hall for a special announcement.

"My Lady, and I - and our children - are most pleased that you could all come to our festival. Let no one's glass go empty."

Freeloading freeholders to the last man, woman and child cheer the idea that for the time being, everyone will drink as much as they please. Mora raises her glass to the crowd and speaks her piece.

"Now we would like to present something special. We shall have a betrothal!"

The assembled masses crow out the approval with the full and certain knowledge that this is truly an occasion.

"Let us retreat to the chapel where we have the ceremony planned,"

54

suggests Earl James.

"The two principals will be our daughter, Honoria, and the newest addition to our household, Bawn MacCarthy, heir to the MacCarthy Mor of Castle Lough!"

In the dull and melancholy world of the Fitzgerald demense, this is a truly hilarious bit of entertainment. Many of the stupified guests are apparently in the same fix and think so, too. There is nothing else quite so daring, and the group rushes out the door and into the chapel. Reassembled there, the wedding party then enters from the side and Honoria is stunningly dressed in a white gown and grinning a bit too much for a modest bride as she is presented at the altar.

Bawn is more or less lifted into walking down the aisle and deposited upright for the moment and holding Honoria's hand. He too is smiling a bit too much, but a permissible smile at that, considering his degree of tipsiness.

Oh, oh and oho. They are now going through the mock wedding ceremony with Lord James and Mora standing in the prescribed positions and helping Bawn to adjust to what to him is a moving floor which is tilting grievously. While the priest is droning on, he is thinking that in order to stand he will require at least a wall, or if he is to sit, it shall have to be in a chair with two strong arms set parallel to the shifting floor. What we have, in Bawn's opinion, is a geometric equation to belie drunkness in a serious degree.

By the time the thing is apparently over, Bawn is grinning ear to ear in the satisfaction, not that he has become betrothed, but that he has neither sunken unconscious nor become ill upon the vests of others. Everyone cheers the couple, but it is the priest who is taking the bows as it is impossible for Bawn to do so and Honoria is too shy a girl for that sort of frivolity at the boundary of a conquest.

Bawn is helped away past Lord James who is still grinning and whispering to the vigorous Mora.

"That ought to do it. He's locked into the family."

To which she replies in equally diminished decibles, "An Drimuin and Siva should be pleased, too. The joining of two great families!"

"Still and all," rejoins the ever thinking James, "I don't think we will tell him right off."

"I hope he likes surprises. The Red Stag of Munster has been roasted before our guests as witness. A piece de resistance, my Lord!"

"We shall see, Mora. We shall see."

In another great hall an Drimuin and Siva are sitting quietly while Walter is near to giving a health and welfare report on their fostered son, Bawn.

"So you are saying you saw him but he didn't actually see you?" asks Siva.

"That is how I view my visit to Askeaton, Lady Siva."

"Well, go ahead and tell us. We sent you there to do that, so tell us, please," urges an Drimuin.

"It was a fine visit, my Lord, my Lady, but I couldn't stand it there much longer. They do put on a party, I'll give them that."

"Tell us all about it, Walter. Who was there and what were they wearing?" asks Siva.

"Well, my Lady, I am not a proper person to ask about fashion, but Lady Bellington had on the most fetching...."

An Drimuin has had enough of the detractions and gets to the point.

"Jesus, Mary and Joseph, Walter! Will you get on with Bawn? Was he enjoying himself or was he not?"

"Sorry, sir, I was only trying to oblige. I would have to say, in my limited chance to make judgement, yes, he was having a good time, though I cannot be sure."

"What do you mean, 'I cannot be sure?'"

"Well, my Lord, there were so many guests there and so much drink being taken that I...."

"He was damn well drunk, wasn't he?"

"I'd have to say, sir that he was not unacquainted with intoxication at that moment."

"Drunk!"

"Drunk as you have ever seen him and more."

"It is time for him to be brought home, husband," declares the distressed Siva.

At that very moment in Askeaton, Bawn is wheedling his way into Fiona's bedchamber on the next night whilst her mother is elsewhere. After letting him, in Fiona has good reason to again change her mind and wish him and the huge dog away and further out of her life. Bawn is curing his hangover in the traditional way and is taking a few from a flask he carries loosely in his hand.

"You are to leave me alone or I will tell my mother what you did last night after the betrothal!"

"You must help me, Fiona. What was it I did last night that put you in this mood?"

"You don't remember, do you?"

"I wouldn't be asking you if I did."

Fiona looks straight at Bawn and excitedly says, "You came in here with your terrible dog, giving out with that King Arthur act and then you tried to kiss me and the dog started to bark at you or me or something and oh, it was just terrible!"

"Me or the dog, Fiona?"

"Both! Now get out of here!"

"I was just doing the damsel in distress parts with Merlin and all."

"Damsel in distress? I'll show you a damsel in distress!"

Fiona bounces rapidly to the bedchamber door and shouts down the dark corridor.

"Mother! Mother! Please come here!"

Bawn is drunk, but he is not stupid.

"I'll just be leaving now, if you'll excuse me."

Bawn and the puzzled dog shoot out the open door without a bow or further bark. "Lord, God!" says he. "I wish I knew what it is I keep doing here!"

Again, an Drimuin and his ever present senachel, Walter, are on their horses and on their way to Askeaton to collect young Bawn. An Drimuin is setting a very slow pace and there can be no doubt that Walter can understand why. This could be the end, but they don't think so.

Inside the castle, Lord James is far happier than he has been in months at the thought that Bawn will soon disappear. His tranquility is suddenly disturbed by the announcement that an Drimuin has arrived. Will the Lord MacCarthy take this dreadful son of his away or will he just be making more false promises of alliances against the Butlers of Ormond? Now he is in the room and with little to be said along those lines.

"My Lord James, I must advise you that Bawn will be leaving your castle and your keep with me. His service with you is ended and I must say it is not a moment too soon for both of us."

"By that, sir, I assume you mean yourself and him."

"Not exactly, Earl James, I meant yourself and me."

"Ah, yes. I take your meaning," says James. He must add something, he knows, but he knows not what. Then he says, "We did our best, my Lord, but it just didn't take."

"That is not an uncommon problem with Bawn. I fear he has a short attention span, to say the least."

"Nevertheless, we have enjoyed his company and he is quite a remarkable horseman. Will you be taking his dog? I'd like that if you did."

"Yes, we'll do that for you. By the way, I noticed young Gerald as we came in."

"Yes, is there something?"

"Well, yes and no. I seem to detect a certain blueness to his colour. Is he eating too many corns?"

"I don't think so. I think he is more blue than white because of his poor constitution. He rarely rides with us and runs more to the music and the drawing than the sword."

"But surely, James, you detect an uncommon appearance, do you not?"

"I see nothing, but I confess that he has a very different odour from the other boys."

"Perhaps then, it is my imagination and nothing more, for he's a finely put together fellow who only needs some sunlight and bog to make his limbs stronger and more able to swing an axe."

"Do you really think so? My, that would certainly be splendid if Gerald could swing an axe! What do you think I should do for the little fellow?"

"Well, there's only one man who can put him right, in my mind. That would be Moriarity. You know the one I mean, the one up in the Boggeragh Mountains?"

"That does seem a bit harsh, but..."

"You must have trust, Lord James. Trust is everything."

"Yes, I suppose you are right..."

Then enters Walter looking uneasy. He has a grasp on the shoulder of the chief's son and is pushing him toward the two.

"Pardon me, gentlemen, but young Bawn is awaiting your instructions, my Lord."

"So he is," replies an Drimuin, sternly putting his command to his son. "Go to your horse and get your silly-looking dog."

"Yes, father," responds Bawn eagerly.

Back-peddling quickly to the door with both eyes on his father and Earl James, in the event they are going to kill him, Bawn leaves the room. An Drimuin and James rise quickly to conclude their meeting.

"What is next for your son? I could certainly use him against the army of Ormond. Young Tom Butler is much the aggressor in my southern reaches."

"That's very kind of you, to be sure, but Johnny Meade is off to Oxford in a fortnight and I'm sending Bawn with him."

"Oxford, my Lord Donal? How unlikely."

"Just so, James. However, perhaps when he is finished or they are finished with him, he will be of some use to one of us."

"That is a faithful and trusting hope, Lord Donal."

"I quite agree, but then Oxford has performed a multitude of miracles in its several years. We'll be off."

And the three of them leave that place without a backward glance.

Chapter Seven

Bawn and Johnny Meade at Oxford

"Civilization and knowledge were all the
while encroaching on the realm of ignoranace."
G. M.Trevelyn

Descended from the great chiefs of the clan O'Driscoll is
the blackguard and smuggler, Liam. Owing an Drimuin back
taxes is nothing new, nor is it uncommon that between the two
of them they can work out an agreement that satisfies both.
Liam liveth in the the town of Baltimore and there his grandfather was saved from the men of Waterford who came to revenge
a more-than-likely oversight when they were swindled out of
their ships carrying wine by the O'Driscoll clan. The lads from
that eastern village surely would have succeeded in their ven-
geance as they sacked Baltimore and would have killed or
maimed the chief. But aha, a clever clansman seeing that the
leader of that Corca Laoidhe sept was chased to the roof of his
castle, shot an arrow attached to a line to grandad while the
later was dancing a lively and hot-footed jig atop his burning
castle. He gamely grasped the rescue effort and slid down to
his friends upon the ground who secreted him away forevermore and Amen.

There are many people who believe this story. Thousands don't.

Nevertheless, as to the subject of repayment and ships of
the sea, Liam is in the line for both, having the brigantine
Deidrie nipping about through the waters in search of items to
pirate or items to land for sale at a greatly reduced price due to
the lack of a Royal Majesty's excise tax.

Yes, sir and you can count on it, my Lord. He will away
with Bawn and Johnny Meade and put them into touch in
Bristol with the fat, sleek Harry Glanville, a merchant with Irish
ancestors and incredible connections.

Leaving the Long Quay at Kinsale Harbour, there is little
contendable motion on the surface. Howsoever, this condition

is changing cataclysmically by the time the Deidrie reaches the Middle Harbour. There are the guns on His Majesty's brig, Bowline, and they are trained on the Diedre and following her most closely. Oh, dear, perhaps too closely for some.

Liam is not a favourite person in the area as he has been known to capture maidens, most of them among the Kinsale willing, that is to say, non-virginal material from both the married and unmarried course of things there.

This is enough to upset some of the British garrison and they are mad to get a poke or a broadside into this despicable marauder whose loins, as well as the many loins of his crew, pose such a threat to the manliness of those living about.

The two are already sea-sick by the time they clear the Outer Harbour and Liam watches them and shakes his head. "Rotten little punks," thinks Liam. "I wonder, could I just sort of push them off into the sea as we pass the Saltees and be done with it?" He ponders only momentarily. He decides the results would endanger his good health and all those who look to him in their already perilous positions in life.

"Instead I will see to some fun."

First he proceeds to position himself so his ears are tuned to the complaints of illness.

"Oh, Christ save me! I'll never disobey my father again!" says Bawn.

"Don't take all of the rail. Leave a space for me!" says Johnny.

Back and forth across the breadth of beam they skate, they slide, they glide and occasionally slither. Gracious mercy and heavenly days, to listen to them one would have to conclude there has never been such a sickness aboard all the ships at sea.

Forward steps our captain with malice aforethought. His manner lacks charity. He will sort these scuts, to be sure.

"It's time for your rations! Salt pork, nice and fresh with the fat and rind still on. Some black rum to wash it down. How does that suit you?"

"Oh, for love of God, leave us alone," the two croak and gag.

Sick they are, but their survival is never in question and they arrive at the dock in Bristol. Such a relief is it that they are soon enough fit, though in weakened condition, when they are introduced by Liam to the man who can do the most. He is Harry Glanville and as such he has been through more than one siege in a busy lifetime dedicated to becoming a scoundrel and the scourgeous purveyor of favours and deeds derring-do.

Harry takes his role most seriously and has the good sense to inquire as to the well-being of his charges.

"Here we are, then. You do look a bit peaked, I must say. Did you have a rough crossing?"

"No, like a mirror all the way. Where are our chests?"

"Liam's bos'n will have them here shortly. I am to let you take two of my horses and give you directions."

"Is that all? No rest and no advice?"

"Oh, there's advice aplenty."

"Other than to stay off Liam's ships, what is it?"

"Simple. While you are up at Oxford, stay out of trouble, speak only English or Latin and take this if you catch the pox."

Harry is in the process of extracting a small box from his waist coat pocket. He sends it by hand to Bawn.

"Be careful of the women there, boys!"

"What is this?"

"Christ, sir, I wish I knew! Eye of the newt? The noses and fingernails of frogs? I don't know, but it works."

"So much for that, then. You said directions to Oxford?"

"Correct you are, young man. Correct you are. And..."

A load of baggage is being unceremoniously plonked upon the dock at their feet.

"...and the names of a few good stews you can stay at along the way. Here's the map I've drawn with all you'll ever need to know written upon it. There are also the names of two right clever men. One in Oxford and one in London who can reach me in case of emergency, if you know what I mean."

"That's it? Nothing else?" asks Johnny.

Down the dock is seen a peeler, walking deliberately and with an exaggerated swagger of over-expressed authority.

"Gentlemen, as much as I'd like to stay and chat, that officious looking swindler coming this way is, without doubt, looking to ask me some questions I have no desire to answer. We should all leave before he gets this far."

"It's a very old story, isn't it, Harry? Thank you anyhow.

63

See you someday!"

The three are quickly on their way, with Harry heading his ample hinder onto the Deidrie and Bawn and Johnny catching hold of their chests and cutting a line to the end of the dock where the horses stand ready.

Their journey is marked by the obvious shortcoming of tender feelings toward Catholic persons. No more are there houses where a priest can rest for there are no licensed priests. The country weather is sad and dreary, and has slowly depreciated into rain and filthy mud, stirred by the tired feet of the poor who wander forevermore in hunger and despair.

"I don't think we dare slow down. There is naught we can do but pity them," says Bawn.

"Will this now come to Ireland?"

"Worse, Johnny. Much worse, but we must now find a place to stay. What suggestions do you have?"

"I'd guess a church ruin, if we don't get to this place on Glanville's map called Swinedon."

"On this map of his it could just as well say, 'There be dragons!' like on your Uncle Friar Meade's old charts."

But find the inn they do, and before darkness they are in the brawling place, chewing on tough beef and eating molding bread.

"This is as bad as the fare at Molahiffe."

"Not quite. Bad, but nothing could be as bad as that was. Do you recall eating on that badger they said was a pig?"

"I'm trying not to. I..."

There is a tankard slammed onto their deal table and a voice unrestrained by modesty or learned decorum.

"You are unfamilar faces. What are you two young pups doing here?"

Johnny Meade is off the mark in a trice. He puts up his lie faster than most.

"We are young men of Christ on our way to see the righteous word against the Catholic cause now being carried out. God save the King!"

Bawn looks at Johnny in wonder and near awe. This lad will surely make a fine barrister.

"You'll have no trouble finding that. We are just readying to hunt down a loose priest spotted nearby if you'd care to join in the fun. He's hobbling about with a broken leg and should be easier to find than most."

"We've had a full day of that, but we'll take a drink anyhow," responded Bawn, fast enough himself on the track of a jar.

"You've a strange accent for Englishmen," says he of the tankard.

"We come from Lincolnshire, friend," says Johnny.

"You don't tell me? That is a far way from here I would suspect. You've come to see the sights."

"So we have, but we're off to bed now, alone, alas," says Bawn.

The priest-hunter staggers off to join his colleagues, sloshing inside and out.

"I'd rather have stabbed the heathen bastard."

"We'll likely get our chance to do that soon enough. Let us be to our beds and be away from here early."

The oats and meat are eaten by horse and men and in the morning the companions press onward toward Oxford. Along the way their necks are stretched, looking at tall places and persons unfamiliar and unfriendly. The map furnished by Harry Glanville has run out at the city gates with only placenames to guide them from that point. They must find their colleges and their lodging,

"What was the name of the college father gave us," asks Bawn of Johnny.

"It's called Brasenose, or Brasenhus, or Brewery or King's Hall."

"A good choice, I'm certain, but Christ's crutches, if it cannot decide upon its name, how in the name of Jehovah are we to find it?"

"I suppose we could ask someone."

So they struggle on, and gape and gaze at dirty signwriting and dirty streets and dirty looks. Suddenly they are face to face with an unknown thing - a crisis so to speak, of unsettling conduct there in the street.

"Hold on, Johnny! What in the name of blue-eyed Rebecca is that going on?"

"I have no idea. It is not hurley and it's not sliter...but what it is I cannot say."

65

"Look at that! Those boys are kicking a pig's bladder!"

"And the others are trying to kick it the other way. Jesu! You can smell that bunch from here!"

"It looks a grand game! Shall we join them?"

"Yes, by all means. We are here to absorb the English culture as your father said!"

Oh, mercy, what a mistake this is to be thus involved. Small boys bodies are thrust aside and cast into the air in the enthusiasm of the two large fellow's unbridled endeavours to gain this object. There is chaos amongst the costermongers. It is rolling this way and that and everyone is now strongly shouting and cursing foul epithets into heaven's air. In his second contact with the bladder, Bawn cries out, "Herdito!" in the most emphatic of Celtic manners and takes a mighty lash at the putrid thing. It bursts. The atmosphere is stiff with the stink of internal organs.

"What in God's name has happened?"

There comes a terrible roar as angry screams go up and cursing chants arise from every angle on the square. Then comes a storm of boys rousting for a kill against the destroyers. Leaping haycock, bailey buckets and strewn stalls, the two catapult themselves away, yelling words in the proper forms in fear for their lives.

"I'd say you broke their toy. Let us hasten to find our way out of this mess!" shouteth Johnny Meade.

"What a terrible stench!" replies the Bawn, and they hurtle to the coda in the great strides of their country backgrounds, scuttling down many yonder streets.

Oh, but soon they find their lodgings and are settled. But, just the one. That is Johnny taking slurps of knowledge and reading the law as it had never been read at Brasenose before him. Left, he is, to scan and skim the iambics of jurisprudence and praemunire. Oh, again, dear scholars, Johnny is a great one for the books and for the speaking and the working by candlelight, whilst Bawn is memorizing only the contours of the female buttocks and his slurping is done to many contours of ladies of all religious persuasions or no religion at all.

Smart eyed whore of fifteen years, Priscilla. Whore in name, lover in the game, voluptuous and energetic to match this Irish stag, Bawn. This is her niche, her calling in the newest expression of the oldest farthings. They are lying abed resting after a fierce round of unrestricted activity.

"My, Pris, where did you learn all of that?"

"Which part, my darling man?"

"All of it! You are magic!"

"Oh, it's nothing, really. You should see my mother."

"I'd love to, if she's half as charming as you!"

"Aw, you're full of it...but, look, it's getting light and I must go home. My old fella will kill me if I don't bring him some money."

"You have a husband?"

"Oh, no. Don't be silly. It's my father down from Glasgow who is after me. It's the gin, you know."

"Yes, I know. I know it quite well by now, Pris."

Principally, times flies, and in a state of alcoholic near oblivion it roars by at an astonishing rate. Hence a year is passing. Now, it has passed and in the lexicon of chancery, the toxonomy of which is periodic boredom, it is infrequently broken. Bawn sits in a lecture hall and sketches a lady whose physiognomy and bum seem equally etched in his brain. Now, he holds the picture at arms length to admire what he is doing. The carbon goes to velum and he is writing what? A ribald verse, of course, to go with the picture. The animus of Bawn yields not to pussyfoot. He is yawning great gulps of torpid air.

"This is all too boring."

"For you, yes. You don't have to make a living for yourself."

"This is the pity of it all. I'm bright and irresponsible. You are dull and studious."

"The only things you have studied thus far, Bawn, are the bottoms of tankards and whores."

Bawn turns the picture to Johnny's eyes and asks,

"When are you finished in this grim place, Johnny?"

"I am as near to done as I can be. In two weeks I shall be searching for new digs in Furneval Inn of London."

"What? You'd leave me here to die?"

"Unless you plan to come along, I will. You will as likely die of the pox in one place or the other."

The Don stares as Bawn breaks into laughter.

"I'd never leave you, Johnny. I think London will be just

the place for me in the spring."

The fortnight passes without note.

As London is to so many, so it is to Bawn and Johnny. A coach clatters to a convulsive stop at an Inn of the Chancery.

Johnny, now a finely dressed gentleman, dismounts and enters the establishment. Already inside, Bawn, is well into his daily program of keeping London's gin industry in business.

"For God's sake, Bawn, pull yourself together. You have an invitation to attend the King at Hampton tonight!"

"Attend the King? What is this all about?"

"I haven't the slightest idea. Something your father arranged, I'm certain of that."

"God's teeth! I've absolutely nothing to wear!"

"Then get something, you great oaf! There has to be something on Portobello that suits you. I'll loan you my lace...if you haven't already sold it."

Stalls are tumbling with unsold goods. Huge Bawn plunges through the line and snatches here and there. Nothing. Not one thing. Ah, the stallkeeper is waving something large. It is black. It is velvet.

"Let me see that one. It seems a bit small and is too much black."

"It belonged to an unfortunate undertaker visiting London from Edinburg who fell upon hard times and then into the Thames. It is quite dry by now."

"Hence, a shrunken suit."

"Ah, sir, but at a shrunken price! Think of the savings you are to gain!"

"I'll have to take it. I'm due to be in Hampton in three hours time. I'm meeting the King."

"I was going to go, too," says the stallman, "but something more pressing has come up. If it isn't one engagement it's another! What is one to do?"

"But, I really am. I ...ah....get the notion you do not believe me. I will pay you next week."

"Next week as you did last month?"

"Well, as soon as I can manage."

"Perhaps King Henry will loan you a few bob. No harm in asking."

Away gallops Bawn and so dressed in black to Hampton he doth go.

Beautifully coiffed, diademed with the royal purple band and looking quite smug is Queen Catherine Parr. She is sitting on her couch while colourfully costumed ladies and gentlemen are standing about in stunningly stupid positions in this brightly candled ballroom. To either side stand footmen and minor Lords hoping for recognition. There, beside our Queen Catherine, is Mary, daughter of Henry. She is plump, ordinary and merry, age, perhaps three decades, staring at what the Court page is announcing.

"Your Majesty, Donal MacCarthy, son of an Drimuin the MacCarthy Mor and the Lady Siva of the Kingdom of Kerry."

This is a problem. Bawn, in his ill-fitting, second-hand black mourning suit dares only a bow before the Queen as deep as his breeches will permit.

"I welcome you in the name of King Henry VIII. He is indisposed with the gout and has taken to his bed. He commands that I receive you and it is with great pleasure that I greet our cousin from Kerry."

"Your Royal Majesty, it is with sorrow I learn of his illness. May I express my wishes for lesser discomfort for our King?"

"Thank you Donal MacCarthy. May we offer you a refreshment? It is a dry and dusty journey from London town."

"I thank you, your Grace.   That would be most welcome."

Queen Catherine turns to her right side and looks at the ladies there.

"Have you been yet presented to Lady Mary, the King's eldest daughter? Mary, show our Red Stag of Munster to the servers. Enjoy the evening, Donal."

"Thank you, your Grace. In such company I will indeed. My Lady Mary, I'm sorry to impose."

"It is my very great pleasure, sir. May I lead you to the entertainment?"

One must bow one's best bow and make firm yet languid steps backward when leaving the Queen's devoted attention and never mind with whom you are. This is what Bawn is doing with the left arm extended to hold up the pleasing hand of Mary, who does a bumpsie-daisy to the Queen. The breeches stretch dangerously north to south, but hold firm and frozen as his sweet smile takes up two hectares of his face. Mary looks again at Bawn's sombre black ensemble and enquires most mischievously.

"I'm sorry, Donal MacCarthy. Was it a relative or a friend?"

Bawn is slow to respond, then cops on and laughs a good one.

"Neither, my Lady. It may have been the death of my Irish innocence, however!"

Bawn and Mary dance the dance of dances to the utmost while eyes are glued upon each other long before Tom Jones was ever known. Oh, blasphemy, blasphemy! You guessed it.

In the soft light of scented candles in merry Mary's copper-coloured bed see Bawn's undulating figure, still poised over the non-inert form of the one on the bottom. Beneath the once pounding bulk, a hand is reaching toward his face. It slowly brushes back his long auburn-black hair, it is tracing his ears, his nose, his lips to the rhythmic, quivering motion.

"You are magnificent, Bawn. More so out of that horrid black suit."

"It was but a temporary thing, Mary. Just something I threw together at the last minute."

There is now some girlish giggling denoting satisfaction and plans for more of the same.

"We'll set the clothes right in the morn. You'll be best in dark blue and red, I think. And, father has more jewels than he could wear in ten years! Oh, this is wonderful."

Bawn's body is now resting on Mary's to some extent, and he is at her again. No. He isn't. Not quite, at least, at this moment. He is resting his broad back by forming a tent above her with his shoulders. See, there, she is peeking awkwardly upward, trying to find his eyes but cannot. Oh, dear. He is so big.

"What is it like to live in an Irish castle? Castle Lough, isn't it?"

"It is not so grand, Lady Mary. It's a raw beauty, over looking Lough Leane. Not much at all. But, it is serene as compared with Oxford and London."

70

"Does everyone speak English there? I'm so anxious to see it."

"Yes, we do speak English there...or Latin... or French. But no Spanish, if you are hunting for our sympathies."

"My mother is Spanish. I will teach it to you in the most agreeable way. Privately; in bed."

Mary is now sighing blissfully and Bawn is taking on the look of one who is being herded.

"My Lady is too kind," he says.

"It is so exciting! I shall renounce my regal rights to the throne as soon as father makes his trip to Bath for his health. He'll be in a much better mood then. I cannot wait to begin making our plans..."

Bawn rolls over on his side as the hair holding the sword of Democles breaks, but misses him. His mind is now two lengths ahead of Mary's cunning.

"Exciting, indeed...and yes, so many plans to be made in so short a time."

"I shall have Hans Holbein do your head."

"My head?"

"Yes, dear heart, your head."

Bawn turns away and a worried look is upon his brow. To himself he says, "Holbein will do my head? Christ's captors! I must...."

What then, is this? Beneath the poorly lighted Boar's Head. It is Bawn and Johnny standing deep within their dark cloaks, huddled against the slimy weather on the dockside at Bristol. Night is everywhere and the ships along the quayside are swaying with the incoming tide. The great hawsers creak and groan in a chorus of protest as the loosened riggings slap against the tall masts. The ships are eager to leave this place and the cryer hurries past the two with his storm lantern raised high against the lashing spray. Furtive is as furtive does, whilst the lads look anxiously for sign of their saviour.

"Johnny, are you absolutely certain Glanville said he'd meet us here at high tide?"

"His exact words were, 'Meet me at the Boar's Head on the dockside at 9 pm.'"

"It won't be Holbein that does my head when Mary finds out I've gone back home. What time is it now?"

71

"That cryer going by means it's 9 pm."

"Hail Mary, full of grace..."

"Wait! Don't waste a prayer quite yet. Hang on! Isn't that him there beside the carriage? Yes! It's him, all right. Hard to miss that fat arse!"

Glanville the fat, sleek, sloth approaches them with increasing speed as his momentum builds slowly in the effort to make haste.

"Bawn, Johnny. A pleasure to see you fine gentlemen."

"And a pleasure to see you, Harry. Especially under the circumstances at hand."

Legal Johnny sees the need for shortening the time in the open.

"You know why we are here, Harry. You said when we met you on our way up to Oxford that you could make us disappear as if by magic if ever the time came!"

"And I take it the time has come?"

Bawn's feet are itching.

"We need to leave without delay and without anyone's knowledge. Is that clear, Harry?"

"Say no more, sir, say no more! You've sent for the right man, to be sure. I am the wizard to destroy all traces of you. I will wave..."

"Stow it, Harry! Just get us out of here!"

Harry Glanville is not offended in the slightest. He is well paid to take abuse upon such occasions and he slips between the two, takes the arm of each next to him and turns them toward the end of the dock. There is a murky sailing ship putting out a gangway and loosening lines. The single oily lamp lights near to nothing as the wind suddenly rises, lifting a corner of the fog that is closing in.

"Here we have the speedy vessel to take you away!"

"Oh, God! What have you done, Harry? It's the Deidrie again!"

"Again you be correct, young fellow, and with the artful Captain Liam O'Driscoll at your service once more!"

"I will kill you one day, Harry! You know that, don't you?"

"Ah, but you wanted away and today. You have it. Why be angry at me?"

72

"He's dead right, Bawn. We cannot ask for swifter service. We will be gone before anyone knows it!"

"Now, if you'll just leap up the gangway, that fat fellow standing at the railing will put you right. Greet your father an Drimuin for me, Bawn. Rumour from Kerry has it that the giant may have the life to reach a century."

"That would be wrong, Harry. Father is not well. He is much upset by the English planters and the Desmonds. He is at war with both."

"Better the Desmond's than the King's army."

"Perhaps so, but I doubt he thinks that."

"Whatever his health, serve him faithfully and well. He is the last of the great chiefs and deserves your attention. As the next Mor you could well be the King of Munster. Mind the step. Have a safe journey."

The crossing to Ireland is ended when the Diedre makes the port of Kinsale at high tide. As the two are disembarking, they are met by one of Johnny Meade's father's stable boys.

"How in the Lord's name did you do that, Johnny?"

"Do what, Bawn?"

"Arrange to have a stableboy meet the ship with horses?"

"Let us just say that the reading of law is a wonderous thing."

"You aren't going to tell me, are you?"

"Never give a rogue an advantage. I decline to answer, sir!"

"Well, bugger you and be done, I say."

"Will you be staying with my family at Ballintubber?"

"That's very kind, Johnny, but I'd best be going. Too many of the King's men in this place."

"Yes. Should they find even me here, they'll ask about you."

"Tell them nothing. Tell them I've left for Spain. Tell them anything you like."

"Which is it then, Bawn, nothing or anything?"

"I'll leave that to you, you conniving charlatan, you!"

Bawn mounts the proffered horse and swings its head to the end of the Long Quay and salutes with his whip.

"Come by when next you're about, Bawn!"

"Not for a while, but when I find out how my father is I'll

do so. I'm off to Castle Lough and home, friend. Stay well."

"And you the same, Bawn. Stay well."

Chapter Eight

An Drimuin's Death: Bawn Falls in Love

That the sons of the king-
Oh, treason and malice -
Shall no more ride the ring
their own native valleys.
                    O'Gnive

Bawn has his sights fixed before him. He is tucking in to some crubeans and cabbage with great enthusiasm until his mother, Siva, catches his fork in mid-air with a penetrating and difficult question.

"Will you be staying here, Donal? Are you again in some kind of trouble? What are you going to do now?"

That is three penetrating and difficult questions, not one. Knife now joins fork in mid-air and then the hands drop to the table and his neck piece is a napkin to wipe his rather greasy face.

"What am I going to do now, Mother? I am going to finish this dinner and then I am going up to see my father. Is there something else?"

"Don't be harsh with me, Donal. I did not summon you home. You came flying in here as though the shrikes were upon you!"

"I'm sorry, Mother. I am a bit flustered, to say the least. What is it you wish to tell me?"

"As you must certainly have gathered by now, your father is dying. I'm trying, but I cannot do everything he wishes."

"And, I can? Is that it?"

"No, that is not it, but you would do well to tell him that you will look after his country and continue his traditions."

"I will do that, Mother, but don't expect me to follow in his footsteps. I have always done things my way. I'll go to see him now."

"Your being able to do things your way was largely at your father's expense. Keep that in your head, if you can."

"I shall think of nothing else, Mother. Now, if you'll excuse me I shall visit him."

Gracious, in a fit he flies up the 27 steps in hurler's time. At the top he knocks a few sharp raps at the heavy oak door and it is opened by his father's bodyman. There is no exchange between them. Bawn approaches his father's bed and there is the ashen an Drimuin. His tired and rheumy eyes follow his son's approach. His arms lie outside the heavy woolen covers. Bawn gently places them under the bedclothes and his hand lingers on his father's shoulder.

"Is it you, my son? I can't see anything in this ridiculous position."

Bawn lifts his huge father's withered and weak body forward and props the pillows up a bit.

"Not so much! I get more dizzy propped up like a silly puppet!"

"Yes, father. Is there anything I can do for you? Would you care to hear some poetry? Perhaps your lute player?"

"To hell with the whole lot of them. They're all a bunch of old women. Tell me about what is going on outside. Are more English coming to Maine Valley?"

"Nothing comes to my ears about new English, father. The crops for the kerne's winter look to be more than fair and the cattle are fattening nicely."

"Is that all there is? Tell me something I can listen to without falling asleep."

"Well, there is news that the Bishop of Cashel has taken a new wife. One of the O'Kel girls from Molahiffe Parish."

As an Drimuin hears this his right hand comes from beneath the bed-clothes and he takes a solid whack at his son.

"Strewth," says he, and with this he rolls over and is dead.

Bawn nods to the bodyman and leaves, hand to mouth.

Such a mournful day in Killorglin's burial place of the MacCarthy clan. The wind is moaning its sadness up over the Cromane bar and the air is bitter at the death of an Drimuin. Here are eight pall-bearers straining their way up the hill to where the rocks have been rearranged and a grave-site made.

Hear the mourners as they wail the Ullaho like banshees. A chorus to the dead is starting much too high and those who are attempting it are perishing for the lack of breath. On the top of the mountain stands Jer McSwinney making a terrible wreck of things on the bladder pipes. Siva and Bawn look about forlornly, hoping no one is noticing the appalling blats. No one is. The priest drones on and on as is the usual case in these parts of Kerry.

A sudden and welcome silence, save for the whistling wind and the sleet is hitting the wooden coffin as it is being lowered to further wailing accompaniment. It is now in the hole and the priest nods to Siva, hoping for something. He starts with a few words.

"Requiescat in pace. Dona eis requiem aeternum...."

Siva steps out to the edge of her now everlasting abyss.

"We, the people of the Cartacht, pay homage to thee, oh mighty ruler, warrior and defender of your people. Why, oh mighty one, are you thus called to the halls of the heroes? Why have you left us here in the mountain wilderness while you hunt with the blessed, far into the mountains beyond the line of the western ocean? Why have you sought pleasure before duty, youth before sagacity of age and strangers before your people? Mighty, virtuous Lord, long may your shadow be missed in the halls of your earthly power."

Siva is facing her son and raises her arm to bring him to the graveside. He is staggering just a touch, having had the one or two taken. A deep breath is pulled from the mountain's clean and bountiful air. He is thinking, "Why in the name of God are we asking these stupid questions? He is just dead." He says,

"A true gentleman. And that's all there is to anything."

He now pauses and stops. He is turning away, anxious to leave. Siva, Elaine, Mhurien and Sabbah are relieved at this and follow him down the drenched boreen to the bottom of the darkening mountainside.

The last great Red Stag of Munster is dead, yes, but is he the last great Red Stag of Munster? Hmmm and hmmm again and again. How are we to know?

Siva and Bawn are sitting by the fireside at Castle Lough, each alone and after so many separated years, uncomfortable with the other's company. Efforts rise to Siva's throat and

77

ahems as well.

"Bawn, it's three months since we buried your father and you're still sitting around moping as though you've been whipped. It's time for you to assume your duties. You're of age and will soon be the holder of the White Rod with the title of MacCarthy Mor and leader of all the MacCarthy clans."

"I'm aware of that, Mother."

"Are you also aware that there are now responsibilities other than giving parties and attempting to impregnate all the girls from the cottages?"

"Really, Mother. And, what might those be?"

"You know right well. You must marry and raise a family. We need an heir. These are things you seem intent on ignoring."

"What are you getting to, mother? Is there someone special in your mind?"

"There is, yes. Honoria Fitzgerald. She is a proper lady and eligible."

"You cannot be serious. She's a Fitzgerald and my sister Elaine is being deceived by that James. One of us going into that family of idiots is enough!"

"I am a Fitzgerald, Bawn, and they are not all idiots. If you disapprove of Honoria so strenuously, there must be someone else."

Triumphant is her wonderous womanly skills of intuition. "A woman always knows. Who is it?"

"Yes, there is another girl, if you must know. Her name is Celia. She is the daughter of our leatherer and sister to my friend, Cormac."

"Our leatherer. A common leatherer? Have you lost your senses? And you having just put down the mighty name of Fitzgerald?"

"Mother, Celia is a fine girl, and quite apart from being Cormac's sister, she is of splendid character and has great beauty. She will be a credit to the name MacCarthy, should she accept me when I ask her to marry me."

"Of course she will marry you! Your head is as thick as the hair on a hedgehog's hind quarters if you don't realize no girl in the kingdom of Kerry would refuse you! And you, of all people, speaking of virtue!"

Bawn is only slightly deflated and wonders at his gene pool.

"I cannot be all bad. I got the way I am from somewhere, Mum."

"Don't you 'mum' me! How can you think of such a thing? Proposing to a cottage girl!"

"Beware, Mother. You are talking about the girl I plan to marry."

Click, click and whirl. Hustle and bustle and odours of horses and golden pot pies. There below is Tralee Fair, colourful and gawdy and wonderous for all to behold before diving into the others of humanity rolling about with the abandonment of their dreary lives. Such gaiety can only be afforded once a year and this is it. Bawn and Cormac on the rise, looking smartly about for signs of dear Celia and her friend, come to meet them, to oggle the crafts, eat a pheasant or two and drink from a keg.

A white, shining head is spotted by Cormac.

"Look, yonder, Bawn. See there by the stall of the weaver Chullen. It's sister Celia and her friend, Eílis Cremin."

The two walk rapidly to intercept these two girls and from his height above the crowd Bawn sees the most beautiful girl he has ever seen in his short life. Oh, yes. Lightning strikes between his eyes, his knees are shattered and not by Celia. It is Eílis. Oh, my God, oh, my Goddess of fifteen years with green eyes, long red hair and precious body in full bloom of Irish beauty! He is dead and gone to heaven, stunned and speechless for seconds. A boar chased by children nearly bowls him over but Cormac jerks him out of harms way and keeps him upright as Bawn then stumbles over a tent post. Cormac introduces the two.

"Bawn, this is Eílis Cremin, the daughter of the captain of the guard at Castle Lough, Frank Cremin. Eílis, this is Lord MacCarthy."

Bawn is gob-smacked. He stutters stupid compliments irrelative to anything current. Stars, buttercups, moonpaths and roses; fathers, sons and Holy Ghosts. Utter garbage. Eílis steps back a bit, hand to open mouth, but smiling. Good natured Celia is giggling.

"Where have you been all of my life, dear Eílis?"

"She has been nowhere but your castle, Lord Donal. She

has been under your very nose except for the fact that you were never there and when you were her father kept her out of sight for every good reason."

"Oh, Celia, that is not so. He is a wonderful father, only a bit over-protective for I have been wanting to meet the new Mor and be of good service as my father has been."

Heaven only knows what is going through Bawn's flimsy head at this point, unaccustomed as he is to kind offers.

"Bawn, you deceitful rogue, you be good and proper to our little Eílis or I shall knock those pearly teeth out of your ever open mouth!" says Cormac.

Wonderous vibrations tear desperately at Bawn's heart. Mentally, he is making great leaps and pirouettes and doing the 12 stations of the cross simultaneously. Never, never has he felt such a surging thrill and exuberance of instant love for any kind of creature, dogs included.

"Well said, brother Cormac," says Celia.

One would think that she might be disenchanted, losing Bawn to Eílis before her very eyes, but that is not at all the case. One can only conjecture that her heart belongs to some other brave man; brave, indeed, if they must pass the muster of Cormac. Bawn hears the warning quite clearly.

"Cormac, my friend, I promise you'll never have the need. I would never befool this fair beauty."

"Such a statement from a man with your reputation, Lord Donal!"

"My reputation was gained before I met you. My swearing before you is the truth!"

"Aye, but where will it go now that you have met me?"

"That will end here and now with a question. I pledge that if you will have me as your husband I will go before your fearsome father and ask for your hand."

Oh's and ah's well around the group, with shrieks of delight in a minor key from Celia as she clasps Eílis to her plunging neckline. Then silence of gigantic levity returns their senses. Wot next, wot next? Celia breaks the spell.

"My soul, I have heard of the lightning and thunder of true love, but this is the first time and likely the very last time I have or ever shall see it! She has been waiting to meet you for ages, it seems and all she had to do was walk in the sunshine and you propose!"

"She walks in the sunshine of my heart, Celia."

"That's the most beautiful thing I ever heard," says Cormac, wiping a tear from his duct.

What can she say? How will she say it if she has the words?

Eílis speaks slowly and clearly, with far more forethought than is normally possible during the epochs of the Tralee Fair.

"If you see my father asking for my hand and if he gives his permission and if you agree to the Brehon Law that a wife may justly leave her husband should he deceive or displease her, I will marry you in the Holy Church."

These people are dead stunned. Look at their faces! There is nothing there. Frozen like a mud pie. Stirring replaces staring and a tiny movement starts in the oversized frame of Bawn. His legs are the first to go. His left knee touches the ground and his right hand reaches for the left of Eílis. It is taken and brought to his lips. Oh, dear God, I'm going to cry. The raw and spontaneous, unaccustomed beauty of it all!

"I more than agree to all you ask, dear Eílis. I shall go to see your father tomorrow if that is not too much a delay. First, let us celebrate!"

"Yes, let us celebrate, by all manner and means!" shouts Cormac.

"By all manner and means!" joins Celia. "I'm starved! Let us have roast fowl and red beer!"

"I couldn't have said it nicer!" states Bawn.

Off they are to the stalls. Bawn buys mountains of flowers and a great white stallion she admired for but a moment. At this Eílis stands upon her tippy-toes and kisses Bawn's fair cheek. He responds by picking her up in his arms and tenderly kisses her upon her red, sweet, springtime lips. It doesn't end there, but this day does. Such joy and happiness may never end for the two of them.

"I must return to my father before darkness. He knows I am to meet you and was most firm that I not spend too much time with you this first day."

"That is as one would expect from a good father, Eílis," says Cormac.

"I will call upon your father at the armoury in the morning."

"I'll warn him, dearest Bawn!"

As promised, Bawn enters the armoury quarters and finds Frank Cremin, Eílis's father and captain of the guard, sitting at a table under a scowling face radiating gloom in every direction, but pointed primarily at his chief, Bawn. A black and white herding dog wanders about, sniffing the strange visitor and rolls over on his back in submission. This is a good omen. Frank's dark mood is not.

"So! You have noticed my little girl, Eílis, at last, have you? And what intentions do you have for her?"

Bawn puts down the bottle of Old Ballybrack, vintage ten days poitín on the table.

"I want to marry her, Frank Cremin."

Frank is not your man for awaiting invitations. He takes the bottle in both hands and pulls the stop with his irregular teeth, holds the bottle up to the light and then takes a very long pull which is followed by a hacking cough.

"That's a fine drink, lad."

He passes the bottle to Bawn who matches the pull, but not the cough, which as the enabler, would be rude.

"Marry my Eílis, is it? She's not but 15, Lord Donal. Marry her and live where?"

"Live in Castle Lough, after a church wedding and all the legal that's asked for. The lady of the castle and all the privileges that go with it. That's my vow."

"And, what will you be asking for the bridal price? There is to be a bridal price for I am a regular man."

"Oh, I couldn't really ask for anything at all, Frank."

They go dumb and each takes another whack at the bottle. Pause. Pause.

Then Frank Cremin squints first this way and then that, surveys the face of his present adversary and future son-in-law.

"Name your price or forget her."

Bawn is not backing off, but he fears the wrong reply would shatter their fragile relationship of the day. Decisions, decisions. Go for high and risk rejection? Go for low and risk insulting a proud man and the family name? Do something, you idiot! He bids low.

82

"Forty shillings and not a penny less!"

Frank is about to lose it with the joy of such a reasonable and well thought-out offer. He uncoils from the chair and his massive shoulders rise in pride. The garrulous Frank Cremin is about to make the deal of the century. He reaches out his hand and takes Bawn's to pump it. Bawn's fingers are numbed by the vice which grips them. He is grinning in sheer pain and joy.

"Done and done, then," issues Frank Cremin.

"And, that herding dog."

"You want Elizabeth there? She don't take kindly to Fitzgeralds of Desmond, she don't."

Bawn's grin speaks as much as his words, which are:

"I know, Frank. All the better!"

But, not the better for the Catholic Church and the robed special emissary of the Bishop of Cashel who has arrived on a visit to Castle Lough. He is angrily lecturing Bawn in the great hall while mother Siva is standing aside and hugely enjoying the moments as they pass.

"Your letter has been received asking permission to marry Eílis Cremin," glowers the visitor.

"That would be correct, your Eminence."

"I am directed to advise you by this notice from the Bishop of Cashel that permission is not granted."

Bawn is struggling to keep his composure.

"And, has the bishop given his reason?"

"He has, Donal MacCarthy."

"What would it be, if I may ask?"

"The complaint filed is from James Desmond, 14th Lord of Desmond."

"On what basis, My Lord?"

"That you were betrothed to Honoria at the age of ten while fostered at their Castle Askeaton. Having been so declared and proven, no marriage between yourself and Frank Cremin's daughter Eílis can be approved."

"This is ridiculous. I was drunk. I am not repsonsible for what was made to happen when I was drunk at the age of ten!"

"I fear, dear sir, that your age and your condition are inconsiderable in the interpretation of the bishop. You were betrothed."

"I do not care how it is interpreted! I will marry Eílis as

planned!"

"The Bishop can only condemn such a wedding, not bless it!"

"Condemn it then! It will change nothing!"

This is way too much for any bishop's emissary to take. Not on your life, he won't. He snatches at his surplice and storms out of the hall. Siva is outraged and approaches Bawn in three meaningful strides.

"You would marry outside our sacred church? Are you mad or merely a fool?"

"Both, Mother. I am mad for Eílis and will let no outlandish tradition or befuddled Bishop stand in the way. I will marry her in our derelict church at Glandore. Then we shall marry in a Druid ceremony at the Standing Rocks and then we shall have a feast at Daniel and Moira Cremin's Ballinohour Castle and I shall bed my bride there!"

"You are so crude, Donal. A fat lot of good Oxford did for you! You had this all planned, didn't you?"

"It was ever so, Mother. I may be crude in your eyes, but in the eyes of my father I would be seen as determined and in a way, righteous!"

"You are also a prat, Donal Bawn!"

A priestless ceremony is not a joke and few would have the temerity to do it. Few, indeed, would dare risk the ire of all the supreme beings in Ireland, not to mention the Pope as can be imagined. Few would have the audacity to add to it a Druid ceremony just two miles from the abandoned church where the wedding is taking place. Only Bawn's stubbornness will carry the sweetness and light of Eílis to altar and sacred stones. Virtual viscera to the power of ten and back again on to the surface of the placid bay below them as the guests pulverize what's left of our church walls. March, sway, walk and pull the cart to the Standing Stones and caustic kilted McSwinneys where Mahoneys once ruled. Oh, vast jars of drink in the afternoon put forth by nine ladies of disorderly affairs! No one could be more attenuated in the art of staying sober than Bawn. He is magnificent and looks it in his silks, his brocades, his lace, his silver, his bonny attitude around the wall of casks spewing amber plonk.

Save your energy as the party is swept unprotesting to

the great castle of Cremin power called Ballinohour where Daniel and his boring and boozey wife called many things, but named Moira, exist. Seated at the table in front of the hoodlums are those two and the other two, the guests just married twice. Moira is in an exceptionally aggressive mode and peers drunkenly down her face at Bawn.

"He's a Norman, that one!"

"Fer Christ's sakes, Moira, that's the chief and he just got married. That's why we're here. We're celebratin' cousin Eílis being wed to him."

"I tell you, he's a Norman! He's what they call an imposter."

"Moira, shut your flappin' mouth or I'll get rid of yez forever!"

"Sure you would. That would be a Cremins for you. First you get me in a family way and then you marry me with a fusil stuck in your ear and now you're going to expose me to the drastic elements by throwin' me out of the door."

"Yes, Moira," says Bawn. "And if you don't quiet down I'll take you home and cook you in place of your father's ten year overdue pig tax. I'll feed you to my dogs, is what I'll do!" says the laughing chief.

"Forgive her, Bawn. She's had everything go wrong here at the castle this week. She'll be just fine once the eatin' starts. You'll see her calm down then, it's sure!"

"Don't be too harsh with my relatives, husband. Don't treat me that way or you'll lose me."

"You tell him, Eílis," says friend Cormac.

"Remember what I told you at the Tralee fair!"

"No need to remind me. I would never let you leave me. Not ever."

"But, Bawn, if you displease me too much, I can leave you."

"Then be assured you will not be displeased," says Bawn as he sweeps her up in his arms and carries her from the hall to the wild applause of these rude anticipants. Up, up and away to the waiting bedchamber where all is lost in meaningful whispers and then terms of sweet silence.

Chapter Nine

Bawn Loses Ellís But Keeps Son Donal

His curling hair is as fair as
*   the leaves' sun and shade,*
His white hands are unbranded
*   by rough shovel or spade.*
O Creator who makest
*   windy weather and still,*
Lead O lead me where none will heed me
*   to weep my fill!*
*   Donal O'Sullivan*

Unto them a child is then born and yet another Donal is he named. The joy, the serenity, the everlasting beauty of child rearing, the games, the dirty, smelly bottoms in pre-talc and diaperless Castle Lough, the running noses, the noise, the confusion, the sicknesses, the unceasing screaming, the sleepless nights, harping against the drink, the peace in taking the latter.

And then another. And then another. And then one night at David Lyster's alehouse in Baltimore, Bawn is cutting a deal with the O'Driscolls. He and his legal arm and lifetime friend, Johnny Meade sitteth on the right hand of the MacCarthy rhymer and bardic poet, the 24 year old Aíne O'Daly. One look and one instantly sees a tall, raven-haired, voluptuous temptress. Look again. Aha. She knocketh back rum in port in quantities unimaginable. The eyes, oh, the eyes of black remain uncrossed despite the assault of the enzymes found in such a refreshment.

Listen. Just listen to the lines she talks in perfect rhythm with good rhyme and for such deep reasons. She is magnificent and she is a target for Chief Donal who is coming undone at the sight and sound, assisted in his powers of decision by you know what. He is near pissed, a state common enough in these ploughlands. Johnny stands ready while sitting with him, anxious.

"Will you look at that one, Johnny. My God, she's a fine

poet and performer. I don't mind telling you she's a fair piece of woman, too!"

"She's a fair piece of woman, alright. It's Aíne O'Daly and she has skinned her share."

"Skinned her share? Why haven't I seen her before?"

"I'd have to say it is because you've always been very lucky."

"So what has she done besides write cracking good verse?"

"Do you really mean you don't know her story...or have you failed to listen, as usual?"

"Honest to God, Johnny. I don't know her from Adam's off ox!"

"It wouldn't take you long to Biblisize her, if you get my drift."

"So, tell me about her and I'll decide."

"She was married for just one day to a distant cousin of yours. It was the great Blind Drunk Daniel MacCarthy Mor. I recall him ever so slightly for he was older than most when he married Aíne and didn't last long after that. One day, to be exact."

"The marriage lasted one day? How so?"

"It's true. He lived but one day. Sadly for Daniel, he was found the morning after the nuptuals beneath the window of the bridal chamber with a stiletto in his ribs, but not a breath of life in his body. No one was ever fined the eric for his murder, the Brehon refused to hear the case and the English avoiding the local political problem, turned a blind eye."

"What happened to this Aíne then?"

"To say a shadow of suspicion hung over her would be the truth, but her next husband faired better for a while. He was a man of the O'Driscoll Baltimore named One-Eyed Lorcan. This handsome Lorcan, a genius of the tin whistle, died of violent stomach disorder six months to the day after he'd wed the widow Aíne. Again, nothing was said, but much was thought."

"You only pause, Johnny! Good God, is there more?"

"I fear there is. The tongues watered and wagged when her next voyage on the sea of matrimonial bliss was with a Glin Fitzgerald. Not a White Knight at all, and not a day under 75.

He had sat a bachelor on his nice little pile of gold coins until this lovely lady bard caught his one good but rheumy eye. It was love, love, instant love, as one could imagine. Here was he, in this room; bald, half-crippled, leaning forward with willow cane and hands tucked under his chin and salivating as Aíne recited her poetry before this very fireplace."

Bawn is getting more excited and his laughter is half in mirth, half in anticipation of Johnny's next words.

"What in heaven's name did she do?"

"It is said Aíne fairly swooned at the sight of this dynamic creature of obvious virile masculinity."

"She married him as well...for the pure love for the man, of course!"

"She did, indeed. Aíne's arsenic must have been diluted as the old codger lived for a year and she was pumping the stuff into him at an astonishing rate. Nothing was ever proven against the daughter of your clan's hereditary bards, but it is certain that she has drunk and gambled away most of the old Fitzgerald's fortune in the few years that has followed his much anticipated demise."

"A fascinating story, Johnny. And to think I knew nothing about her until now!"

"And, as your friend and legal adviser, I'd say your best bet would be to forget you ever did know anything about her!"

The enchanted Bawn rises from his bench and stretches to his full length. Her recitation stops without finish and her hand goes to her glass, her eyes bang up against his and reel back coyly to downcast position.

"She seems quite sweet, really. Quite demure, so to speak."

"Fold it, Chief Donal. She holds all the better cards and you have a wife and three lovely children waiting your return."

"Maybe so, Johnny, but I am here and she is there. Eílis will never leave me."

The folly of women in season and men of position and wealth! It is hard to believe what those two, Bawn and Aíne, were to conceive doing. Conceive, certainly so, for over the next three years they have two children, one an absolute idiot, Frank, and the other, not so absolute, but an idiot in most cases, Cormac. The diabolical iniquities, the tragic overtones and undercurrents bring disaster faster than religious zeal, which is what Aíne caught one day from a visiting priest. Her poetry goes south, her soul goes north to Limerick and in the belief that she too can walk upon the waters, she sinks in Roaring Water Bay and drowns as surely as any one mortal person can do.

Frank and Cormac, Cormac and Frank. Nearly inseparable and with but one IQ to cover the two, they come to live with Bawn and Eílis, young Donal and the two sisters at Castle Lough. This does not look to work at all. This does not work in the slightest and Eílis is quite distressed. She is talking about all the work and drudgery she has to endure without any help from the big one and then to bring two of his love babies, stupid ones to boot, home to Castle Lough is more than she should be expected to bear. She doesn't.

"In a fortnight's time the first day of February arrives. I shall take my rights at that time."

"And what rights do you think you have, Eílis? I don't recall Johnny preparing any papers for you which bestow rights."

"The rights are there without Johnny's papers. The rights of decency, my husband, is what I am referring to. On that day I will leave your bed and board and take Donal and the two little girls with me."

"Just where do you think you can go?"

"It is already arranged. I shall go to Carbery first and to my family there."

"You've planned this ahead of time? Without any consideration for my needs?"

"Your needs seem always to be well met."

"I can change, Eílis, honest to God, I can change....and I will, if you will stay."

"I've heard that too long, Bawn. You cannot and will not change. That is your nature and it is mine to raise your children as best I can."

Bawns' hazy brain is making a mull of flashbacks and he is finding no point of reference or peg to hang his past sins upon.

And, lamely, "But this is all happening too quickly."

"I told you when we were betrothed that I would leave you if you couldn't mend your profligate ways. It has become unbearable and with the Fitzgeralds proclaiming our children bastards, I've no choice."

"What of Donal, my son and the next Mor?"

"You make no mention of the girls, but if you will continue to educate them and give them proper manners, I can agree to their staying with you for that. The moment I hear differently, I will collect them and you shall not stop me. And as long as I am unmarried, you will support them."

"You will not stay unmarried for long, that I know."

"If God wills me to have a decent man to be married to, I will do so. It cannot be a question of love."

"Nor will I love again, dear Eílis. My heart will always be yours."

"Your heart is mine? Perhaps that is so, but the rest of you is shared from here to Dursey. I shall go. Do you agree with what has been said?"

"All agreed, of course."

She is off and Bawn is off her plate like cheap cheese.

Agony upon agony, flagon upon flagitous flagon of wicked drink. Self incrimination, apology and words spoken in the poetry of death. The acts are great acts and some acts are no acts, but come from the neglectful breaking heart and at the centre of all is his uncertain false pride. Woe, oh woe is me.

Now that Eílis is gone, now that she is no longer there to calm him, to sooth his fits, to love, honour and obey him, he is easy prey to onslaughts with vivid fantasies of anger and self-pitying mania.

Bawn raises taxes, is paid back taxes, now takes black taxes and hires bonnachts to aid himself and his kernes to raid and pillage even his own people. He attacks the Fitzgeralds. He attacks the Ormand legions of Black Tom Butler. He stretches the boundaries of his ploughlands, he steals his own tenant's cattle and raids others for theirs. He gambles away what money he has. He mortgages his castles and castles not his own. He borrows and loses. He borrows and he loses again. He lives on guts and smuggled wine. In three years time he is tipping over the dark edges of abuse and an abysmal proposal. He will marry Honoria. The decision is taken against groans and fierce banging of the head upon the soaked table.

After three years he is in a near state of perpetual

oblivion and he finds himself in Muckross Abbey being married. No, wait again. He remembers only when they are leaving that stone-cold place.

He is saying to Honoria, "I never thought I would be going through this pageant with you twice in my lifetime."

She is saying to this, "Well, you wouldn't remember much of the first time, now would you?"

And, he is right in saying, "I probably won't be remembering much of this one, either!"

Look! Bawn is slumping to the ground!

So Honoria will throw out the bastard children; 1, 2, 3, 4, 5, and start some legal ones, she thinks. A daughter Ellen, full of it all her life as is expected with such unusual parents. Tadgh, a son. Sickly, disinterested in titles and duties, surety bait to the Crown, prone to early death in France at the hands of a dislikeable Barry boy.

Oh, dear me, the porridge is spilt.

All the while there is healthy, robust, cheerful, handsome, not so little Donal, age six, his son by Eílis. He is a sober copy of his father, Bawn, and one who would rather live in caves than castles, dance with the woodlands creatures and ride his horse by his knees.

Which is what he is doing. He is cavorting through the thick forest on trails only he and his father's black herding dog, Chance, know. They are merry and having a wild time of it. Donal slashing with his wooden sword at brush tops and imaginary enemies. Chance is busiest marking his territory as Donal tops the rise above the road around Muckross Abbey. Suddenly he sees a troop of Stanley's English cavalry headed by a brash lieutenant who is anything but blind. He instantly sees the half naked Donal, all right.

"What have we here? See the lad on the horse! We shall catch him and see who he is."

"I think not, sir. I'd say that's Lord MacCarthy's son. He'd be very upset if you unsettle that boy!" his lead man tells him.

"That drunken lecher? What in hell's name could he do to me?"

"You'll find out if you take the lad, that's certain."

"I'm bloody terrified! We'll see what comes about!"

Cruel man, he jabs his horse's flank hard with his steel heel and takes off after young Donal. Behind him follows the reluctant troop at a canter. Donal smiles as he sees the officer approaching. He teases a pause, then whistles for Chance who barks loudly and dashes directly at the oncoming lieutenant as if to herd the troop down the shallow valley. Donal turns his horse away into the forest as the dog leaps at the officer's horse and nearly unseats him.

"Get down, you lousy cur! I'll chop your mongrel head off!"

Chance springs once again and then takes off low to the ground, cutting through the underbrush and easily escapes. The dog stops and listens. There is another whistle and the dog wags his tail and jaunts off to where he sees Donal waiting for him.

"Good boy, Chance."

In another forest in another time, nine years later, Donal has made it to age 15 and he is riding this time with his half-brother, the fearless Frank, his father and the aging Walter. They are hot-hoofing it and criss-crossing to avoid contact of an evil nature with those who are pursuing them. Those determined persons are John and James Fitzgerald and their depleted army who have nevertheless cleverly positioned themselves at the head of a valley into which the MacCarthy group has managed to find themselves. They are entrapped. This is certainly not a reflection on the planning power of either Walter or Donal. The flank of Fitzgerald's force has pressed the three forward without threat and those worthy folk now face the brothers. Full stop.

"We have been trailing you for the better part of the afternoon," says John Fitzgerald. "Well, Bawn, you have gotten along quite handsomely since last we saw you."

"And, you don't look any better, John," replies Bawn and adds quickly, "quite truthfully, we knew someone was watching us, but we thought it was the Butlers of Ormond."

James is not taken in by Bawn's falsehood. "There would be no Butlers this far north and west, MacCarthy. You knew it was us and you knew why we are after you."

"The tribute, is it? No need to worry as you shall get yours when I get mine."

"Either you pay your debt or we massacre your people. No question we can do it is there?"

"We are hardly in a position to argue that."

"You will also furnish us with 20 of your kernes..."

"Me furnish you with 20 of my kernes?"

"...as well as yourself, Donal and that strange looking creature over there strizzling in the stream whilst I am speaking..."

"That would be our Frank, over there," says Walter.

"...and Frank over there. And you will return to Castle Lough, Walter Tibbet, to collect the horse and men and meet us at the Timoleague Abbey."

Now is the time for all the MacCarthy clan to start to worry. The decision is in Bawn's hands, the warriors are 15 year old Donal and 13 year old Frank and the kernes will be poorly armed, poorly mounted, ill prepared and totally knackered by the time they reach the Abbey.

"Do you fancy a bit of action, Donal?" asks his father without enthusiasm.

"Better yet, we'll just take your son Donal with us. It will be a fine education for him to see how real gentry fight," says James.

"Never!" shouts Bawn.

"It is also a bit of surety on your part, old man. You don't desert us and sweet Donal here keeps alive. It's a once in a lifetime opportunity for him."

"You've got me at the straddles, Fitzgerald. But I will not do a deal with my son's life."

Then the sun rises in his eyes. A billiant thought has burst through the fog in his head.

"You wouldn't take Frank or Honoria for surety instead, I don't suppose? Sure, now, you'd be far better off taking your sister."

"She's your wife, you murdering twit!"

"Ah, yes, so she is. Hmm. Right. The offer stands for Frank. I'm firm on that."

"Don't be ridiculous!" a chorus responds.

Bawn's shoulders slump a good bit and he is looking like he is about to take his leave.

James and John both draw their swords.

"Don't move or you're bad memories. I'd be delighted to kill the lot of you here and now, but it's your son Donal or all of your lives. I want your answer to that right now?"

"I just offered you our Frank. He may not look a proper soldier, but I assure you he can quickly maim any man you put before him. He is what you would call a natural born killer. He is, so."

Frank is through shaking his willie and joins the group, curious at what it is he is being bargained for. "But Daddy, I'm only six years old. I don't want to go with those funny smelling men in them balloony frocks," he says.

"He's a bit fuddled, Lord James," says Donal. "He's not a great one with the numbers but he did kill his first kerne Wednesday. He is a trifle forgetful, I fear, but he has always been told to stay away from strange men."

He turns to brother Frank to reassure him.

"Those are called pantaloons, Frank, but you're right in not wanting to go with them."

Turning to his father, this sensible young fellow takes his young life into his own hands, having suddenly tired of having his father bungle it.

"I'll go. That poor craythur doesn't know skirts from pants, he wouldn't last the day with this lot. Be dafter than he is in minutes."

"This hardly solves your problem, James, as I have been given to undertand," says Bawn to the Fitzgeralds. "You two killed Sir Henry Davells in Tralee and the Crown wants your heads for that. Surely Charlie McTigue has been put under orders to take you out!" says Bawn.

"Sir Henry was an accident. This is not. You will join us or we will finish you here," replies James.

"I think it means we must join him," says Donal.

"Christ, you are a wonder for a MacCarthy! Did you hear him, John?" says James. "He 'thinks it means we must join him.' Yes, bastard, it means you are to join us immediately."

"The three of us, with Walter gone to the castle?" asks Bawn.

"No, you sot! Donal with me, you and this Frank are with John."

"You cannot split my son and me."

95

"We just have. Let us get on with it."

Seldom would one see such an expedition as the one on which Donal is now taking part. Catastrophe follows catastrophe and ill will accompanies everything. This troop of mounted officers and gallowglass is slowly pressing up the creek bed toward anticipated battle.

Hang on, there is Pat Spleen, now in the pay of the Fitzgerald folk. A Scot, he is that, and at age 16 he has a strongly built body and an attitude to match. For two days they go a-marching and for three days the officers are smacking at the brandy and for three days the soldiers are emulating their leaders and doing their best to eliminate the mead. It is hotter than a buck-sheep's arse in a pepper patch and derogatory comments are frequent. Donal complains.

"What's the great hurry? In this condition we'll only be killed when we meet Charlie McTigue! We may as well take a rest and live for a few hours more."

"I'll have no MacCarthy giving orders here. I am the commander."

"So, when do I get to command? I should be riding alongside you."

"You're only 15 years old."

"I may only be 15, but I have been a soldier for my father for 6 years. You're only 22 yourself."

"That's right. I am 22 and the commander and you are 15 and a common soldier."

So there you are. James rides away with the brandy flask at his lips.

New-found friend Pat Spleen shakes his head at both.

"Would you stop your forever carping about how you should be riding and leading a troop?"

"Have we any drink left?" asks Donal.

"Oh, yes, for his lordship, yes. For anyone else, no."

"Now you are at me! Is it not enough Sir James is on me? God, if that stream was deeper I'd gladly drown myself!"

They slog along. The heat and the mead are taking a hard toll.

"I deserve a command. I can get us through Charles McTigue MacCarthy's country without a loss."

"I don't care about casualties among you. I want to cut

96

through him and we will."

"Great leaders, these Desmonds. Horses' arses, every-one," observes Pat.

"What was that, Spleen?"

"I was just sayin' how much I admire your horse, Sir James."

Chapter Ten

Donal is Captured and Held as Surety

Eternal God
there are two in Munster
who destroy us and our property
namely the earl of Desmond
and the earl of Ormond
with their followers
who at length the Lord will destroy
through Christ our Lord
Amen.

Bishop of Cloyne
1381

The lack of preparation is a boring thing one would have to agree, but what follows immediately after Pat Spleen's remark about the Fitgeralds was anything but boring. Just as Bawn predicted, the Queen has sent her soldiers to capture or kill the Fitzgerald Desmonds just as she has eliminated the power of the Fitzgerald Kildare near Dublin.

Oh, there was action, to be sure, and the fearfully familar face of the high sheriff of Cork, Charlie McTigue, looms imminently from some past scubas and his underpaid minions are at the drink-subdued group. There is no pity shown for aching heads or for the aching hearts of those who love them. Oh, my goodness gracious, you have never seen such an uneven affair. There is roaring and slashing aplenty, mixed with unrepeatable oaths and curses of a most horrendous text, but with more near misses than hits. When the day's work is done it is Charlie McTigue 22, Fitzgerald 0.

James is given a frightful axe wound to his left leg and is falling from his fine horse. He and his two stone medieval shield land upon Donal, knocking him colder than a frozen pud, a state just one drink away, regardless of battle conditions and results. Pat Spleen, a wise lad if ever one came south past Hadrian's Wall and not as silly as the others, dives face down

99

into the aforementioned stream and becomes quite still.

"I will be looking dead to them," he thinks.

High Sheriff Charlie is sweating like a Zulu warrior and riding up and down the stream looking for further exercise. James is loaded on a horse in a most rude and uncivil manner and he is bent double, holding his throbbing and gushing leg. He is not at all as confident as he was seen so shortly before to be.

What is this? There is a strapping lad still groaning and breathing poorly underneath where James had lain. "This cannot be," thinks Charlie, "Tis my strapping cousin, the natural son of Bawn. What could he be doing? Oh, for the love of Mary," he thinks further, "That fooking father of his has sent him off to battle with this inept group. I must get him out before...aha, I know what I will do. There is a haphazard appearing Scot lying there in the stream next to Donal trying to look dead. I will put the two of them together in the Cork jail and save Bawn's son in that manner. Now, then, where did I leave my sword. Oh, yes, there it is in that dead man's head, held there by the crevasse in his helmet."

Rump, tiddy rump, tiddy rump, rump, rump. They ride to the Cork jail where Charlie must report and file charges for trespass or whatever and he gives James over to the salivating lads of the attitudinal adjustment team. Donal and Pat, along with 12 others are booted thumpity-thump, pall-mall down an exceptionally long and hard stone stairs to a dungeon cell far below. Donal is still less than crisp in his procedures and only wakes up after an hour. Pat sits with him and the others in a urine soaked, straw-filled area with the gray carcasses of dead rats and excrement aplenty. Donal is shaking his head, trying to clear away the unkind thoughts he is having.

"So, you're alive then are ye, wain?" asks Pat.

"Only just. God, what a headache. Where are we?"

"We're in the Cork gaol, that's where we are, and lucky enough to be alive with all your insane ranting and raving. Out of your mind, you were."

"I was drunk and sick and somebody fell on my head. Is there no water in this stinking hole?"

"A few hours ago you were asking for my last drop of mead and now you want water. Give it up, Donal. That's your lunch in front of you."

"That's a dead rat in front of me."

"Exactly. That could be your lunch."

That is quite repugnant, one would have to agree. It is even more so for the drink-suffering heir. The future Mor need not take such unrespectful treatment.

"Guard! Guard! Let me out of here. I don't belong in this place at all. Don't you know who I am?"

"For the love of Jesus, be quiet Donal! If they do find out who you are they will take you up to the chamber where they have Sir James, wounded leg and all."

"What are you going on about?"

"Don't be stupid, Donal. Would you ever just listen? They have all the officers up there and on the rack, wounded or well. Raleigh will have Sir James drawn and quartered soon enough."

"Raleigh is here?"

"Raleigh is everywhere there's blood to be let."

"But officers cannot be treated in such a way!"

"You might wish to remind them of that when they break you on the wheel. I'm sure they will be pleased enough to be corrected by a 15 year old prisoner from the troops of the Geraldine Rebellion!"

"That cannot be! What about my cousin Charlie McTigue? He knows I'm here. It was he who captured us."

" Aw, fer God sakes, you twit! Use your pathetic head for something besides a place for James to land. Your bleedin' Uncle Charlie put you in here to save your mouldering arse, and for no other reason. Of course he knew it was you! That is why you're here. That's why I'm here, too. Shut up, Donal, and stay shut up."

"I don't have to take that from a gallowglass in Desmond pay!"

"You know what? You really are a bastard at that! And, you know what else? You just do as you think fit and you'll be as dead as that rat in an hour's time. Go ahead! Shout all you want! You are a disgrace to stupidity."

Now, this seems to catch his attention. Yes. See him now think. He is thinking there could be something to what Pat is saying at that and that is, "Oh, my. I am in a pickle, all right."

"Still, you could be right. So, what do we do now?"

"To tell the truth, I don't know."

After all the gas has passed from Pat's mouth you would be right to expect that he'd have some plan of action. The perfect plot: A well-conceived and developed plan to escape through some tunnels and sewers, perhaps? Not a chance. He is a single cell amoeba and although a brave one, not much more than that.

There is naught to do but wait. They go silent in their separate thoughts. There soon comes the sound of boots on the stone steps at the other side of the gaol door.

Two crusty English officers are being led down to the cells by an Irish guard. One has one hand to his face. There is a kerchief. It is becoming obvious that there is an odour of supreme esterification about. The condition has not escaped Flower's notice.

"Coor, you catch the reeking pong in this place!" says he. "B'god, I thought the Irish soldiers kept themselves clean. What a stench!"

"What did you expect? This is a damned gaol, not a French brothel," says the other.

"Let's get on with it. How many of these Scotsmen will be ready to change sides and fight for our Queen?"

"If they have any sense, all of them will."

Keys are rattling officiously. The guard opens the cell door and in waltz these two butchers.

"Don't you people ever muck out your cells? I am Captain Bostock and this is Captain Flowers. Are you all Scots here?"

Pat springs to his feet and answers.

"We are, sir. All bonnachts forced by the Desmonds to fight against our Queen."

There is a nudge and then another. Pat is urgently trying to communicate the need for Donal to join in the discourse.

"We are!" says Donal.

"Of course you are. And you haven't been paid in months," says Flowers.

"You know the situation better than anyone," says Pat.

"How many of you are there in here?"

"There be 14. All soldiers of fortune and available immediately, if you know what I mean. Isn't that right there, Angus?"

Donal is getting quicker by the second. He knows who Angus is alright.

"Och nue Willie, all born Scots and all born fighters!"

"I'm sure you are. Guard! Take them all out of here and see what you can do for arms and clothes. They look like they've been starved. Bring some stirabout to the yard for our Scottish bonnachts."

"And make sure they wash down before we leave!"

The boys are urged to leave their cell and are joyously splashing about with a bucket bath and gulping stirabout in great hunger, safe for the moment from the death they have anticipated.

They are keeping well up-wind, these officers Bostock and Flowers. They are tossing garments here and there and having a look-see at their prospects.

"I don't know, Bostock. In the daylight they all look a poor grade."

"Charlie McTigue said they'd be good soldiers had they not been more drunk than usual."

"So be it. We've come for soldiers and this is what we get. Some days gives better hunting than others."

"We've collected only a few horse. The MacCarthys have near cleaned this area out. We're lucky to get a few garranes. Most will have to march."

"Then let us make the most of it and get away from this despicable place."

And they do, setting a slow pace through Youghal and up the coast toward the city of Dublin. Donal and Pat are riding side by side. Bostock and Flowers are at the lead and the others are strung out, catching rides on carts if they can.

"This is a damn poor way to make war against the English, Pat," says Donal.

"Consider yourself lucky to be alive. Enjoy what you can, I always say, and don't forget you're meant to be a Scot. If they find out who you are you will be ransomed in an instant."

"I'll do what it takes. I'll play the Scot and fight for England if necessary, but the day will come when we can make it right."

The march progresses north. It is a poor example of

much of anything.

Then, at near last, the Dublin Castle is in view. Now the troops are entering into the courtyard where there stand the toadies and English persons to do politics and the swindles of land. The small groups so arranged notice there are strange persons coming into view, escorted by soldiers. Of those to notice are David Barry, a major member of the fraticidal Barry clan, and a corpulent and fifty former treasurer of Berwick and now the Queen's surveyor, one Sir Valentine Browne. The two are chatting quite amicably as the governor strides to meet the arrivals and singling out Bostock says:

"So you've finally gotten here. How many did you bring?"

"We have a grand total of 14 able-bodied bonnachts, sir," says Bostock.

"They don't look able-bodied to me. What in hell has happened to them?"

"Well, first they were with James Desmond, and I won't say God Rest His Soul, and they were then smashed up by Charlie McTigue and then they spent ten days in the Cork gaol. It has been a trying few days for them, Governor."

"These are trying times for all of us, Bostock. Just get them sorted out and put to quarters."

While all of this breathtaking excitement was taking place David Barry has sidled up to where Donal and Pat are standing awaiting orders. His demeanor is most camp and he is picking at the lace of his sleeve while fluttering in excitement of seeing a friend now in bondage. One would do well to keep an eye on this fellow at the front and back doors of all existence.

"Donal, my dear boy! Is it really you? I cannot believe that you are here and I am here and we are all here at the same time!"

"You must be mistaken, sir. I am but a poor bonnacht in the service of the Queen."

"Don't take me for simple, Donal. I know it's you. Who else could look so devastating in that awful garb?"

"David, for God's sake, be still. If the governor finds out who I am I will be in custody against my father's conduct!"

"And, what is that to me, my dear? I am in no position to gain or to lose by your predicament."

"You have always done well through your pretended love of the English. You never hesitate to use them."

"As a true believer in the Mother Church, I have no choice, nor will I hesitate now!" He waves his kerchief to the East. "I say, Governor!"

Donal is doomed. He bolts toward the open gate. David Barry has his quarry well measured and slips a neatly booted foot into his flight path and Donal goes sprawling. From the other side of the yard Valentine sees the action and comes chugging toward the downed one. He plows his way through the crowd as Donal is rising to his feet.

"What is going on here? Why this raucous conduct in the governor's castle?"

"Just a bit of fun with the strangest Scotsman I've ever seen, Valentine Browne."

Valentine takes another look down his big cheeks.

"Hold on there! Who do we have here?"

Valentine circles Donal as he rises to his full height. If he was doomed before, he is double doomed now because he recognizes the man who recognizes him. Oh, the irony of it all!

"My God! I know this young giant!"

"And so do I, Sir Valentine, so do I!" says David, the little viper!

"This be the son of MacCarthy Mor. What is he doing here?"

He waves excitedly.

"Would you kindly step this way for a moment, Governor?"

This worthy disengages and fumbles forward at his leisure.

"What is it now, Valentine?"

"Governor, sir, we have before us Donal MacCarthy, the base son of the MacCarthy Mor and his favorite to succeed him."

"You've been spending too much time in the bogs and sniffing their gases, Browne. The Mor's son, Tadgh, is inside doing his sums."

Now, we knew about Tadgh, but he has been forgotten, hasn't he? It is just as well as he doesn't last long on this overly green part of the planet.

"Excuse me, Governor, but Sir Valentine is absolutely correct. I've known Donal for badger's years. Say something in MacCarthy for the governor, Donal," states David Barry.

"You rotten spoiled little pup! You are a traitor to your family!"

"See! What did I tell you. That is pure Kerry MacCarthy!"

Valentine, seeing his point for recognition drifting toward the centre-forward of the Barry clan, pushes his line forward.

"Be a good lad and go bother someone else while the Governor and I discuss the situation."

"Oh, all right, but just remember, it was I who first recognized him. Should there be any reward, I ask that I be considered."

Governors never know where to stand with the Barrymores and Barryroe inhabitants. With the Brownes and MacCarthys, he is more sure.

"David, I'll promise you nothing, but believe me, you will always be kept in mind. Now, kindly do as Valentine suggests and leave us for the moment."

David is many things, but an interferring idiot he is not. He smartly exits the scene.

"If you wish, I shall be glad to take this upstart off your hands," says Valentine.

"Not so fast, Browne. Now that we hold both the Mor's sons we can cause him to submit to the Crown. We must immediately notify his father and inform him of Her Majesty's demands against further disturbances in Munster."

"My father will ignore you!" yells Donal.

"Not so, Donal," says Valentine. "He loves you more than all his others. He'll submit, all right and I'll have peace at Molahiffe Castle."

"Molahiffe Castle? What have you to say about Molahiffe Castle? It has been our holding for centuries."

"Your father fails you again, I'd say. It is no longer your castle. No indeed. Molahiffe is ours now and will stay ours long after the MacCarthy clan is forgotten."

Now, this is shocking news to Donal. It would likely be shocking news to Bawn as well, him having ignored most of the loans and mortgages he has taken in the past. He is, one could say without fear of being wrong, a simply horrible manager of tangibles and is lost without Johnny about to steer him.

Oh, there is worse to come, be certain of that. An instance of this is the exhortation concerning the decrepit and decayed institution called Bawn's marriage to Honoria.

These two, Honoria and Bawn, simply do not get along. Never have, never will. Still, they are sitting at the table in the Great Hall in Castle Lough and the remains of a meal are pretty much still in evidence. More evident are the carcasses of several dead wine containers. Honoria looks tired at 35 years of age and she also looks quite put-out with her husband, to be sure. He does not look great himself.

"Is that all you can do? Sit there like a dumb animal? You drink away your probelms while your son Tadgh rots away in Dublin Castle."

"He's not rotting away. He is probably better looked after there than he would be here. And, don't you forget, my son Donal is there, too. You cannot pretend he doesn't exist because you wish he didn't."

"Neither of them would be there if you hadn't squandered away everything we own on your wretched gambling. How much more must we lose before you come to your senses?"

"I have my senses, woman, and I would thank you not to suggest otherwise! You are my wife by necessity, not by choice."

Honoria is now glaring at her depreciating husband with the look that comes from hundreds, perhaps thousands, of years of Fitzgerald Desmond practice. It could very likely put the ice-cap on Snowden or the Italian Alps to shame.

To her, the emperor stands naked before the facts as she recites them.

"Suggesting seems to be the only thing I can do these days. I suggest you stop drinking for one minute and try to decide what we are to do to get my son out of Dublin Castle. I suggest also that you stop gambling away our hearth and home. I suggest further that you stop using my inheritance as your personal security. I don't take kindly to being used as a pawn in your game. So, if you have your senses as you say you have, I suggest you finally start using them and to be quick about it!"

107

"Damn you! If Eílis hadn't left me I never would have had to honor that ridiculous betrothal at Askeaton when I was ten! You don't like being used as a pawn? How do you think I feel? Your game is more deadly than mine ever was!"

"Maybe so, Bawn, but I'm winning my game and you continue to lose yours! That is all you are and all you ever will be. A loser from start to finish!

Chapter Eleven

Donal Escapes Dublin Castle and Meets Ethné

The tale of Ethné also involves St. Patrick.
Ethné was a lovely and gentle maiden, even
though she took no nourishment of any kind.
The rest of the household fed on the magic swine,
which were eaten one day and alive again for
the next meal.

Ronald Pearsall

In the Dublin Castle three years whirl past with Donal still pondering just how to go about breaking loose. He is primarily a latitudinarian and wants away sooner rather than later. Bawn is a bit slack in his efforts. If three years seems excessive, one should hear the hair-brained plans which could have been installed and precede the one coming up. Harken to Donal's friendly keeper.

"Do you have any friends or relatives with a missing leg, a wonky eye, stinks like a sty and seems perpetually nervous?"

"Not to my knowledge, Declan. Could be anyone. Why do you ask?"

"Well, there's somebody like that sitting on what looks to be a dead horse outside the gatehouse and he wishes to talk to you!"

The lad is quite certain it wasn't his father. Of curiosity he consents to see him. This person is Richard Cremin, a willingly forgotten brother of his grandfather Frank and obviously thought by the castle-keepers to be no great threat to taking him out by brute force. Donal nods upon sight of this stark creature.

"Ah. Yes. I do know you. You're the brother of my grandfather. What in God's good name brings you to Dublin Castle in such filthy weather?"

"Immediately, you are right. I am, indeed, Frank's brother Richard, and I must say, this is a fine set-up you have here. I remember back in '42 when I was summoned here...well, not exactly summoned, I was near murdered for what they said was poaching, but then again we all have our ways of catching the wily game, don't we? As I recall....."

"You do have a reason to be here, nonetheless? That was very interesting, I'm sure, but you must not have come all this way to... Is it something about my family. Is it a message for Tadgh? If so, I will gladly have you see him."

"No, sir. This messasge is for you and you alone. It will, without doubt, effect your life for some time to come."

Donal waves a dismissal to Declan and urges this poor, wet man to sit down. Donal hands this Richard Cremin a large flagon of port and sits facing him beside the fireplace.

"Please then, by all means, do proceed!"

None of these bold hints faze Richard, who seems determined to give Donal all the family news first. He begins by telling him his detestable and intellectual cousin, Florence MacCarthy Reagh had been in a grand fight with David Barry Buttevant over who had founded the Timoleague Priory and who had first call for burial rights.

"Richard, as for corpses, that's what Tadgh and I will be before we're shown the other side of the walls. Get us help, damn it! Get us out!"

"We're workin' on it, we're workin' on it. Don't get your trews in a clutch, sir! Your mother Éilis and your father's people have it as good as done. Not to worry. I'm sorry, but the word on Tadgh is that he stays. Yes, sir, he stays. Your father has to leave a hostage for the English and he's the one to be kept on deposit. Better him than me, I always say. Your father did try to use Honoria again, but her market value is well down as you can imagine and them authorities is on to that game of good riddance so that is not an option open to your father. No sir, not an option at all. His good wife is definitely not going to volunteer. Oh no, and is more than a little put out that your father would consider such a plan. She's determined to outlive him and see him gleefully into his crypt at Muckross, I do believe. Not an option, no, no, not an option at all, sir, more's the pity."

Richard pauses and his good eye waters somewhat in all the heavy pondering.

"Richard, all of this is fascinating, but just what in God's name has it to do with my getting out of here, if that's not pry-

110

ing too much?"

"I'm glad you asked that, sir." said Richard, fumbling and twiddling his cloak clasp passionately.

Then, of a sudden he hoarsely whispers, "Be ready in the mornings at 0300!"

"For what?" asks Donal in exclamation.

"That Jezebel Lee, the turnkey's wife you've been busy bonking has agreed to open the door at that time, heh, heh. She'll be making as to see a certain elderly and plump English gentleman by name of Browne whom she has been servicing with amazing regularity considering his age. The guards on the outer bailey will let her through, like as always. Old Finnerty Lee, her husband will be out cold as yesterday's mackerel. Mistress Lee has been adjusting his drinks for as long as she's been on the game. She has this soft spot for you and she is lending you her best frock to wear to smuggle you out. She'll take you with her and you are to be her cousin from Sneem. You'll have to scutch down sumhut, I'd wager."

Bewildered by the torrent of near meaningless rhetoric, Donal can only mutter.

"Yes, fine, go on, Richard."

"She's leaving old Lee for Nibblet Grimes, a small land-holder in Drinagh," he confides.

"What, may I ask, has that to do with anything?"

"Well, sir, you'll be her protection in her dash to little Nibblet and it's sort of romantic and I didn't want to leave anything out, sir."

"Right, Richard. 0300 it is! On some morning!"

"That's it, lad! You have it all in your brain. Some morning at 0300!"

And this is the extent of the planning for the incredible jail-break. More gas and dark clouds and mirrors than common sense. Belay that! Perhaps not so incongruous! Only a few days are to pass and then:

Donal's youthful appetite is there, his hulking figure is there as is the perfivid attention to detail in the bed. He is predictably in the kip with the slightly plump wife of the castle turnkey. They have just polished off a bottle of wine and each other. This is not so bad at all. It is better than that. It is the fine efforts of this Jezebel Lee to do her bit to make the night as little dull as possible and she thinks him about as good as it gets. This toothsome, red-haired, 34 year old, buxom and experienced yummy-yum-bum, speaks in a contented voice.

"What wonderful times we do have here!"

Donal, at eighteen, has spent the past three years under such bedclothes and conditions. Some persons never learn to appreciate the ambiance and benefits of their current environment.

"Jezebel, you darling tart! I don't know what I would do without you. You've been such a pleasure during my stay."

"The pleasure is all mine. Will you have some more wine?"

"Thank you, yes. But, not if you have adjusted it with sleeping potions I'm told you've been doing to your husband."

"Would I do that to you?" says she as she slips out of the bed and is now slipping into her dress.

"You need not leave so early."

Watch her as she rummages about in her rummage bag. She is turning back to Donal. He is hunching up upon his haunches with bareness to the waist above the coverlet. He is punching at pillows. As was said, this is not so bad.

"I have a surprise for you!"

Donal has heard this terroristic approach before.

"Oh, no! Dear God, you're not....?"

"No, no, deary. Nothing like that!"

She turns about and tosses a frilly garment onto his head.

"Just this. It's too small, I know, but it will have to do. I've let it out everywhere I can."

Donal increduously holds the flowered frock before him. His worst fears have come true!

"A frock. A flowered frock. What am I to do with a frock? Not that it isn't a lovely frock...it's just that I seldom have the occasion to wear a flowered frock, you see, Jezebel?"

"I'm taking you out of the gates at 0300. You are to wear it, dearie. You will be my cousin from Sneem."

"This is preposterous! I could never get away with it! I should have told old Richard that!"

"You can and you must. It is all so outrageous that we won't be questioned when I leave to go to see Valentine Browne. It's all your mother Eílis's and your father's plan!"

The frock drops to Donal's lap and he looks at Jezebel. A slow smile crosses his face and then...and then the two of them burst into wild laughter.

He puts the frock out in front of him again to size it up and gets out of bed while so doing.

"I'd say you'll just have to hold yourself in."

"I wish you were larger, Jezebel"

"Try to be more serious, Donal. Much as I'd love to stay, this will never do. Now, come along. Don't make us late. Your mammy will be waiting with a cart in Dalkey."

"Will my father be with her?"

"I have my doubts. Oh, Donal, you will be shocked when you see him. He's losing his castles and money to everyone. First it was Molahiffe and now he is in danger of losing Castle Lough."

"I haven't heard that story, but nothing could surprise me as regards him."

"It's being said around Dublin that he's likely to lose your family home. He's borrowing money again and this time from your handsome cousin, Florence MacCarthy Reagh."

"He's gone that bad, has he?"

"And, small wonder, dear one. Your father has been nine tenths under the hatches since your mother walked out on him."

She pauses, distressed with herself. She has blatted too much, she thinks. "Why wouldn't I?" she asks herself. "I've always talked too much." And, as always, she recovers her senses to give directions and assistance in the project at hand, that is to say, getting the frock on Donal.

"Ah, you'll do just fine. I wish we had something besides your boots. Praise God, it's dark. Don't forget that you are my cousin from Sneem. Use a high voice and scutch down sumhut. Now, put the shawl over your head. That's it. Come, then. You're ready for your first night out."

She puts a plump and reassuring arm around his still elevated waist and leads him to the door. They are out the door and into the courtyard. It is darker than Toby's underpants. It is difficult, this scutching. Now they are at the gate. A guard hails them.

"Stop in the Queen's name. Who goes there?"

113

"It's only me, Timothy."

"It's you then, is it Mistress Lee? Going out to do your bit for the good of humanity?"

"Just you shut your big mouth and open the gate as you were told to do, Timothy. I don't wish to hear your comments."

"Of course, Mistress Lee, of course. And, who do we have with us this morning?"

"We? We have no one. I have my dear cousin from Sneem who is here to visit me and perhaps to make a few bob in the process."

"She's a biggun, isn't she? Let's have a feel of your boobies, darlin'!"

"Have you no decency, Timothy? I know she is larger than most Dublin girls, but she is full of love and joy. Say good morning to Timothy, cousin, and we'll be on our way."

Donal is ducking his head even further and trying to take smaller steps to accommodate the strict confines of the tightly stretched frock. In a falsetto voice he hopes denotes a shy girl, he pipes,

"Good morning, dearie!"

Timothy is far from the brightest of the castle guards or he wouldn't be on the dog watch. He sees no hope for morning romance and opens the gate and in his head he cannot now imagine being in bed or against the wall with any girl this large. He merely shakes his head and bids the ladies adieu. Out of sight and hearing of the castle gate, Jezebel loosens a still restrained gurgle of mirth.

"We've done it. Christ's cuspids, you were the grandest of ladies."

"Well, thanks to you, Jezebel. You weren't so bad yourself!"

"I must say, though, that for a man who loves the ladies you show a distinct lack of understanding when you impersonate one!"

"I've always loved them more than I've understood them!"

"Oh, you wicked boy, you. Let's be quick. Your mammy should be waiting for us."

"You are coming with us?"

"No, dear. Only until we reach Eílis and then I must

meet my darling Nibblet Grimes. He's not half the man you are, but he loves me and has promised to take care of me."

"That's the most of the matter, dear Jezebel. I shall miss you very much and will always be in your debt."

"Nothing of the sort, love. One gets what one gives, you know, and you have given me much."

"You are a tart, Jezebel! A delectible and sweet tart!"

As the sun begins to cast high shadows from behind them they hurry as best they can toward Dalky. There is a large and threatening dark object beside the narrow paved road. Donal's boots are making heavy noises against the cobblestones. His frock is swishing. Never mind, it is a cart. In the cart is Eílis. All is well. The escape is near complete. Tight and long embraces are passed around most willingly.

"Thank God you are safe, Donal. My, how you have grown since last I saw you! Your father will be proud of you."

"But, not proud enough to come to meet me."

"He's been like a madman since this whole plot was hatched. He was much afraid that Honoria might learn of our plans and notify either Valentine Browne or the governor."

Jezebel disappears behind the cart to gather the clothes Eílis has brought. Now she is coming out with a bundle.

"Donal, here are some clothes so may I please take what is left of my best frock. I fear the repairs may be too much."

"I'm sorry, Jezebel."

"It was well worth it just to see you with your mother. Perhaps Nesbbit will buy me a new one. I must be off."

Eílis is also eager to take leave. It is her thought that perhaps now Donal's father will take charge and do the right things in the right places for their son. In some ways she could be right, but not in many. She is a dreamer in that respect. How did she ever get into such an unsatisfactory situation? God only knows. Her bubbles of thought fizzle out. She is back.

"Thank you, Jezebel, for everything. It was a good plan and it worked."

"Twas my pleasure, Eílis. In a way it is good to see him away from there."

The horse is slapped out of his dozing stupor and the leather tightens on the shafts. The cart starts to move and they are clop-clop-clopping along toward the west.

"Where are we going, Mother?"

"To your father's demesne where your friends will keep you safe. You are an outlaw now. We will meet him in the Fieries Caves near there."

Well, it takes nearly six days across mountain and bogs and Donal walked it all beside his mother in the cart and the horse pretending she weighs twenty stone. There be danger everywhere and more than once Donal must slither under the hay in the cart box for curious glances are given by royal men on heavy horses.

They travel at dusk and dawn and goeth they through mystic counties of Anglo-Normans called Meath Liberty, through the lands of Plunket and Preston and finally into friendlier hidings of O'Connor, O'Molloy, O'Dunn and O'More; then great chunks of moon-mad O'Carroll's to O'Kennedy. Carefully do they skirt the Butler of Ormand holdings and as swiftly as possible, past the Slieve Bloom heights they pass. Suppressed monasteries in the gloaming. Oppressed townlands at Thurles. Inside and north of the Galty Mountains they coast southward down the hills. Especially and chronically deadly dangers of The Earldom of Desmond, slaughtered Fitzgerald and soaked by Roche in payment for their incredible rising. In a final slough they arrive in that of Munster called the Kingdom of Kerry and its king is still MacCarthy Mor; Bawn, soon to be Earl of Clancar. The River Maine, Molahiffe Castle, the Fieries Caves.

In near exhaustion, they slowly move and slowly talk.

"What can be left of father's lands and properties, Mother?"

"There is still much in holding, but nothing in wealth. The cattle are taken. The kernes are leaving to join with the Brownes. Many others have been killed either by the English or by Fitzgeralds and it is much the same everywhere. There is great starvation as you have seen. Many live on roots and watercress or not at all."

"It is not much that I come home to, but it is better than being a cat in a cage."

"You shall soon know, Donal. This is where I am to leave you."

They are near to a thicket hiding the entrance to a little

known cave.

"Where will you go, Mother?"

"I will be with my husband in Roscarbery. For tonight and the next few days I shall be in a cottage near here with loyal friends."

She is weeping and brushing away the tears with the back of her hand whilst holding the reins in the other. She is gorgeous. Seeing her thus, one would like to roast Bawn's hazelnuts in a roaring fire. How could anyone...?

"Mother," Donal says, also wiping a tear or two with his head turned, "I will see you as often as I can. I would like to know my sisters once again, but I am fearful that there is much to do to keep me away."

"It would be a wonderful thing altogether if you could see us now and again."

"That damned father of mine! He has ruined himself first and all those who love him. He has destroyed our country."

"Don't be too hard on him, Donal. He loves you as I do."

"I truly know he does love me, but dear God, he has such strange ways of showing it!"

"He has said that he will be here at eventide. I must go, my darling son. I cannot bear to see him and you together and then leave."

"It's such a waste of wanted love. He could have done it all, but has done nothing but the worst."

"As I said, Donal. Don't be too hard on him. Goodbye and farewell."

They embrace once more and he hugs his mother most tenderly as he kisses her. The tears are flowing most rightly at this point and she is fearful.

"Goodbye, Mother. Will I greet my father for you?"

There is no answer. Eílis turns the weary horse away and the cart starts westward once again. Donal stands and watches it slowly disappear down the lane to the tiny nothingness of the forest.

He is sighing. A sob escapes. His shoulders hunch under his meager cape of wool. He shrugs once and then again as he turns toward the cave. He sees a weak and flickering light coming from within. This is not supposed to be.

117

"What have I here?" he asks.

Chapter Twelve

Bawn is Summoned by Queen Elizabeth

No wonder that the Irish despatches should force from Queen Elizabeth the exclamation that, "she was weary of hearing them."

Lord Burghley

Donal stoops to enter the cave. He is peering past the firelight. There is a young girl cooking meat and humming an unknown song. This is most unusual, but it gets more so. She sees him and is not surprised. She is just a wisp of a little girl. She is thin and dressed in long brown sacking. She looks at Donal, smiling as she pokes the meat to turn it over the fire. She is something else. Count on it. It is silly and Donal must be, too.

"Hello, young miss. May I come into your cave?" he asks.

"You may, sir, and welcome you are, too!"

"Thank you. You are most kind."

Donal is looking about suspiciously, expecting demented others to pop up or out from the crevasses and holes contained herein. He is moving forward toward the sweet smelling meat and the little girl moves from behind the fire to meet him. He is standing with his mouth four feet above her upturned head and with a smiling face she is winning him.

"You seem so small and fragile to be here in these dangerous caves alone. May I ask your name, please?"

"I am called Ethné. You must be starving. Will you have something to eat?"

All this hoodoo-voodoo, black magic, sorcerers, and tiny person thing. Is she going to try to poison him? No. Not now or ever. This is truly a good little girl and that is the sum and total of it. He is wonderfully comfortable. He thinks this is just fine.

"Oh, thank you. I am famished, but there appears to be

only enough for yourself, Ethné."

"Well, Donal, I don't eat. It is for you I made the meat. I drink only the milk from my cows."

"How is it that you know my name and what in the world are you doing here? Do I know you... have we met somewhere?"

"Oh, yes. We have met through your father when I sang at Askeaton. This cave and others are my hide-aways from people who fear me. They think me evil because I see the future."

"You see the future?"

"I do see it, but I cannot alter it."

"What is it you see?"

"I see more death of innocent Irish at the hands of the English usurpers. I see famine and plague. I see powerful lords and their men doing nothing to help those so tormented."

"You speak the truth."

"Believe then that your future holds great things in store for you. You will take up the cause and fight for the good of the people. Your life of hardship will be rewarded."

Ethné pauses and senses the air. Not at all timerous.

"Your father is here. Go and greet him."

Bawn really is arriving at the mouth of the cave. Donal is wondering the eternal five again. Who, what, where, when and why? And how? The how is very important to him, but not so important at this very moment when Bawn, his father, is entering the cave. He is no longer as fit as Donal remembers him, but he still has much about him of the heroic. He is carrying a massive sword in his right hand and in his left he has a dirk. His eyes flash against the firelight, still with the power of youth though the rough gem of his manhood is less obvious.

"Are you here, Donal? Call out if it is you in here! Let me see who it is by the fire!"

"Yes, father. I am here with Ethné."

The two stand against each other, taking in their sights. Bawn drops his sword and dirk and embraces his son warmly.

"It is you, then, is it? God's knees, you are a fine looking young man!"

"Thank you, father. I'm glad to see you!"

"Thank our Lord you made it. How are you?"

"Tired, but well. Thank you for coming here."

"I am very sorry I couldn't be there for the escape, but I'm in a spot of trouble with the authorities in London. They seem to think they can govern my country for me simply because I have submitted."

He pauses only long enough to look around.

"That's odd. When I entered this cave you said you were with someone. I see no one else here. Am I mistaken?"

"No, not at all. Come and meet Ethné. She was here to meet me. For a moment's time I thought you had sent her ahead... but she is so small... never mind what I thought. She was the one who cooked the meat."

"Donal, were you knocked in the head while leaving Dublin Castle? There isn't anyone here. No one."

Donal quickly looks around. The meat is still there on the spit and turning itself ever so nicely. There is nothing like meat cooked on the rotisserie over the coals of an oak-wood fire for that wonderfully blended flavour of meat and natural fat. You get the same sensation from a properly oak-aged cask wine.

Ethné has disappeared.

"She was here just a moment before you arrived, father. She said you were here and now..."

Bawn's jaw has not fallen open. He has gone all his life expecting and getting into these episodes, drunk or sober.

"What name did you call her by?"

"She said her name was Ethné. She said she didn't eat anything, that..."

"...that she 'lived on the milk from her cows?'"

"Then you know her?"

"I saw her once before when I was yet younger than you."

"At Askeaton, where she sang."

"At Askeaton where she sang the night I was... never mind. I know of her, yes. You are very fortunate, Donal. She is myth. She is legend. She's the foster daughter of Angus and Mananan. Let us not refuse her hospitality."

The spit stops as they turn to it. Bawn first disappears himself and then is back with Donal's weapons, his sleeping robe and some oat cakes. A lovely salade de Coquilles St. Jacques et Topinamabours a la Vinaigrette Parfumee a L'Huile de Noisette would be very nice, but there you are.

These two large folk take up a considerable bit of the length and breadth of the cave as they stretch out and roll into their blankets. They are still catching up on who has emerged from the slime mold of plantationism over the past three years in which Donal has been absent.

"What of Frank and Cormac, father? Are they as well as can be expected considering their disadvantages?"

"Oh, I'm glad you asked. I have almost forgotten to mention them, haven't I? They are, as you say, somewhat impaired in the communication skills, but I must say they have developed into rather unbelievable soldiers. Regular warriors, they are. Cormac's brain is working very hard and he is doing good things and wouldn't you know it, Frank has become an able field commander. He has taken to horse and sword with uncommon zeal and slashing. I'm very proud of them."

"That is great good news. What about my sister, Ellen?"

"Who?"

"My sister, Ellen. Your daughter by your wife Honoria."

"Oh, yes, that's right. I have a daughter by the name of Ellen, you know. Very pretty, I must say. She has her mother's face and tongue, but other than that I find that she can be quite attractive and intelligent. In a limited Fitzgerald way, of course."

"She is fourteen now, is she not? You must be looking about for a proper husband soon."

"One would not believe the bother of having an eligible daughter, Donal. No one is good enough according to her mother and if they are they don't please Ellen. We have chased off more twits than you can imagine."

"Who? Would I know them? Would I know any of them at all?"

"Well, let me see. There was the lieutenant governor of Cork, Tom Norris by name, but he is already in love so he bid no trump and exited in the first round of stakes. Then there was one of Lord Stanley's people, I think. Killed at Yellow Ford in lasts season's finals between Desmond and Ormond. Fine, fine young man, he was, too."

"That is the whole of the list?"

"Oh, no. Not at all. That insufferable Valentine Browne who swindled me out of Molahiffe for a paltry £66.40s on a mistaken debt has a son named Nicholas."

"I had the misfortune of making the acquaintance of Valentine Browne when I was first brought to Dublin Castle by Bostock and Flowers. So, what does his son think of our little Ellen?"

"He is not impressed, to speak honestly. His father, however, sees a vast improvement in his many positions if he finally convinces his son Nicholas that marrying her is the correct and intelligent thing to do."

"His son likely has nothing to say in the matter, has he? If his father wants Ellen to be this Nicholas' wife and the bride money is right, he'll have to take her, won't he?"

"Not so, son. It is Ellen and her mother who must be convinced it is the best. Ellen is young, as you've pointed out. She believes in love."

"You believed in love when you married my mother, Father."

"Yes, I did, and in my own way, I still do, though it is much less expensive and much more convenient not to. Nonetheless, it will be some time before any decisions are taken. The sooner the better, though, I would have to say!"

"Father, I hesitate to ask you another question, but I do have one."

"As long as it isn't about your mother, speak up. Then I will bid you good night. I am weary, Donal. I have been without drink for the six days of your journey here and it has taken a great toll."

"It is just that Jezebel Lee told me you had taken a loan against Castle Lough. And, that it was a loan from Florence MacCarthy. I know he is handsome and wealthy and is legally wise, but by the waters of the holy wells, isn't that very dangerous? He's a shrewd man, from what I'm told."

"Oh, that! Yes, I did do a little deal with Florence MacCarthy Reagh. I was short of the ready and he was making funds available at the most reasonable of rates, so I took it, yes. I took quite a bit, as a matter of fact. Took quite some time to get rid of all of it, but I succeeded."

"It is all gone, father?"

"Yes, it is all gone, but don't worry. He is very wealthy and I could get more should you need any of your own. I am given to understand by Johnny Meade that when his father died the money simply gushed into Florence's hands. Has a lovely place down in Carbery, you know? You must see it some time, Donal."

"He's quite the gentleman, isn't he? Great respect all around, would you say?"

"Yes. That would be a fair sizing up of the man. Having said that, I must add the caveat that although he is my nephew and your cousin, if I could choose another to be a relative I most certainly would. In a trice, I would."

"Why do you say that Father?"

"I think you must find that out for yourself, Donal. Now, Good Night!"

Outside the cave, the wind takes up and howls its welcome home to Donal. Inside, the cave is snug and the blankets warm. These two are asleep in each other's company and assurance of saftey from elements and the hunters of the British forces who are searching for this outlaw. There is no sound from the horses outside. No danger is forthcoming on this night of freedom in his father's country. In these regions of Kerry the hunters are in more hazard than the hunted.

The gray dawn. There is no sparkle in the air. It is pissing rain and improper planning has provided no dry firewood. The few remaining oat cakes have gone missing. Donal suspects his father might have become hungry in the night. Bawn thinks Donal ate them. The rats did, but never mind.

It is time to get to and on their horses. Donal thinks they are headed home. They are not. Bawn has a bright idea coming on, impelled by sobriety. He thinks this is a simply grand day to call upon Valentine Browne and see about a few rent coyne. This is not possible. He no longer rightfully owns Molahiffe, just a few short miles away. Not on the route to Castle Lough, but close enough not to mind the added distance. That alone is enough to overcome the fact that he has lost the castle to Browne. Perhaps something will be shaken loose from his son, Nicholas. Worth a try, worth a try, worth a try, indeed!

"Donal, if you are ready to travel we shall go."

"Yes, Father. On to Castle Lough and home at last!"

"There is just one short trot over to Molahiffe. I must see Valentine Browne about a most urgent matter."

"Money, father?"

"Well, ah, yes. Money."

"You cannot expect much from Valentine Browne, father, if he has Molahiffe fair and square on a defaulted mortgage loan."

"Well, now, I wouldn't say 'fair and square' there, Donal. Let us just say it is in litigation with Johnny Meade. It will be more a social call than a threatening one. You know what I mean?"

"You are 'a bit low' as I have heard you call the condition before."

"In truth, Donal, you are correct. I cannot recall when I was holding sufficient coin. But, enough of that. We must make our plans for your safekeeping and decide what we are going to do to get

124

Molahiffe back from that pretender, Browne."

What can Donal say? He is in a hopeless position. He cannot just say, "Come on Pappa. We're going home." It simply wouldn't work. He must go along with what his father says and go to Molahiffe. He is glad enough to be in Kerry, but he isn't at all happy to be trying to tidy up his father's imagined accounts on his first day back. Oh, well, life is short. Besides, he wants to meet this Nicholas Browne who might be compelled to marry his half-sister, the lovely Lady Ellen.

As if to overcome the dismal day anticipated, the sun breaks out of the clouds as they scud away northward on a brisk spring breeze. Onward they ride back to the north and east and there at the gateway is a young fellow of about 20, light hair, fair complexion, sturdily built at 5'9" in height and dressed in trews and working leinte. Coming as they do up the lane from Fieries, they are close to him before the sleeping dog awakens from his dream-pestered madness. The dog is embarrassed and covers himself and the countryside with barks and jumping about. Does my master think I should have given him more warning of the approaching strangers? Yes, it seems he does. Nothing I can do now but bark. I've got to get more sleep at night.

Nicholas straightens up from his task whacking at a stupid post with his adz. What he was trying to do we will never know. There is standing evidence he doesn't either. He has about had it with Molahiffe after moving house from the comforts of Dublin, hauling and heaving horse and brainless oxen across rough rivers with carts full of the nonsense of his sister's etagere and curlers.

He is glad enough to be interrupted.

"Gentlemen," he says. "May I be of service to you?"

"We seek Valentine Browne," says Bawn.

"He is not here, sir. I am his son, Nicholas. May I ask the reason for your inquiry? Perhaps I..."

"We are the MacCarthy of Castle Lough. This is my father, Donal MacCarthy Mor. It is a matter of debt."

"Debt, sir? I know of no debts owed between your family and ours. What manner of trickery is this?"

"Trickery? It was by trickerey that this castle was taken from me on an overlooked piece of paper!"

"That paper, sir? I was told by my father when you needed money a loan was made. This castle and land stood as surety and you failed to repay. I do not call that trickery!"

"Repayment? If it is repayment you want you shall get repayment! Run him through, Donal!"

This is strong language, to be certain! And, this is a courageous young block of granite at the gate. It could be deduced from his next action that he lacks patience and conversational skills so apparent and evident in some young English gentlemen. He could be a stupid oaf. He now acts as though he is a stupid oaf. He lunges with great speed for his sword hanging from the gatepost . Great speed gets one nowhere in the face of incredible speed. This is what old Bawn still has and in a nanosecond this Nicholas Browne is pinned by his leinte sleeve to that same post by the sword Bawn was not even holding the last time Nicholas looked.

"I wouldn't ever try that if I were you, Nicholas Browne. Drunk or sober, he is still the quickest sword in Munster!" says Donal with very much due respect for his father's abilities.

"So I see. Now loose me, sir. I am not your enemy. Your quarrel is with my father. I suggest you take the matter up with him at Dublin Castle. In the meantime, take yourself from this land. You are in trespass!"

This is impressive. This Nicholas Browne is with but a few kerne and no gallowglass and he is pushing the most feared man in Munster to get out. It is difficult to believe, but Bawn loosens him and sheaths his sword.

"We will let you go this time, young Browne. Another time, however, you will be less lucky. Tell your father we were here. I want naught to do with Dublin Castle."

Bawn turns his horse.

"Let us away from here lest I change my mind."

Donal turns away, but over his shoulder he offers solid advice to the young Englishman at the gate.

"You are lucky, my friend. Had he been less sober he would have killed you for your impudence! Farewell, Nicholas Browne. You will see us again soon. If not my father and me, then me, assuredly!"

Mary and Joseph, if this isn't enough for one day! Hear now the sound of furiously beating hoofs upon the ground. What can this be?

What it can be is a lone horseman from Cremin's forces at Castle Lough, the familiar Pat Spleen, riding like the gates of hell are about to close upon him. The horse is lathered and the lad is dusty and road beaten. Bawn recognizes him from the riding style and the huge horse he is seemingly suspended above.

"That would be Pat coming. I wonder just what in the name of hell he is in such a hurry about?"

"I don't think it will be long before we find out at the pace he is setting!"

"Let us hope the English haven't word of your whereabouts."

Pat wheels into their presence and the horse rears up very nicely as he is reined to a stop. Bawn's and Donal's horses try to look unimpressed by this big, black beauty. "I could do that," they say to each other.

Donal is delighted to see his old gaol-mate and hails his arrival. Pat in turn grabs Donal in a hug and then must quickly report to Bawn.

"My Lord, a messenger of the Queen has arrived at the Castle with a request that you come immediately to the Court to arbitrate the differences between the Ormonds and the Desmonds."

"My God! For three hundred years those idiots have been warring between themselves and now she wants me to put it right overnight?"

"She must think you can, father. She puts great faith in the power of the MacCarthy."

"That may be so, but it is primarily because our country lies between the two," says Donal.

"That has never stopped them before. If it wasn't for the Desmonds I would not have ended up in Dublin Castle in the first place."

"The Queen is not stupid and she knows there is little I can do. There must be more reason for her command than a truce between the two. Could it be that she has heard of your escape? That would be impossible."

"That would be impossible, yes. There has to be something more to it."

Pat is still standing there looking anxious. Bawn sees this, thank God for that!

"Is there something else, Pat?"

"Yes, my Lord. There is."

"Well, what is it. Out with it!"

"Yes, sir. As I was riding through the valley past one of your small tenant holdings I caught sight of one of those bastard English Eaglets. Your cottage was being rampaged."

127

"And you didn't stop? You did nothing, Pat?"

"I was told by Lady Honoria that my message to you was very important and that I should stop at nothing to get it to you, my Lord!"

"Donal! Go with Pat and sort out this Englishman! I'll leave it to you. In the meantime, I shall get back to the castle and then head for England. I won't be gone long, lad!"

And other such flimsy tales.

"Yes, Father, I'll do whatever is necessary. Safe journey."

Chapter Thirteen

Donal Kills an English Murderer, Bawn Settles a Mortgage and Florence MacCarthy Reagh Enters Everyone's Life

Although Florence MacCarthy Reagh had not
succeeded in the Captaincy of Carbery, and
therefore , though an inheritor of vast estates,
he was of no political importance. A few years
later the keenest eyes of Munster watched his
slightest movement, and then it was discovered
that "he had long affected the company of
Spaniards, and had learned their language; that
he had so won upon the affections of the old
Lord de Courcey as to obtain from him vast
portions of his lands, and especially the fortress
of Down m'Patrick (the Old Head of Kinsale),
which commanded the harbour of Kinsale and
mostly tending toward Spain"
                                    Daniel MacCarthy Glas

Donal and Pat are riding like their hair is on fire. Into the clearing and off their horses. There, before the door of the stone and thatch on the packed dirt, lies the body of the tenant, Fynan. He is stabbed through the chest.

"God forgive me! I should have stopped!" says Pat.

"You would likely be lying there, too, unarmed as you are."

Now comes out a man pulling at the strings of his breeches. He is quite calm and composed. He is bloodied but unhurt. From inside there is the shrieking voice of the tenant's wife.

"Kill me now! Kill me!"

Donal is at him.

"What in the name of God has happened here? You! Who are you and what are you doing here?"

"I am doing nothing here. That fellow there on the

129

ground attacked me whilst I was asking directions."

From the cottage the shrieking turns to wailing.

"Pat, get inside. You, sir, step aside!"

"Who tells me to step aside?"

"I am the son of MacCarthy Mor, the keeper of the land you stand on. Who are you, you fat scum?"

"I am Bentley of York. You are most insulting. Why would a young pup such as you want to know?"

Pat is coming out of the cabin. He carries the hysterical wife of the dead tenant. She is torn and ragged. She sees Bentley and is screaming at him. Donal pulls his sword from the scabard. The tenant's wife has courage now.

"You murderer! Where is my daughter?"

She now screams at Donal.

"He killed my husband! Where is my little girl?"

"Take her to Castle Lough, Pat! Give her to the care of the ladies there. I shall join you soon. Now, go quickly! Tell the castle guard about this."

"Why the great fuss, sir? These people are but kerenes and fit for nothing else. Why waste your time on them?" asks the Englishman.

"How dare you talk in such a way about my people?"

"Oh, for God's sake! Be "serious"!"

Next comes something one would hardly expect from Donal, him being as he is, pro-life and like so. He drops the tip of his sword and lunges forward, running Bentley through against the door of the cottage.

"Is that serious enough for you, you English pig?"

Donal steps back and withdraws his sword. Bentley slumps to the ground and is dying on the spot. A wry smile crosses his lips as his head now begins to fall forward and his worthless life leaves him.

"You surprise me, sir."

He is absolutely dead in seconds. Donal sheaths his sword and glances skyward.

"He deserved no better than he gave, Lord!"

Donal is looking about. Nothing to be seen in front. He cautiously walks to the back of the cottage. His eyes go instantly to the body of a dark-haired girl, dressed in a white night shift, hanging from the branch of a tree by a halter made

130

of her own hair. In horror, he realizes it is Ethné. He is heart-broken. Blood is still dripping down her legs and the front of her shift is torn and bloody.

"Hail Mary, full of grace..."

He cuts her down with his sword and he gently gathers her frail body to his chest, holding her carefully, his left hand behind her beautiful head, pressing his face into her neck and laying her gently on the ground. He is weeping and crooning.

"May the Lord have mercy..."

Stricken with grief, he is. He finds a shovel and starts to dig. Numb, he buries the bodies of the father and little girl. Stones on top and a cross of branches. He wanders in a daze and gathers flowers to put beside the cross. He is nearly over-come by what has happened to this innocent, young family. He is kneeling beside the grave. A quiet voice comes from his rage.

"You foresaw too well, Ethné. I will not allow these foreign intruders to rape and burn Munster. Those who try will pay with their lives. I will fight to my last breath and in dying let me inflict such a wound as will not heal, but fester 'til the bearer pleads for an end. To you now, Ethné, and to every child in Munster, I vow to become your avenger. If the murdering English wish to take the whole world into madness, then I swear on your grave that I will die of fighting them."

It is time to leave. He slowly mounts his horse. There is nothing here left alive.

Except a sweet puppy. A golden wolfhound puppy which comes crying from a back corner of the cottage, unnoticed before. The puppy is frightened. He whimpers. He looks forlornly at Donal, pleading to please be noticed. He is. Donal dismounts and picks up the nervous and crying little fellow and hugs him to his tormented chest. He remounts with the puppy in his lap, kissing his face.

"Come along, then, friend. Not even you should have witnessed what happened here today. I name you Kaigengaire."

That night at Castle Lough passes in torment. Pat and Donal talk in the castle guard quarters. There are ten other men roughly dressed in mantels of dark wool. These are gaunt, hard and haunted looking men. Some are armed with swords. Some have only pikes and staff. All are listening to Donal.

"You have done well to gather these men, Pat, but I see none of my father's castle guards."

"They will answer your call as well as these men. They have come from all the nearby ploughlands. They too have been evicted by the English and came to see you when they heard you had escaped."

Donal turns toward the glowering heads.

"I have little or no money as yet, but that will soon change. I plan to ride the country to raid the planters' stolen land and houses. They will pay for every inch of ground they have taken from you. We shall take two lives for every one they have killed. We are few now, but we shall grow in number and strength."

A ragged and dispossessed O'Mahoney clansman speaks in response.

"Sir, my brothers and other loose swords will surely join you once they know for certain that you are returned. They are eager for revenge."

"And they shall have it! Will you all get the word to the others who are so in distress?"

The voices quietly mumble their pledges and leave the quarters.

When all have left, Donal looks to Pat.

"How many will come?

"Many? There will be many, many, sir!"

On the other hand and ten days later, not many and certainly no one with his senses about him disregards or delays his visit to the Queen when summoned. Especially when that Queen is Elizabeth. She has a reputation for insisting on punctuality and severely impedes the progress of those who cause her to sit and wait. She simply will not stand for it and so the umpteenth time, everyone who was supposed to call upon her at Hampton Court does so and does so with alacrity and studied good timing.

So the MacCarthy Mor, or Bawn as he is called here, arrives not only at the hour but has arrived sober as a Bishop's page. With him is his great friend and legal adviser, Johnny Meade.

Remember when an Drimuin was taking Bawn to Askeaton years ago? Of course you do. He had asked James

132

Fitzgerald, the 14th Earl of Desmond, if his son Gerald was eating too many corns? Said he was a finely put together lad but that if he was his son he'd send him off to Moriarity in the Boggeragh Mountains to be trained so he could possibly swing an axe some day?

What an Drimuin really thought was that if Moriarity got hold of the scrawny little toad he would have killed him from over-exertion or he'd be drowned in an ice-cold stream. There would be one less heir to trouble the MacCarthys if that were to happen, but unfortunately, that is not what happened at all. Nothing like it. The little bugger thrived on the regimen, climbed every peak, swam every river and, yes, managed to swing an axe. Swing an axe, indeed! He swung his axe in a most menacing manner, lopping off the arms and legs and an occasional head of friendly kernes as well as those opposing his opinions.

As you can imagine, this sort of behaviour leads to disagreements of all kinds. Put that together with the fact that the often referred to Ormonds and Desmonds hated each other's bloody guts and have done so with enthusiasm and painful results for several dozen decades. They are having at each other and Gerald is busily practicing his acquired skills and calling upon Bawn to join in the fun when the complaints to the Queen cause her to call this meeting. Gerald is "in rebellion" and "causing wars" and all manner of other harmful disturbances. It is Tom Butler who is calling upon her to equalize the conditions and you know, of course, that she is most sweet on him. Calls him her "Irish Husband" and all that. "Black Tom," too. Of course, she gets Bawn in attendance to stand in the middle of things and declare right from wrong. That is how bad things are. Bawn is going to set things right. Fat chance, eh?

"Gentlemen! My Lords Ormond, Fitzgerald and MacCarthy. Would you be so kind as to step forward that we might all hear each other in comfort?" asks the Queen.

Well, that is what they do. Not crowding around, but in an uncomfortable and gentlemanly way.

"You have been given a notice. You are constantly in conflict over territorial rights. I have summoned Donal MacCarthy Mor to Court to act as arbiter to settle this matter once and for all. Is that clear?"

"Perfectly clear, your Majesty. Be assured of my continued compliance," syrups Tom.

"It is all very clear, your Majesty," says Bawn.

There is a period of silence. You have already decided who is not answering in the affirmative.

"And you, sir. What is your reply, Lord Gerald?"

"I see no need for a further agreement as to the rights of land and castles. I am, your Majesty, most displeased with the way the Court has adjudicated territorial settlements."

"Begging your pardon, your Majesty, but Lord Gerald has rampaged through my southern ploughlands and caused great distress and damage," says Tom.

"You lie, sir! I have never taken anything that was not mine..."

"Both of you will do well to be calm. My government rules Ireland with justice."

This dolt Gerald just keeps on talking:

"...nor should I be put at any disadvantage by English standards of equal status in Ireland."

"If I could speak a word here, your Grace," says Bawn.

"This butchering gambler who asks to speak has no say in the settlement of anything!" shouts Gerald.

"You will calm yourself, sir, or you will be taken to your quarters until such time as you can speak sensibly," states Queen Elizabeth.

Gerald is sensitive about words such as "sensible" and "balanced" and "reasonable" and "sane" as one can imagine. He goes mad. He pushes his own attendant out of his way and lunges at Tom. As directed, Tom is calm. He steps out of the way. Bawn is not calm. He steps in between the two and flattens Gerald with a single sweep of his arm. Gerald goes quickly to the floor and Bawn is seen to be kneeling beside him as though he is surprised and sympathetic. Ho, ho, ho!

"Now, either you submit to the Queen's decree or I will do more than just mediate the settlement," whispers Bawn in Gerald's ugly ear.

Fiesty. That is Gerald, all right. Stunned, but fiesty. He thinks he will resist a bit. This is not probable in the least as Bawn has got a hammer-lock on him in what appears to be a helping hand.

"Do it now or I will end my role by murdering you, you maniac! I am serious."

Bawn is looking into Gerald's wild eyes which are watering a bit from the pressure-created pain.

Bawn now does slowly raise Gerald up, tipping him to his feet as one would place perpendicular a tent pole, all stiff and rigid with anger. But Gerald does speak as he is being stood.

"Very clumsy of me. I am prepared to submit immediately, your Grace. I wish to apologize and would deem it an honour to make such an agreement with my fellow landlord, Lord Thomas Butler."

"You, Tom Butler, and Donal MacCarthy will then meet my representative here tomorrow to sign the memorandum of agreement. I shall speak to Earl Desmond now in private as he seems impatient to recognise our authority."

What is this? The Queen is smiling at Donal and Tom. There is a hint of amusement in her eyes, praise God.

"I think you should be advised, Donal MacCarthy, that tomorrow the Crown will reinstate the well-earned title of Clancar upon you. You have my leave to retire."

In less time than it takes to tell about it, Bawn and Tom are walking down the corridor arm in arm. Johnny Meade is strolling behind with the other members of the two parties.

"You crafty old devil, Bawn. Thanks to you I didn't have to kill the bastard on the spot. And, you now have a title again! Dear, oh dear me, Clancar, is it?"

"Don't you ever dare call me that to my face!"

"No chance, old friend. How is it you seem so sober? Would you care to join me for a drink?"

"I am perishing for the lack of it."

This is a great idea, but it is not going to happen for the simple reason that there is someone waiting in an alcove to cause a visit. It is a very tall, elegant and handsome gentleman. It is Florence MacCarthy Reagh, tanaiste of that sept. He is dressed in tasteful opulence and bears the unmistakable polish and poise of a person of breeding, education and intelligence. Someone you could spot a mile away in an ordinary crowd. With him is Gullepatrick, his fencing instructor. Finigan is moving with exquisite stealth into the corridor to intercept.

135

"Uncle! What a wonderful surprise to see you here and how convenient for both of us. Am I to understand that you are being bestowed with the title of Clancar? There are no secrets from me in this place, you know!"

"Finigan. What brings you here?" asks Bawn.

"My name is Florence, as you well know."

He turns to Tom to engage him as well.

"My uncle always tries to annoy me by using that barbaric name when he knows I insist upon my proper name of Florence. Good day to you, Tom Butler."

"Hello, Finigan. You always seem to magically appear when there is trouble. I hope it's just a coincidence this time," Tom replies.

"I must confess I had hoped to find Bawn here. One might say that I have been waiting for a chance to catch you."

"We were just going for a drink, Finigan. Would you care to join us?" invites Black Tom.

"I'm afraid there isn't time, thank you very much. There is an urgency to my seeing the MacCarthy privately and immediately."

"Aha. Then I shall leave you two gentlemen," says Tom as he turns in unison with his coterie and they leave in step, hut-2-3.

Bawn knows he is trapped. Nothing good is going to come of this.

"I'll want Johnny Meade to hear this."

"Above all, Clancar, you will want a legal adviser."

"There is no need to assume a threatening tone, Finigan. Let us just have our little chat."

These two frauds enter a small anteroom with Johnny. Gullepatrick, Florence's swordmaster, and Fynin McCormick McFinnin, his retainer, enter closely behind. Gullepatrick thinks this is a good time to examine his rapier and holds it in his hand while backing up to the door, which he closes.

"This better be important, Finigan."

"Nothing could be more important at the moment."

"Has something happened to my son?"

"Nothing of the sort, Clancar. Your robber baron of a son has been sighted at once in every county of your country, but he's uncatchable. Thus far, I hasten to add. This is a matter of

136

finance."

"Finance?"

"The money you owe me to repay the over-due loan of £300,000."

"Are you mad, Finigan? I don't owe you £300,000. What are you talking about?"

"The money I loaned you two years ago against Castle Lough. It is a year past due and I would be repaid."

"I don't have £300, say nothing of £300,000! Where's the paper on the loan?"

"Oh, I have a paper, all right. It is right here."

Florence flourishes a rolled-up document and hands it over to the flap-mouthed Bawn.

"It clearly states the terms. There are no mistakes about it."

Bawn takes the paper ever so reluctantly. It is hot in his hands.

"I cannot believe this! Johnny! Have a look and tell me what we can do."

"Oh, you did it all right. Now I need the money you owe me."

Johnny is quickly going through the document.

"It's clear enough. I find no misstatement or errors," he says.

"It cannot be. I refuse to give up my Castle Lough."

"I fear you might have to if you cannot raise the money."

"That's ridiculous! I haven't any way of getting that amount!"

Florence is savouring every moment of this.

"I feared as much. Oh dear, oh dear. What shall we do?"

"For a start you can stop that mocking sarcasm. It doesn't do a thing to help solve the problem."

"It is not a problem for me. It is your problem, or so it would seem," says Finigan as he turns away to stare out the window into the garden. Johnny sniffs a decomposing rodent. It is Finigan.

"Is there some way we can have more time to settle this?"

Finigan turns back to the two. He looks from one to the other and pauses. He has their attention.

"Well, there just might be something."

"What is it? What are you saying?"

"I will be fair; more than fair by all standards. Grant me the hand of your daughter Ellen and I shall cancel the mortgage."

Johnny doesn't even glance at Bawn.

"That is ridiculous. What would Honoria, her mother, say to that?"

Bawn suddenly has this instant and gratifying vision. He waves his hand at Johnny to belay further complaints.

"Be quiet a minute, Johnny. My dear nephew Florence may be cleverly on to something here."

"Oh, it's clever enough. He takes the girl and when you die she gets the inheritance, Florence gets Lady Ellen, Castle Lough and all your other holdings that may be left and your son Donal gets nothing, as usual."

"As for Honoria, gentlemen, I think she will be most pleased. When the Queen's men find your son he will be hanged or worse, for murder. As for me, I just want repayment."

"Murder? What in the name of God are you talking about?"

"As I was leaving Kinsale the word came down that Donal was wanted for killing an Englishman named Bentley of York."

Bawn is surprised. Not stunned or shocked, just surprised. Then he becomes pleased. However, there is no denying the fact that he is now a wounded and weakened dealer.

"You are a heartless man."

"No need to lose our tempers here, gentlemen," says Johnny.

"It seems I must accept your proposal."

"I'm sure you brought papers for that, too," says Johnny.

"I did, indeed. If you would be so kind as to sign the marriage agreement I will cancel the debt. Johnny Meade can sign the witness. It is imperative that you say nothing to anyone until I send you word that I am at Castle Lough and proposing marriage to Lady Ellen in Honoria's presence."

The papers are quietly signed and Bawn heaves a sigh of relief interchanged with disbelief. He is now stunned, to be sure.

Florence is quickly away, stuffing the papers into his leather pouch as he hurries out the anteroom door. Bawn and Johnny are left standing.

"I really can't quite take all of this in," Bawn says. "What did I just do?"

"I'm afraid you've done a great deal. You've just settled a dispute, you've become titled once again, you've gotten your mortgage cancelled and you have gained a wealthy and powerful son-in-law. What you haven't done, and this is truly amazing, is have drink taken. Lord only knows what your conniving mind will come up with once you have one!"

"I cannot imagine what you mean, Johnny, you sly devil. Let us go find out."

Chapter Fourteen

Florence Sweeps Bawn's Daughter Into Marriage and Donal Kills Another English Eagle

"That, as the Mariadge of Florence McCartie
to the Earle of Glyncarr's daughter tendeth to the
disturbance of these partes yf it not be prevented,
so, as great and as dangerous troubles will growe
otherwise if it be not looked into in tyme"

Sir William St. Leger
12 June 1588

At Castle Lough there is a giddy atmosphere about the place. Get this. Florence is now sending his favourite spokesperson to the Castle ahead of the deal-making in London. Florence knew this was going to turn out his way so Donal O'Sullivan Mor is there to get a little turmoil and excitement into the old place. Honoria and Ellen are now the complete subjects of O'Sullivan's propaganda campaign to win the ladies over to this gallant. He is going on and on and on about what a fantastic knight in shining armour this Florence creature is. God! If they only knew the truth! That is neither here nor there at this point. The great specimen is arriving on his own to take up the proposal of marriage.

As was said, the place has a giddy air to it. All the servants and so forth are tweeting and gushing as though Florence was some kind of great star visiting from our heavens. Honoria is very excited as you can guess. She just knows that this fellow with all the money and land and everything else is going to make everyone deliriously happy and solvent. She is eager as only a Fitzgerald can be. Ellen, well...well, Ellen is wet.

The three, Florence, Honoria and Ellen, are seated in the main reception room and doing a good deal of complimenting and talking nonsense. Florence has just moved up to the edge of his chair and is listening intently. Ellen is watching every quiver of nostril on the handsome face. She is a bit awed in his presence and aware of the haste he has made in coming to Castle Lough. The inside muscles of her thighs are starting to quiver. Oh, Christ's wine, he is a charmer!

Honoria can cope, believe you me!

"We were surprised and delighted to learn that you would be paying us a visit this day. It is too seldom that you are able to take the time to come to Castle Lough," she says.

"Indeed. It was just a year ago that I was last here and that occasion was the birthday of your lovely daughter, Ellen."

"We remember. Do you recall that Florence asked for more than his share of dances with you? We couldn't keep you apart."

"You should not have tried, mother," says Ellen.

"You are very kind, Lady Ellen. I shall never forget the evening."

"That is why you have stayed away from our castle for so long?"

"Don't be rude, Ellen."

Honoria is walking on eggs. She does not wish to offend Florence nor does she want her petulant daughter to foul what looks like a lifetime of comfort and free lunches. She smiles a warning with a tiny shake of her head toward Ellen and grasps the moment.

"You stated that there was a matter you wished to discuss with the two of us?"

"This sounds exciting, Lord Florence. Will it be of interest to me?" asks Ellen.

"Don't be so bold, Ellen. Be patient. He has travelled far to visit with us and he shall tell us in his own time."

"It is I who must be bold, Countess. I have come to you with one purpose in mind. I fear my heart will no longer be silent, for I desire the hand of Ellen in marriage."

Honoria is onto this like a hawk on a hare. Her talons quickly close on the subject.

"You what? You wish to marry little Ellen?"

Ellen is even faster.

"That is what he said, mother. He wants to marry me!"

Florence reads the reaction he wanted and expected and plunges forward.

"Exactly! I want to marry Lady Ellen immediately."

"Did you hear that, Mother? He wants to marry me immediately!"

Honoria thinks she is losing control of the situation as Ellen's mother and the ultimate director of finance. She must slow the process or the whole unwritten bill of benefits will be lost.

"I heard it all right!"

"Oh, Mother of God! I am going to marry Florence MacCarthy Reagh, the most handsome, wonderful man in all of Ireland!"

"Oh, I wouldn't say that, exactly, Ellen. Munster, perhaps, but all of Ireland?"

"We must consult her father. He should be returning from England shortly and he can give us his counsel," says Honoria.

"If I may again speak boldly, I am to tell you that Lord Donal has been consulted and the agreement to marriage has been made. He is delayed in returning by the importance of his work there. His legal assistant, Johnny Meade was his adviser and in my presence, approved the documents."

"You are saying that my husband is fully aware of your proposal to marry Ellen? How can that be?"

"Oh, mother! If the tanaiste of the Reagh clan says it is so, it is so! What are we waiting for? His word is good, I'm sure."

"I was not doubting his word, dear. I only meant to make certain...when do you want the priest to perform the ceremony?"

"I think this being Monday, Saturday would do very nicely," answers Florence."

"We cannot possibly be ready by then. There are the guests, the reception, the dinner, the gifts...oh, dear me, there are just hundreds of details to attend to."

"Mother, if he wants to marry me on Saturday I think he must be willing to forego the formalities and just marry me. I think it is very sweet and impulsive!"

"It would have to be at Muckross Abbey. Ardfert has been done by the English as you know," states Honoria.

"Muckross would be my first choice, Countess. I would marry Ellen anywhere, in the lanes if necessary, but Muckross is

143

splendid, be assured," replies Florence.

He's got her. Florence has landed the greatest prize in Ireland.

The wedding will take place on Saturday as was asked and it will be unattended by outsiders, those being anyone and everyone who might have an objection. Ever so many do have an objection, but they are not being heard in the immediate area.

There is always a however.

You know how many of the Castle Lough tenants and kernes were deserting the MacCarthy and joining Browne at Molahiffe for thoughtless considerations such as food and coyne. You also know the staff in the castle is excited by Florence's visit. As always, this sort of conduct and excitement results in the phenomenon of word of mouth. Horses cannot travel as fast. How does it happen? It is similar to dust on the wot-not. No one knows.

In the case of Florence coming in to marry Ellen, the "however" is Valentine Browne's determination that this wedding should never take place. Valentine and his son, Nicholas, are having a conversation about the whole of it. Valentine is highly agitated. Nicholas is calm and disinterested in the threats against Florence and Ellen.

"I tell you, Nicholas, this is a diabolical travesty! Florence swooping in here to marry Ellen before anyone knows it!"

"Father, anyone with enough money could have done the same. He only did what he wanted to do and what everyone should have known he would do."

"Anyone? Anyone? Do you not remember that I offered £500,000 for her to be your bride? Bawn was fairly drooling at the thought of all that money! So what has happened? Why has he sold her to that cad Florence or Finigan or whatever he is called? The Queen is furious!"

"If something is to be done it is the Queen who will have to take the action. I suggest you simply forget you ever made an offer for her and get on with it," says Nicholas in a spurt of intuition.

"So you are perfectly content to let Florence get away with the most sought after girl in all of Munster?"

"I don't wish to be obstinate, father, but it appears that

144

the deed is as good as done."

"Not while I am still able to do something."

On such short notice it would appear that "while I am still able to do something" really amounts to nothing. But, that would be if you didn't consider the nature of a surveyor. A surveyor must, in the end, look at the bottom of the triangle as well as the top. What he sees, then, is that the law and the awesome power of the Queen are at the base of what is to be done. If She Who Must Be Obeyed didn't want them married in the first place, preferring, of course, an English husband for this potentially powerful girl, then do something locally. Tom Norris, the non-runner for her hand, had let Florence travel in the country where he should have been forbidden. Let the guilty and regretful Tom try to make amends. Send some men of the high sheriff's force.

No one is to say, you see, that his plan is worth the pucker in a pig's arse. The dubious Nicholas enquires.

"Just what is it you think you can do, Father?"

"I am going to ask the governor to take the two of them into custody until the marriage can be annulled. I will have the Lady Ellen brought here to Molahiffe and when it is sorted out, you will marry her in a proper ceremony."

"I doubt anyone will listen to that argument, but I know you want this for my benefits. It matters little to me either way."

"I sometimes don't understand you, Nicholas. You just don't seem to comprehend the value of a proper marriage in these times."

"I don't fancy her. She is tall and angular and froward and I dislike tall and froward women, father."

"She is a prize to be sought and I intend to do all that is possible to obtain her for you."

"And, you will bring her here? To Molahiffe?"

"I will indeed, if Tom Norris gives the support I need."

The priest is now finishing the wedding ceremony at Muckross Abbey. The wedding couple is coming down to make its exit. Ellen is radiant. Florence is looking smug. Honoria is looking smug, too. She is also happy, but not radiant.

There is a loud clatter and the doors of the Abbey fly open. Standing there is the high sheriff and four of his guards.

145

They all bare their heads.

"What is this rude intrusion on our wedding day?" asks Florence rather exitedly.

"I beg your pardon, my Lord. We are sent by the governor to take you into custody for having proceeded with the wedding without the Queen's consent." says the high sheriff.

"But, I have the papers giving Clancar's permission to marry his daughter. There is no reason for arrest."

"I'm only carrying out my orders, sir. Please understand that you are not under arrest. I am your escort to Cork City."

"And, what is the difference between arrest and escort?"

"I'd have four more men if you were to be arrested, sir."

"What follows the journey to Cork City?"

"I believe the Queen wishes to see you. You will be transported there to the Tower of London. Lady Ellen will remain in comfort in Cork."

The wedding party can do little but obey and off they go.

Did our Ellen remain in comfort in Cork City? No, she stays but a fortnight and then one dark night, she slips out of town with one of Florence's retainers, a fellow named Fynin McCormick McFinnin. She is whisked, well, no, because you simply cannot whisk someone for over 245 kilometers and expect them to survive. What really happens is that she is transported to the estates of friends of friends, the O'Rourkes in Donegal. She has no plans at present to return to that city of ingrates, Cork.

The high sheriff is entirely right in his surmise. Florence is soon away to London and passes through the water gate to the Tower. If you have never been to the Tower of London, you are most surely under the impression that it is just another gaol. It is not. It is quite nice, actually. Drafty, yes, but the apartments are large and and as long as you can afford it, the meals are catered. You have the freedom of movement up to three miles from the Tower and approved visitors are permitted to enjoy life with you there. One is never certain about the arrangements for linen service or laundry or the possibility of room service. Theatres, of course, for this is Shakespeare country. Still, it's not like it's your home and things can and will go amiss.

146

There is one thing about Irish life in these days. If you have some property and your neighbor has property and if the property consists in part of some nice fat black mountain cattle you go get them. Or, you try. The way you do this is to get a whole group of friends or employees together and perform a raid. Is it legal? Not exactly, but everyone is doing it and if everyone is doing it, then who is going to complain except the victim and if you're a victim, then you must be the weaker of the two parties and therefore no one is going to listen to you anyhow. So that's it. It's just a part of the process and you must try to live with it.

Which is what, in his own way, Donal is doing. He has these people who think he is anointed following him everywhere at anytime he thinks it's a good idea. It is a simple plan. He will make use of these loyal and until now unpaid devotees and go raiding so they can get some cattle and turn them into money so Donal can pay them and get more soldiers to do more raiding to get more money to pay more people and then he will be able to fight off the inevitable challenges of his half-sister's husband, the chap in the Tower of London, Florence MacCarthy Reagh. What one has to keep in mind at all times is that Donal is going to be his father's successor as Mor, or the big cheese, as they say. But, not if Florence has his way, which is one of the reasons he is married to Ellen in the first place. He is cancelling Clancar's debt of £300,000 on the strength of this probability. £300,000 is old cabbage in this game.

Donal is very much in a revenge mode for the killing of Ethné and Fynan and nothing will do but to raid the English planter Clarke who is nearby. He and Pat are leading their rag-tag band of sword and horsemen toward the hovels of one of the abused tenants of Clarke. As they approach they are not confronted, but briefly delayed, by a troop of Irish soldiers in the pay of this very rough English adventurer. They recognize Pat with Donal and do not stop them or warn Clarke.

As Donal and Pat come into view of the tenant Collin's hovel, they hear cries of agony. The two push through to where they are suddenly watching this Collins, a shaggy-haired, thin and bloodied relic of the system. He is getting the English Protestant new and improved interpretation of the Spanish Inquisition from your man, Clarke. He is swacking the life out of this man with the flat side of his broadsword and has nearly accomplished his intentions and is making some comments on the way.

"You worthless little pip! You are here to care for the cattle, not sit on your stinking arse and watch the trees grow!"

"I was only taking a rest from gettin' the cows away from the bramble, sir!"

Clarke has taken no notice of the newcomers, so intent is he on his work on the head and shoulders of Collins.

"You were sitting on you arse beside the stream and the cattle are wandering everywhere. You are a worthless, lazy lout!" screams Clarke.

Collins is in poor condition from the thrashing. His face is gashed, his head half-scalped and his pitiful skinny legs no longer hold him up. Clarke now begins to kick him with his booted feet.

"Have mercy upon me, sire! I have a wife and four children with nothing to eat."

"I'll kill you, you skinny little toad!"

Donal has seen more than enough. He pushes Clarke roughly and Pat helps Collins to his feet and to a nearby stream for water.

"Just what in the name of God do you think you are doing to this poor herder? Can't you see he's half starved and now you have beaten him close to death! You will do no more against that man!"

"You'll tell me no such thing. Who in hell do you think you are, coming here? He is my property and I do as I like! He who tells me I cannot had best be prepared to die!"

"You would be foolish to try me, Clarke. I know you well by your reputation."

"And who addresses me with such vulgar familiarity?"

"I am Donal MacCarthy."

A murmur runs through the Irish soldiers of Clarke. The name of MacCarthy is repeated around the circle. Donal's own men are moving into position to assist Donal and Pat. Something huge has to happen.

"I have heard of you, boy. You will not live another day. I will make you but another victim of my skills. Then Collins will be my next."

Clarke circles Donal and calls to his soldiers.

"Keep the kernes of this bastard away whilst I severe his head from his oversized body!"

Clarke's men make no move but to back away further from the circle that now forms the arena.

"Your audacity is even greater than your stupidity, Clarke. You are an English planter on Irish soil and in no position to taunt me further."

"Enough, I say! Back it up!"

Clarke lunges forward and slashes with his great sword, but his attack is easily thwarted by Donal's instant reaction. Donal drops his sword to his side taunting,

"Is your sword too heavy, Clarke? Or perhaps your strength has been wasted on Collins?"

"Not so tired as to be unable to finish you!"

Clarke slashes again at Donal's head and catches him high upon the shoulder, the blade glances off into Donal's chin, drawing blood.

"You have cut my face, Clarke. You should not have done that."

"Your eyes are next, bastard!"

"I would doubt that."

Donal isn't getting fancy, but he does effectively use his sword as a rapier, totally confusing Clarke, who takes two wounds, one to the stomach and one to the neck. Clarke's look of surprise changes to horror as he realizes he is being bested.

Donal dances forward and again wounds Clarke two more times with a punishing pause before the last one. Clarke is now kneeling and dying. He makes an effort to rise, but falls back, dead. Pat rushes up to Donal to help him. No help is needed.

"First Bentley of York and now this Clarke. How many more?" asks Donal.

He turns toward Clarke's men.

"Will any of you take his body home?"

No one answers and no one moves. Their eyes are cast downward.

"We should leave him where he lies, Donal. Someone might care enough about him to come looking in a day or so."

Donal again turns to the Irish soldiers of Clarke.

"What will you do now? You have seen your leader killed."

The soldiers stir about, then one finds his voice.

"If you will have us, Donal Nonthus, we will join your troop."

"What do you mean, 'Nonthus?'"

Pat knows immediately what the soldiers have decided.

"If I may answer for them, Donal, you are called Nonthus in the honor of great soldiers. They have given you the name and the title. There is no one before you who was as you are now."

There is a another murmer, this time of approval of how Pat has put the name to Donal.

"Thank you, men. I shall do my best to live to such a title. Should you wish to join us you will be treated as our brothers, not as traitors."

He walks with Pat to the edge of the stream where Collins is still sitting. He splashes water over his own wound.

"What say you, Pat?"

"I'd say it's a good day's work done already, sir. One more dead English planter and ten more men for the cause."

"What about Collins? Will he survive?"

"Yes, he will survive. He's a wily one. He has no wife and no children. Nobody would have him. He was just telling Clarke that to try to keep him from a further beating."

"Fair play to him, anyhow, Pat. Have the new men gather the cattle here and we'll be on our way."

And on their way they are, again and again, for Molahiffe Castle and it's fantasy treasure are not to be forgotten. Donal and his men assault Browne with ferocity and regularity. Does Nicholas Browne give in? He does not give in, for he is as stubborn as an Irish landlord and gives nothing. Stubborn being a common term for the both of them, Donal gains a great respect for Nicholas as does Nicholas for Donal. It is such a shame when friendship is ruined by hatred.

Chapter Fifteen

Donal Wins Kate O'Sullivan and Nicholas Browne Takes Sheila as His Wife

*"These purposes Sir Owen (O'Sullivan Beare)
did so pertinently pursue, that within daies he
entered into a league with his greatest enemye
before, Donnell McCarthy, the Earle of
Glencarres base sonne, thence came to Kerrie,
and concluded a marriadge between his yonger
daughter and the Knight of Kerrie's sonne and
heire; hopinge, no doubt, that they two should
drawe untoe them all the evill disposed of Kerrie
and Desmonde..."*

Sir Warham St. Leger

Good fortune comes in clumps and one day Donal and his followers are riding along the Roughty River when the thunder of hooves catches their attention. When one is out riding in the countryside with a rather sizeable price on your head, you learn to pay heed and thundering hooves are not that hard to hear.

Here come Owen O'Sullivan Mor, Lord of Beare and Bantry and his escorting soldiers stumbling over the plentiful rocks. You've all heard that verse, "Who thundering comes on blackest steed, with slackened bit and hoof of speed." Well, it was a bit like that, but not much. The standard being carried is that utterly ridiculous pig banner that denotes who and what they are.

Donal's men whirl about to face them, but in recognizing them, relax and shout rude exchanges as soldiers will do. Donal is pleased to see a friend in this change of venue.

"Chief Owen. Well met. It has been a very long time since I saw you last. Where are you going at such a rate?"

"We are now returning from a journey down the home country to where my nephew Cam is trying to re-take the land his father put in my care before he died. Cam says the land

151

should be his now! I tell you, Donal, some of these young people today have no respect for the law!"

"Nor do some of the older ones, Owen, my father being one of them."

"You're right on that, Donal. We must all of us get back to the castle today and set ourselves to work. Have you heard we are having a few games and contests at Carriganass next week? Can't guarantee Cam won't show up looking for a fight, but there you are. Join us if you will."

"Would you by chance be looking for alliance against Cam?"

"I would, indeed."

"And, husbands for your two beautiful daughters?"

"I am indeed."

"May I ask how your eldest daughter, Sheila, has taken the news that her promised husband, Florence MacCarthy Reagh has done a bunk and married my sister, Ellen?"

"Ah, our dear Sheila, yes. It has broken her heart, but she is young and strong and will survive to wed another, I feel certain of that!"

"Will Valentine Browne and his son Nicholas be present? They've had hard shocks as well with Florence stealing Ellen away."

"Nicholas will be with us, but I doubt Valentine. He's been struck with the ague, but what about you? An outlaw and eligible! That would seem to be a challenge enough for most young ladies hereabout. Certainly my daughters are no exception!"

"I know, Owen, and I have met your daughters before, remember?"

"I do, and they are still talking about the attractive but unkempt young man who made them swoon."

"And, who would that be, Owen?"

"I'm speaking of you, as though you didn't know! Will I have an answer from you or are you only going to play shy?"

"Oh, I shall be there, thank you. I must warn you, these men with me could eat half the cattle we've just taken at one sitting."

"That will suit the cooks at Carriganass just fine, Donal.

Tuesday a week, then."

"Tuesday a week it is, Owen, and thanks again."

Have you ever heard of such a set-up before? Here is this great Owen O'Sullivan Mor, commander of fleets, owner of castles and cattle, keeper of his brother's land from his dangerous and twisted nephew, but not so busy as to neglect the possibility that a potentially powerful man such as Donal might marry one of his daughters! Or bringing into play an English gentleman for the same purpose, though Browne had no soldiers left at the castle after the Queen reneged on the financial support for her planter's protection and took them away?

What could the Queen be thinking? She sends her armies out but leaves no one to protect those who have chosen to stay! A poor policy, all English concerned say. There is more to land than that within the Pale. The Irish are licking their lips, but it is far too soon to enjoy the feast of fallen landlords. When the ten days pass, here is Donal and his troop arriving at Carriganass Castle. These are not very well disciplined people travelling with him, as you can imagine, having got them off the glutted killer market when prices for gallowglass are at an all time low. One simply cannot tell what one will get under such circumstances, but it was ever so. It appears, however, that his luck is holding. "For the moment," as they say.

There is a great additon to the spirit of good feeling. That poor little puppy he picked off the ground at the scene of Ethné's and Fynan's death is showing signs of appreciation and growing up a proper boy. And big. He is not just a large wolfhound dog, he is a big wolfhound dog. If you were measuring the dogs those days as you do horses now, you'd have to say he 'stood 17 hands'. But you see, a hand in dog measurement isn't a full hand like it is with horse's measurements. What you have to do is turn your hand sideways and use only the first three fingers, minus the thumb. Then you have to divide by....Let us just forget it. His name is Kaigengaire and he is a big one.

"You men will have to make do here until the festivities start," he tells them. "Remember, we are the invited guests of O'Sullivan and there will be no plundering while here. I shall go and present myself to our host."

"You heard Donal Nonthus. Bed down only the wenches that come to you," instructs Pat.

153

It is easy to imagine what kind of an impression this makes. Oh, my goodness, the grumbling and the pissing and the moaning is right fierce.

"Let's have less of that and more cleaning up and making yourselves at least appear human. Remember, you are getting free food and you don't have to do any fighting for a few days," adds Pat.

These fellows don't know dickey-boo about manners, so they more or less have to listen to their champion, who is Pat. Oxidized by failure, they are, the poor lads.

Carriganass courtyard is already crowded with servants and soldiers putting things in order for the contests. There is an air of the occasion which indicates a good celebration, i. e., oodles of drink. Donal gives the reins of his horse to one of the grooms and walks toward the keep.

There is a great volume to be someday written about the girls of the O'Sullivan Mor clan. The beauty of Irish maidens is well known and well documented in song and verse, so what is it about the O'Sullivans? The 'what about' is that they are stunners. Absolutely, no question about it. Well developed mind and body is what it is. Sharp and seductive without forcing it, if you get my drift.

Imagine what Donal is coming up to when he walks only a few steps further and there is Kate, Owen O'Sullivan's youngest daughter. She is 15, gorgeous and a vision of innocence and purity. She is medium-tall, full figured, but still slim and... Aurgh, Christ!, the kind when you see them makes the backs of your legs tighten up. She is watching the building of a stall, but that is just a pose, as she has spotted Donal and her reaction is rather poorly hidden. Donal, on the other hand, is being quite casual.

Sure he is.

"Good Day to you, mistress Kate. I trust you remember our having met before?"

She is giving him the most dazzling smile in her repertoire.

"I do, Donal MacCarthy. I see you have not succumbed to the trends of fashion," she says, running a quick scan over his motley ensemble.

"I'm sorry to be so ragged and filthy. I have only just

154

now arrived."

She is really going to give it to him now. She clasps her hands backward in front of her, arches her shoulders, sighs deeply and flutters her eyes while shaking her head so the long flame of hair is doing the toss. What a great show. She is smitten with Donal, you can see it, plain as day.

"I have looked forward to seeing you again."

"And here I am, Kate!"

Bastard according to the law or not, Donal is his father's son. There is no denying a proper genetic pool and this youngster is proving it in spades. He may not have the polish of good home castle time, but he is well away from the caves and bogs in which he has hidden as an outlaw. His teeth are very good, too.

"Will you stay with us in the castle? Father said you were to have a room here. You'll stay inside, won't you? Not out there with your men. I would like to have you stay near."

Unseen, Owen comes from among the workmen and quietly approaches the two. They are completely oblivious to him or anyone else within sight, hearing or memory.

"I would like to stay near you, too, Katherine. You are one of the finest looking girls I have ever met."

"Thank you kindly, Donal MacCarthy! You are the most handsome boy, ah, er, well, at any rate, the most interesting boy I have ever met, I think, but first you would have to remove those terrible...but I suppose that's a disguise while you are hunted by the Queen's men for murdering Englishmen. Would you have a bath, please, and then someone should look at those old wounds. I can do that. I'll tell my father. I suppose I should tell my mother, too. She is very strict with me. She isn't so strict with Sheila, but that is because she is older. I'd rather not tell Sheila you are here or she will want you for herself and I should very much like to keep you for my very own."

This is not in one breath, but some people can talk ever so well while they take in a deep breath and Kate is one of them. I'm sure you know someone who can and will do that.

Nevertheless, Kate is quite out of breath from her speech and she sighs with the pleasure of having gotten such a nice bit into play, shakes her hair, tilts her head and unloosens a minor barrage of lashes at Donal. She is pleased, as well she should

155

be. There are only a few 15-year-old-ladies who can get away with such a pageant.

"I should very much like to be with you, too, Katherine, but first the bath and then I must see to my horse."

As he regains consciousness he becomes vaguely cognizant of Lord Owen's presence.

"Oh! Good day, my Lord Owen!"

The mouth of the Mor of Beare and Bantry has been open in awe of such a spectacle, never once before seen or heard at Carriganass.

"My god, you two! That was fast! Go on about your business, Donal, and when you have been seen to, come to the hall and meet my wife, Julia. And some of the others, too."

"Thank you, Owen. I will do that and Katherine, I shall look for you there."

As they separate Kate turns to her father a bit unhappily.

"Father, did you mean Sheila when you said he was to meet 'some of the others?'"

"I did, Kate. But don't worry. I think you have captured that one already."

It is in the nature of frivolity that festivals of sport and game are held. Most of the guests to Owen and Julia's gathering are there to eat and drink in excess, however. Such practice leads to other games. Anyhow, there is music playing from a trio in the corner, the servants are passing through the hall serving these well-dressed people and Donal, already bathed and changed, is coasting up to his hosts. He looks quite smart, actually. A vast improvement over his condition upon arrival, which brings us to the subject of whatever in the world sweet Kate sees in him. As the saying goes, "he cleans up nicely" and having said that, one soon becomes aware that he does, indeed. Nice cut to him and although "the handsomest boy I have ever seen," was downgraded to, "the most interesting boy I have ever met," there is the fact remaining that he is truly wonderfully handsome when fully clothed in proper fashion. Which he is now. And, clean, to boot.

Julia and Owen are more or less in the centre of the hall and beside them is no surprise at all. It is Nicholas Browne and he has a frozen smile upon his puss, the kind that says to a determined observer, "Oh, oh! What is this I spy? 'Tis that bastard Donal Nonthus who intends to harm me."

Owen notes this not at all, but proceeds to warmly welcome Donal.

"Julia, this is Donal MacCarthy, son of the Earl of Clancar. He will be staying with us for the festival. Donal, this is my wife, Lady Julia."

I don't understand where Donal gets all of this charm, raised as he was half here, half there and with Frank and Cormac as his formative companions. He is bowing and scraping the front foot back again like a genuine court dandy. This is not lost on Julia, who is surprised and a bit taken back by this nice young man with good manners.

"It is an honour to meet you, Lady Julia."

"My great pleasure, Lord Donal," returns Julia.

Behind Julia, but far from hidden, are the two daughters, Kate, the one you met, and Sheila, whom you have not. She is a black-haired beauty, no less so than Kate, but with a more reserved personality. The kind one gets from having been taken advantage of by Florence and then ditched. Still, take nothing from the fact that she is one of those O'Sullivan girls that should have a book written about them. Kate bubbles with youth and innocence. Sheila simmers with maturity. Mind you, she is but eighteen herself, but she has already been through phase one. Short fuse, well-hidden.

"May I present my daughters, the Lady Sheila and the Lady Katherine?"

"I have met your daughters before and it is good to renew the acquaintance."

Julia is saying to herself, "Just what does he mean by that?"

He means only that he has been introduced before, Julia, so don't get excited by misapprehensions.

"I believe you already know Nicholas Browne as well?" asks Owen.

"Yes, Owen, I do. At our Molahiffe Castle, wasn't it, Nicholas?"

"It was, as you said, at our Molahiffe."

"I'm sorry, I simply cannot get it into my mind that it is yours."

"Try harder, MacCarthy. It is ours all right!"

157

Right here is where O'Sullivan steps in between the two.

"This is the first time for Nicholas at Carriganass Castle. I trust that you will make it a habit of coming now, that we've all met."

And so forth. Placated by platitudes, a meaningless and peaceful conversation ensues and is being carried to the extreme until interrupted by the ever gaudy David Barry. Up until then, there had been some hope on everyone's part that he wouldn't show up. No such luck.

"Nice to see you free and enjoying yourself, Donal. I wish I had been present for your escape. Dear me, I would have given my best doublet to see you in a frock!"

"You were happy enough to see me held as surety at Dublin Castle. Are you planning to betray me once more?"

"Not at all, dear boy. I admire what you've managed to do since you're free. I'd much prefer you to be my friend than my enemy."

Donal is no dolt. He knows very well, and always has, that this Barry, loyal to the Crown or not, loves his rocks and bogs and pig sties as much as the Irish and can be a useful ally.

"Well said, David. I would much value your friendship."

At this Owen and Nicholas exchange surprised and unbelieving glances. Have you ever tried to do that? Exchange glances? Very dodgy bit of eye movement.

This is the first clear indication that anyone can get along with David. He is not a very nice man and there is a history of fratricide within that clan. Did in his granny. He is not, nor are the other Barrys, persons with great knowledge of poisons, but they are fond of the process involved and the lack of a scientific background does not stop them. They often confuse toxic materials with herbal medicines and this totally confuses the intended victim. You can imagine how they feel and what they think: "I feel great. Ran a mile this morning, but I know I am dying." One of David's relatives has had considerable practice and has often gotten the formula nearly correct and deadly. He is still working on perfection. His name is William.

In the master plan of things, Donal is more than just fundamentally aware that Lady Julia is David's auntie. There are some things to be gained by the fact that blood is thicker than water.

So here are David and Donal, face to face and acting most strangely while the gathering crowd around them is beginning to pair up for some deb dancing. Donal has now got other things on his mind than having a chat with this flakey young fellow. He turns back to Julia and Owen.

"If I may take Katherine from your company?"

"Of course you may, dear boy."

Lady Julia takes a short but analyzing look at the dandy David, then turns back to Nicholas Browne. He is obviously put out by having been out-manoeuvered.

"Nicholas, why don't you and Sheila join them?"

Nicholas is an English gentleman and as such does not kill Donal on the spot.

"I would be delighted. Would you lead on, Lady Sheila?"

What follows is as you would expect and likely do if it was your story. Donal's time at Dublin Castle was not spent in a dungeon. He has taken the French, he has been injected with Latin, he can find his way around a map. And, can this lad dance? He is terrific. I don't mean that he is terrific 'for such a big man,' hell, this fellow could be a lead in a ballroom group on London's West End. He is doing steps that Florence's dancing master has never heard of. Kate is aglow and doing some very impressive things with her little feet.

At some time one must take a break, which is what Donal is doing while Kate is off some place refreshing herself or something. Owen is offering a drink and bits of polite talk. Kaigengaire is laying there having a little snooze and being very furry and good. Owen is leading up to something.

"That's a fine dog, Donal. Kaigengaire, is it?"

"Yes, Kaigengaire is a prince among dogs, but I doubt you invited me here to talk about my dog."

"Well, you have me in the corner there, Donal. I wanted to ask if it is true that you have had your sister Ellen's new husband put away in the Tower?"

"It's true. He is in the Tower, but I cannot claim full credit. Valentine Browne brought a case against him as well. Florence is safely put away and we hope to keep him there. The Queen is quite keen on his proximity."

"You realize what that has done to my poor Sheila. She

159

was, as you know, betrothed to Florence and now she has no one. I'll not have her marrying some weak chiefling."

"I'm glad you brought that up. I would take your daughter Kate's hand if you'll grant it."

Owen was certainly hoping for this sort of reaction to Donal coming to Carriganass, but his greater hope was that the proposal would be the jilted Sheila. Anyone who can keep Cam in check must have good speed in body and mind and Owen had both.

"You are looking for a reply tonight? My God, Donal, it is such a surprise and came about so fast I don't know how I can give you an answer."

"Oh, I think you could coax an answer to come out, Owen."

Owen is wondering if he dare approach the business of armed assistance, but realizes quickly that the marriage proposal is the finest assurance of Donal's allegiance he could possibly get.

"You're dead right. It is coming to me now. The reply is yes, of course. Take her if she will have you. A happier father you'll never find!"

The ladies are returning from the toilet. By "toilet" you get the idea that this would be a sort of grooming centre. However, what you have at Carriganass is a little less than that. That kind of facility is only alluded to. Ever look at those pictures of castles where they have some sort of flat-bottomed extrusions along the upper parts of the castle wall and overhanging the moat if there is one? Well, those are toilets. Very tidy, actually. You could brush your hair in there, too, if that would please you.

Nicholas and Donal find themselves alone together for the first time ever. It isn't a comfortable situation at the start.

"You're either very brave or very foolish to come to this castle while your father is ill and alone. I could be sending more men against Molahiffe at this very moment."

"Perhaps I am, Nonthus, but I am also shrewd enough to know you have your men here and would never attack my castle without you being there yourself."

"You're right. Foolish, brave, but shrewd. That will get you everything."

160

"I don't want everything. I want my castle and I want Owen's youngest daughter, Katherine, to be my wife."

"Ah! I see, but it is already too late, Nicholas. That's the girl I will marry before the summer is ended!"

"You're planning to marry Katherine? When did this come about?"

"Just an hour ago."

Nicholas is about ready to go home.

"What have you to offer? A life in the bogs and caves, chasing dirty cattle and wondering whether the Queen's forces will hang you before Florence does you in?"

"Kate knows what she is doing. I will have the castle and the title of Mor when my father dies. I will also have Molahiffe and the hidden gold as well!"

"That old story again. Treasure hidden in Molahiffe! How many more years have to pass before that rumour finally dies?"

"Oh, it's there for the right man to find, Nicholas."

"And I suppose you are the right man?"

"I am, Nicholas Browne. I am indeed."

Chapter Sixteen

Donal and Kate's Wedding: The Honeymoon at Gougán Berra.
Nicholas Browne and Sheila, too.

> *Gouganebarra Lake is set in a dramatic glacial*
> *valley and is the source of the River Lee. The*
> *valley's name means 'St Finbarr's Cleft', after*
> *the patron saint of Cork. It was on a tiny*
> *island in the lake, under mountain crags and*
> *surrounded by pine forests, that the saint set*
> *up a hermitage in the 6th or 7th century,*
> *before moving down river to build his*
> *monastary at Cork City.*
> Borde Fáilte

The dancers are again in place with Donal and Kate at the centre and Sheila and Nicholas having quite a nice time together over on one side. At no time do Kate's eyes leave Donal's face. He is also blinking delightedly at her. She asks the dreaded question.

"How long will you be able to stay with us?"

"Just the three days of the festival, Kate."

"That is such a shame. But we will be happy for three days, then, won't we?"

"Three days and three nights, then?"

"Three days and evenings. I told you my mother is very strict with me."

Donal feigns a crestfallen look. His shoulders droop in mock despair. Kate puts her fingers to his face and smiles up at him. What this young girl does naturally most women would take a six weeks charm school course to learn.

"Three days, then. What will I say to your father?"

"Tell him you want to marry me, Donal. Tell him that if you dare!"

"Oh, I dare, dear Kate. I have dared already!"

163

Kate's arms drop in surprise, but in less than a blink shrieks in delight. They swirl away as a huge castleswell of dingyness overcomes them.

A short distance away in the deserted foyer, a slightly inebriated Sheila and an intoxicated Nicholas Browne have come to rest and are seated together under the stairs and comforting one another. It is obvious to all who would see them, if they could be seen, that they have spent far more time at the refreshment table than on the dance floor. Nicholas is leaning back and away from her, trying to grasp a focus but not exactly executing it with precision and grace. Now, as his weaving and circling orbit again comes near her he asks:

"Are you happy, Sheila O'Sullivan?"

Sheila was only taken from the shelf and placed on the market a year ago and in that time she has been spoken for by Florence, rejected without sufficient cause to satisfy even the most meager-brained idiot on the Beare Peninsula and now she's back on the shelf, returned as damaged goods. Tonight, for the first time since the ordeal of hearing her only true love has found another, she is feeling better. She is somewhat flattered that this English gentleman; this slightly loop-legged English gentleman, is paying attention to her even though she knows she is the second feature on the menu and at a reduced price at that.

"I am only slightly happier than I have been in some time. Are you being happy, Nicholas Browne?"

"No, Lady Sheila, I am not. In all honesty I was hoping to find that Kate might fancy me. It is not to be. Donal has stolen her heart."

"I know. Poor Nicholas. You and I are dealt a loser's hand in this. I once thought I loved and was loved, as well."

For three months she hasn't been able to say the word, "love" without a catch in her throat and a sob. Just now, there was neither and this is a very good indication of the temperature of the times. She is a bit surprised at herself.

"That cur, Florence! The one who jilted you for Ellen MacCarthy!"

"The very same."

Nicholas is feeling quite sorry for her at this point. He is also quite randy, what with all the stimulation he has taken on

164

board. He is moving on her now and she is not flinching. Aha! Aha and aha! He reaches to wipe a tear from her face with his linen handkerchief which has found his right hand from his left sleeve. Sheila is now moving closer at his tender touch. Look! Nicholas is putting his arms around her and she is cocking her head, encouraging his kiss if he can just locate her lovely lips. He does! He does so magnificently and with great ardour and the scuffling of back feet as he puts forward his energy into a five star feature! She is kissing him back quite fervently, it would seem! Now what? They are sliding to the floor in a dazzling display of acrobatic romanticism. This is incredible stuff we are witnessing. They are getting into a compromising position ever so neatly, all bits conforming to the other and all that. They are now....

Lady Julia, unnoticed, of course, descends the stairs in very nice fashion and spots them. What she sees is not quite right. They are very nearly in her path. Her regal bearing is quickly disappearing. Here is her eldest daughter about to become engaged. Humph and haw and an authoritarian clearing of the throat is just the start,

"Hold on there! What in the name of the Holy Father is going on here?"

Nicholas rolls over onto his right shoulder and hip and looks up blankly at Lady Julia. A sheepish grin crosses his rather plain English mug.

"Lady Julia! How nice to see you. We were just about to console each other."

"Console each other? Console each other? That is not what I have just....Sheila! Sheila! You let go of his breeches this very minute!"

"We were just comforting each other as Nicholas Browne was saying, mother. I think he would be very good at consoling."

"Both of you! On your feet and make yourselves presentable! You can thank your lucky stars it was me and not your father who came down the stairs!"

"I'm in love with your daughter, Lady Julia! I wish to marry her!"

"You've been drinking, Nicholas. You hardly know her!"

"I know her well enough to know I wish to have her

165

hand in marriage."

"This is most uncommon. I honestly do not know what to say."

"Mother, please. If he is in love with me he should be heard. He is a very nice gentleman."

"Wait until your father hears him. Then we will know what is to be done."

So straighten themselves up they do and Nicholas goes to address Sheila's father. He is quite sobered by the experience. He tells Owen what he has just said to Julia. Owen is impressed by the speed of the young Englishman, not to mention the fact that this should also help him in his strivances. Trust me. Strivance is a word in these times.

An hour goes by. The word is passed around the hall and the music stops. There is an announcement to be made by Lord Owen. Lady Julia is still whispering in his ear.

"Lords and ladies, guests and friends. We have an announcement which we are pleased to make at this time."

There is a steady murmur and the crowd closes in.

"When we had asked you to join us here we had no idea that our castle would be the scene of such a romantic conclusion to the festival."

"Go on with it, Owen. Tell them! Tell them!"

Lady Julia hasn't been this excited in a long time and if you were married to Owen you could see and understand that there just isn't that much going on in their personal lives at present.

"Very well, Julia. We would like to advise you that wedding plans are being made!"

You know what kind of turmoil this causes. Especially amongst the ladies. And the men being as they are, nudge and wink and raise their eyebrows in anticipation of something really..., well, you know.

"That is correct. A wedding will be held in two weeks time. One wedding, two couples. Both of our daughters, Sheila and Kate, are taking husbands. Sheila will marry Nicholas Browne and little Kate will marry Donal MacCarthy. Be prepared for a lengthy celebration."

As the days pass and the wedding hour draws near there is some apprehension about Nicholas Browne. Poor, poor

166

Sheila. "Not again, they say!" Donal you could count on, but Nicholas? He has made the excuse that it was necessary for him to return to Molahiffe for some personal reasons. Has to get proper wedding attire or some such delaying action. Could it just be that he has changed his mind and has sequestered himself there forever?

Not to worry, here he comes now. He is arriving in tatters, looking unusually dirty and unkempt. The crowd now parts to allow him to walk his horse into the centre of the courtyard. One wall of the enclosure is lined with barrels of drink and most of the men are at it. Donal's father, Bawn, has arrived for the ceremony and primarily, for the celebration and to test each of those barrels. He sees the arrival of Nicholas and has Donal by the arm.

"I see your fellow bridegroom has made it safely. He seems a bit the worse for wear, however."

He calls to Nicholas.

"Here, there, Nicholas. You are very nearly too late. What has happened to you?"

"We lost our way and then we ran into this band of your ruffians who seemed intent on stopping our progress!"

Bawn is laughing at his appearance.

"What happened then?"

"We quarreled with them They were determined to tie me upside down and backward under my horse, but in the end they just left. What are you laughing at, Nonthus?"

"The wedding clothes!"

"These were not meant to be my wedding clothes. Those scoundrels took those!"

"Then we must get David Barry to outfit you. He always carries more clothes than brains."

"I'll not wed in togs of yellow and red and purple or whatever he has!"

This does David's sensitive feelings absolutely no good at all and he is peeved. Both of the bridegrooms have now put their feelings about him into the air and everyone has heard their remarks. He is starting to do one of his famous saunters away from them when he is spoken to.

"David! Could you come back here a moment, please?" calls Donal.

"Yes, dear boy. What is it?" he replies.

"You would please me greatly if you would go to the wardrobe chest that always seems to accompany you and find an outfit for Nicholas to wear at the wedding services."

"Oh, he is a bit of a mess, isn't he? I think I have just the thing. This will be great fun, my dears. Let me see. I think a nice oyster-coloured jacket over a leintl of white linen with brown breeches would do you for the occasion."

Bawn is developing a sudden softness in feelings for the beset Nicholas. However, it could just be those barrels along the wall.

"I think you are dead right, David my boy. Would you see to him then?" he says.

"Oh, I will, I will! For my Lord Clancar, anything he wishes!"

"Watch your tongue, David."

David pays no attention to the threat from Bawn and disappears into the crowd which is gathering to gain information on what in heaven's name will come next. Owen O'Sullivan and wife Julia come out of the castle and tell everyone who can cram into the chapel to do so.

The O'Sullivan's have not given a great deal of attention to the upkeep of some of their properties and the chapel is a clear example of neglect. It is a drafty old thing and it is steaming with people. It is August and the over-heated bodies are stuffed into the seats with people standing in every spare space. The drink that has been taken has done little to calm the spirit or emanating odours of those inside or out. It is as noisy as you have ever heard and the wedding parties are hard put to hear the priest. Kaigengaire has found his way in and is trying to find Donal but cannot get to him, so he howls his plaintive complaints. Donal's half-witted half-brothers, Cormac and Frank, unencumbered by either good sense or a reserved nature, are having a simply splendid time of it and are hooting their approval and bashing each other in the glee of all of it.

The priest is unimpressed and goes on about his business, digging his way through the solemn ceremony. Both of the girls are radiant and flushed by the heat of the day and the excitement. The grooms are somewhat nervous, fidgeting and anxious to get out and away. Unbeknownst to the largest part

168

of the rowdy crowd, the ceremony is ended and the two couples are starting back down the aisle. Then, when this knowledge has pierced the surrounding alcoholic fog, all hell breaks loose. The audience is cheering and shouting and making rude remarks as is the nature of such rural assemblies. The wedding party escapes into the castle and Owen and Julia O'Sullivan stand on the steps of the chapel looking victorious and extremely relieved.

"Hold on, then. The brides and their grooms will join us in the hall when they have made ready for their journey. Don't try to follow them or you could be sorry as Frank and Cormac MacCarthy have been told not to allow any trespassers on their privacy."

"And you two see to it that your father, Clancar gets to the hall and is vertical. I'm sure he will want to say goodbye to them, if he is able."

"We'll have him there, Lady Julia. Unless he doesn't want to come," says Frank. "Then we could have some trouble."

"You're right there, Frank."

Cormac turns back to Lady Julia.

"Unless he doesn't want to come, Lady Julia. You can count on us two!" says Cormac.

"Count, Cormac? You know I can't count!" exclaims Frank.

"You'll have to excuse Frank, ma'm. He's a bit tiddley."

Lady Julia's eyes go heavenward.

When the couples reappear, the bloody pipes begin again and the noise from them and the crowd is deafening. They take the toasts and congratulations and Kaigengaire is delighted to be re-united with his master and rushes around with his tongue hanging out of the corner of his mouth. Then the great dog is suddenly put off. He knows this gorgeous creature of a Kate has taken his place in Donal's feelings. He is no longer so important. He is, as they say, playing second fiddle! He will have none of it and goes to the wall of the chapel and sits, all hurt and inferior feeling like. He puts his head back and won't look at them. You've seen dogs doing this kind of thing a dozen times.

Donal knows what it is and is immediately apologetic.

169

He goes to Kaigengaire and consoles him. He puts his arms around the fellow and squeezes him up.

"You've every right, my friend. But you must trust me. You will soon love your mistress as much as I do."

Very nice of him, with so many other things on his mind.

Garlands of flowers are put upon the horses the two couples are to ride away upon; Nicholas and Sheila toward Glengarriff and Donal and Kate to nearby Guagán Berra.

Bawn is upright and splurting inane Latin phrases as the couples mount their horses. David Barry is concerned about the loan he has made.

"When will I get my clothes back?"

"When I'm done wearing them, David Barry! Perhaps after tonight."

"You are such a teaser, Nicholas."

The couples move off at a fast clip.

In the primal forest surrounding Guagán Berra there is a little, rustic cottage. It is just the thing for a secluded and very private honeymoon couple in the throes of it. It is cooling quickly in the high air of Keimaneigh Pass. They are standing in embrace at the doorway, looking over the lake. The sun is setting softly over the mountains of the west. Kaigengaire has already found a place in front of the cold hearth. The horses are feeding alongside the cottage and wander toward the lake for a drink. Kate shivers, snuggling nicely into her husband's arms. Donal encloses her and looks down at her.

"If you're cold, I'll light the fire now, darling Kate."

"I'm not cold, my dearest, only excited about the day. Our wedding day."

She pauses. Schoochee, schoochee, she works herself closer to him.

"I thought it went splendidly, all things considered," she says.

"It's a day that will be remembered in your father's country, that's certain. I've never seen such joyous chaos in my life."

"Nor me, Donal. Your family was hilarious, most especially your father. Is your family always like that?"

"Only when I get married, dear. Would you like some wine and something to eat?"

"Not now, dearest. I want you to teach me about love, the kind the story tellers go on about."

"There should be nothing to teach, my dear. It is said to be natural."

"Has it always been natural for you, Donal?"

"I cannot answer that, Kate. I've been with girls and women before, as you know, but I've never been in love before so you must rely on how I feel about you."

"That seems a fair risk, Donal. I know nothing about the act of love...except that how I feel tells me I shouldn't be afraid, nor should I worry that I won't please you. And, dearest, I'm not afraid of anything with you."

Sweet Kate slowly disengages herself from his embrace and turns to the bed, located at the side of the room. She turns down the bedding and then returns to him.

"Would you like for me to leave while you prepare for bed?" asks Donal.

"Oh, no, Donal. I want to see you all the time. I want you to undress me and to kiss me and caress me and be my first and forever lover, my husband."

"I will, my dearest Kate. I shall be as gentle as the down from the pillow."

And he is. They kiss ever so tenderly. He is most patient as he caresses her and removes her clothing and slips easily from his own. Her closed eyes open wide as she feels him against her and she coos and nuzzles him, but without haste or the fury of getting to the act of love. They are both savouring the delicious feel and taste of each other and ever so naturally they move to the bed. No hurry. The darkness falls.

You're all probably familiar with the rest of that scene and it's just so difficult to describe! Anyhow, after all the thrilling and sensational sex things, they fall asleep. Yes, they do. It has been a long, hard day.

There is total darkness in the cottage. It is silent and peaceful save for the sounds of the mountain night birds. Suddenly there is the sound of a dog's dream from the hearth. Kate wakes.

"Donal, darling. What was that noise? Is there someone in here?"

"No, dear Kate. It's only Kaigengaire dreaming," he

171

replies.

"Praise God for that. He frightened me."

"Just wait until he starts to snore. That is what should frighten you!"

They are laughing and resume the process that made them tired before. There is bound to be a good deal of that going on with these two, you can rest assured!

Kaigengaire senses the sounds of love, rouses from his dream and takes an interest in the goings on in the bed. He stretches and yawns and stretches again. He sees that his master's bum is somewhat exposed from under the light covers. This huge dog moves to the bed and cold-noses Donal. Donal explodes.

"Yikes!" he shouts. "I'll kill him!"

"You'll do nothing of the sort, dear Donal. It was a delicious thrust you made!"

At Barely Lake on the mountain top near Glengarrif, a faintly similar scene is taking place with Nicholas and Sheila, but without a dog to help them.

Chapter Seventeen

Kaigengaire is Killed by Florence MacCarthy's Henchman. Donal and Nicholas Browne Track the Killer

"The same day we buried Kaigengaire
under a tree on the west side of the castle
we hanged O'Flavey...Then the Earl's son
returned and all we his people, bathed and
changed our clothes and we entered the
great hall and lit many candles, and ate,
and drank, and the Earl's son spoke comfortably
about Kaigengaire, and related certain
of his feats."
                               Standish O'Grady

There are those who say that weddings and marriages and the like have a calming effect upon the human male. Don't you believe it for one minute, at least in the case of the MacCarthy clan of Kerry. It has done nothing for Bawn in the past and it is doing very little for Donal, who it seems, has inherited the lust for raiding, if nothing else, from his father. And then there those other two sons of Bawn's relationship with Aíne O'Daly, Cormac and Frank, who excell at that sort of thing and can't seem to enjoy themselves with much else. They couldn't pour piss from a boot unless the directions are given on the heel, but then Bawn was always a great one for giving directions. Not that he himself ever took any. He didn't have to, being Mor and a hell of a warrior chief, but he delighted in playing the roles of Cormac Mac Airt and even named the one son for that mythical high-king. My God, how he did go on about those adventures and often pushed his sons into things no normal father would ever consider. Those high minded thoughts cause him to ruminate about past events and how those events have charted his life.

173

Then, of course, there is the thing with the Spaniards landing at Smerwick and their slaughter by Raleigh, with Spencer the poet looking dispassionately on, which is bothering Bawn greatly. How could the English be such unthinking Christian soldiers while giving off such a false tone of personal integrity? Those poor visiting hidalgos with Sabastian San Joseph had been promised cultural immunity and a quick trip home or something. Even after their interpreter Plunkett had explained they'd be killed if they laid down their weapons. My God, all right.

Now, that had all started with those Fitzgerald creatures killing the Magistrate Davells, a provost marshall named Arthur Carter, and uncle of Johnny Meade, and Raymond Black at Tralee and you can imagine how that got up Bawn's nose! Then they drove all the English out of town, for heaven's sake! Whatever it was that really happened made the English excited and they did in the 500 "Italiens" as they called them and in turn, this got Bawn excited as well and he was sending out his two eliminators, Frank and Cormac, to burn and pillage every English planter they could.

By this time Donal's troops are getting to be pretty good fighters, poorly paid or unpaid. Newly married or not, Donal's job is to see to it that his half-brothers didn't whack too many of their own in the process.

So, here they are, going up to Cosby's demesne with a little mayhem well planned, namely they are going to burn his fields. They are split into four attacking forces of 6 men each on horse, and each horseman carrying a torch. They ride to the far reaches in order to take advantage of a nice westerly wind when Cormac recognizes the terrain.

"This is that murderer Cosby's land, isn't it, Donal?"

"The very same. The one who has the hanging tree in his garden for Catholic mothers and their children."

This upsets Frank, who is, if he is anything, a kind person to animals and little things. Women, he is none too sure about.

"Can I have him, Donal, please?" he asks.

"We are only here to burn his corn and chase his cattle about a bit, Frank. He is an inviting target, though, and perhaps we will let you have him another day."

"Just ignore him, Donal. He's been on the mead all the

174

way from Castle Lough," says Cormac.

He is a well-meaning fellow, is our Frank. Let us get on with it.

"Take whatever horses Cosby has loose and set the fires. This Englishman will be most surprised to see the soot flying."

Cormac's eyes light up. He is most keen to get the flames running toward the castle.

"It's my turn to give the command, isn't it Donal?" he asks.

"Yes, Cormac. It is your turn to give the command."

"Circle and burn! Set everything alight and get to the north side as fast as those horses will take you!" Cormac shouts to the raiders.

There are other forces at work against Donal. It is not all slash and burn and have a good time. That night, whilst everyone is asleep in bivouac between Castlemaine and Molahiffe, there comes an intruder. It is Tómas, a sleaze bag if ever there was one. You know the kind. You can tell he is a worthless slob just by looking at him. And, he is considerably fatter than needs be. This fact will come out later on.

The camp is silent and the moist air from the hay, the straw and the horses' breath is heavy. Donal and Pat, along with Frank and Cormac are sleeping on the riverbank, away from the others. Here comes Tómas, and fat or not, he can slither along very quietly when he has to. That is what he is doing, slithering. The dog boy is lying in the straw, sound asleep and Kaigengaire is very comfortable and unconcerned about things. Tómas clubs the boy and knocks him senseless. Kaigengaire quickly awakens and lets out only one bark before Tómas's cloak covers him and he stabs the dog three times through the stomach, twisting the heavy short sword each time. He is left for dead. The assassin vanishes.

A few hours later and a few kilometers away, Nicholas Browne, his wife Sheila and the chief of the castle Molahiffe guards, Jack Willis, are sitting together discussing just what in the name of goodness one can do to protect oneself when all your soldiers have been taken away.

Jack is saying they need a new defense plan because Clancar is on the rampage again and there will now be little they can do. Just then one of his guards rushes in saying that

175

Nonthus is on the ground and wishes to speak to them!

"Nonthus is here? Where is he?" asks the flabbergasted Nicholas.

"He is outside the door, sir. He is alone," answers the guard.

At this, Nicholas is looking at Jack very hard.

"How in the name of heaven did he slip in here?" he asks the guard.

"I couldn't say, sir. The girls from the scullery came running to tell me and said he is there, and he is!"

"Tell him to come in. Jack, you stay right here."

Donal enters in a hurry, makes a nod to Sheila and approaches where they are sitting. Jack circles behind him and signals for the guard to leave. The front of Donal's tunic is covered in blood.

"So, Nonthus! I see you have been at it again. What is it you want to see me about?"

"I am here, Nicholas, to ask for your help."

"After all we have endured from you and your father, you have the audacity to come to me for help? I am in no mood for false appeals!"

Sheila is considerably more sympathetic, sensing in a moment that Donal has never been so distressed.

"How could we possibly help you, Donal, and as my husband says, 'why?'"

"I understand your disbelief, but I am in need of Nicholas, if he is well enough, and your tracking dog."

"You what?"

"Forgive me if I am distraught and incomprehensible at the moment...."

"Go on, Donal," says Sheila.

"Florence and Ellen are back from the Tower and he is at me in every way he can to destroy my power. This I can manage, but on this occasion he has sent one of his sept's paid killers to hurt me personally in the lowest and most vicious manner."

"What has happened, Nonthus?"

"My dog boy was bludgeoned and Kaigengaire was stabbed three times through his stomach. The one who did this was Tómas MacCarthy Reagh of Carbury. I'm told it was him by one of my young kerenes who saw him leaving. The boy had no idea that anything had been done."

"Is the boy all right? Was Kaigengaire killed outright?" asks Nicholas and Sheila together.

"The boy is fine, praise God. He is a very sturdy lad, and no, Kaigenaire lives, but not for long, I fear. I've carried him here and he lies in your stable now."

"In this case, we must help Donal, Nicholas."

"I doubt we can be of any help, but we will try," says Nicholas.

The four of them hurry to the stable where the stable boys are tending to the dying Kaigengaire. Seeing the attention the dog is getting, Nicholas is concerned about their loyalty.

"You seem to still hold some power here at our Molahiffe."

"We are all Irish, Nicholas."

Kaigengaire is lying on the stable floor, with one of the stable boys trying to make him more comfortable. Kaigengaire tries to wag his tail when he hears Donal's voice as they enter.

"You see, Nicholas and Sheila. He is helpless and dying."

"How can he still be alive?" asks Sheila.

"I think it had to be his love for me. He wants desperately to live."

Sheila is kneeling beside Kaigengaire and the other three join her.

"I think he is gone, Donal."

"He is, yes. I must ask another favour of you."

"What would that be?"

"Could we bury him in your churchyard?"

"Here?"

"Yes, and he'll be the best of the dead there. He's never willingly harmed anyone. I doubt that many of the others could say that."

"You could be right, Donal. I'll see to it. You said you needed my tracking dog, Nimue?"

"Yes. I have a mission for her and the two of us. Four, counting the spirit of Kaigengaire."

"I have a bad feeling about what you are going to say," says Nicholas.

"Yes, it sounds most dire," adds Sheila.

"I want you to ride with me to track down the killer of Kaigengaire."

"And, pray, what will you do when we find this assassin?"

"I shall kill him."

"You cannot do that!"

"I can and I will."

Sheila is hopefully doubtful.

"The life of a man for taking the life of a dog? That's most unreasonable!"

"Perhaps, Lady Sheila, but it is also just."

"Jack, what do you think?" asks Nicholas.

"This Tomás MacCarthy deserves nothing better. It was he who was the killer of the young herder who strayed into Carbury country last season. The boy was first tortured and then hanged."

"So, Donal, you will kill him for the wrong crime?"

"I will kill him for what he has done to Kaigengaire. I cannot judge him for another murder."

"Jack, ready my best horse and get Nimue. Some grain and some meat as well. I feel we will be gone a few days."

Sheila tells the stable boys to help her with burying Kaigengaire and lay him to rest. Donal and Nicholas put Nimue on a lead and ride westward to where the camp had been the previous night. Nimue is taken to the spot where the dog boy was clubbed and Kaigengaire was stabbed. She becomes very interested in the details of the place and the scent she needs is found.

"He will take the shortest route to the coast and hope to hide away with his fellow clansmen in Reagh country."

"Pray it doesn't rain tonight. If it does, she will lose the scent," warns Nicholas.

"Let her have her head. I'm ready," says Donal.

The dog makes a bee-line to the southeast and the two men come along behind her, neither hurrying or withholding her. After trailing the fugitive all that day and crossing a valley floor they come to a ravine where they find a loose horse with a rope bridle.

"That would be his horse, Nicholas. I'd bet on it."

"The horse has broken down. Gone lame in the front.

Too many hills too fast for the old fellow, I'd say," says Nicholas.

"So Tómas is afoot and fleeing. We have him now."

"You actually sound as though you are enjoying this. Tell me, Donal. Are you?"

"I'm not. It's a matter of getting a job done."

After camping the first night they arise at first light of dawn. The eager tracking dog is released.

Nimue hastens along the rim of the ravine, most anxious to resume his search for the new trail.

"I know this country. The valley leads to the sea. I've had to hide in this area more than once when I myself was hunted."

"If it's another day's travel we must rest the dog."

"I'm almost certain it's within the hours of daylight we have. This will take us to the land of Septimus Boggs."

"Is there really such a man? I've heard of him, but I didn't believe he actually exists."

"Oh, he exists, Nicholas. If he isn't away snooping in some old burial ground he'll know we're on his land and you'll meet him. He calls himself a scientist."

Nimue is fairly loping along in great leaps and bounds and the two men on horseback are moving rapidly forward. She soon breaks into a full, nose-down run across an open patch of ground and enters a heavily wooded area in a glen in sight of the ocean.

"We have him now," says Donal.

"Yes. I see him. Look there, he is trying to get out the other side."

Without command of either, Nimue is now surging between the trees and through the vines, catching up to the sweating, swearing, pleading Tómas. Tómas is a man you would recognize immediately upon sight. His most distinguishing feature, or lack of it, is his left ear, which for the most part, is not there. It has been lost; chewed off in some brawl somewhere along his way. His clothing is torn and hanging from his fat body and he's begging for pity. Donal and Nicholas dismount and approach the dog and Tómas. The hunted killer is somewhat apprehensive about his treatment after capture. One would have to say that most killers are quite apprehensive when they are captured.

"Have mercy on a poor farmer! Call yer dog off! He's killing me for God's sake!"

"You fat swine, you killed my dog, Kaigengaire!"

"I didn't do nothing to no dog! Now get him away from me before he tears my throat out!"

"You killed my dog, you bastard!"

"Christ, MacCarthy! Yes. I only stabbed him a few times. I can't help it if he died!"

Nicholas is observing all this with part curiosity and part horror. He leashes Nimue again.

"You are a pathetic creature, Tómas MacCarthy Reagh!"

He gives a sharp tug on the leash and separates the dog and the man.

"Back, Nimue! Stop now!"

Nimue stops, but stands salivating over the cringing Tómas.

"I think your bitch Nimue knows a dog killer when she's caught one. She'd fair love to finish him."

Nicholas is standing over Tómas. He is getting into the spirit of the catch.

"And, did you kill the herding boy last year? The one who was hung for trespass?"

"I did no such thing! I only came across him after someone else had strung him up and there's no crime in that."

"It's alright, Nicholas. The one crime is enough for me."

Suddenly, the amazing face of Septimus Boggs looms, emerging from a deep crevasse ten feet away, above the side of the glen. Septimus has the incredible ability to pop up almost anywhere and scare the blue-eyed crap out of everyone. He is, to put it mildly, a wild sight to behold with his tall, gangly structure, the lank of hair, slim to the point of emaciation and with the strange ictus characterised by the constant movement of his large, shaggy head and tripping gait. He is wearing spectacles which he himself invented while staring through a flask of alcohol. He wears a floppy hat and a cloak tied at the middle by a length of rope. His legs are nearly bare with only traces of trews, his feet are in sandals and he is carrying a piece of parchment and a stub of carbon marker. He has been disturbed while conducting an earth-shaking experiment on a eowu. Ahem and hmmm. But then again, what is one to expect

180

from a direct descendent of Curcóg, daughter of Mananán, I ask you? I tell you, some of these blow-ins from Brugh na Bóinne!

"Oh, it's you, is it Donal Nonthus? Haven't seen you in ages. What is that dog eating?"

"Septimus! Where did you spring from? This is Tómas MacCarthy, recently in the pay of Florence. This gentleman holding the dog is Nicholas Browne who occupies our castle Molahiffe."

"What in the world is Tómas doing here, Donal? There hasn't been a Reagh in these parts since last year."

"We have just now run this one to ground and now I shall hang him."

"What did he do, Donal, if I may be so bold as to ask? It is my land, you know."

"Last year he hanged a boy for trespass and just three days ago he killed my dog, Kaigengaire."

"This man killed Kaigengaire? Hang him!"

"I fully intend to. Do you have family, Tómas?"

"Oh, yes sir, I do. I have a wife and two small children. Spare me for their sake!"

"I will spare you for no one's sake. But, I will give a bag of coin to Septimus who will, I'm sure, be glad to find your wife and give it to her so she can at least have a dowry for when she marries someone else."

As Donal is talking amicably with Septimus about the up-coming hanging and the price of gull's eggs, the outlook for goat's cheese etc., Nicholas is re-arranging the dog's life and calming him down considerably. A tracking dog can have such a one-track sort of activism and in such a mode they frequently must be reprogrammed or they are hopeless the rest of the day.

"Come along, Nimue. Your work is done. Good girl!

He turns to Septimus and asks,

"What will you do, Septimus?"

"I will likely make more goat's cheese as it is thought to be a cold winter coming."

"I meant about Tómas, sir!"

"Oh. I beg your pardon. What will I do with Tómas, eh?

"Yes. What will you do with his remains?"

"Well, sir, as a scientist I will observe the hanging and make certain it is done under the Brehon custom. Then I shall make a study of his physiognomy, if that is what you could call that lump, take the body and measure it all over and then drop it off with his widow."

"You can actually do all that without any feeling?"

"Oh, I shall feel him, alright. He seems to contain a good deal of puss. I'd have to say he is a bit pussy, isn't he? Yes."

"I meant without it bothering you. Without any anguish?"

"I have feelings, Mr. Browne. I feel that most dogs have noble pretentions, but I don't recognize that in human creatures. Not, at least, among those who visit here."

The head of Septimus Boggs is bobbing quite nicely now with a fine rhythmic bounce to it. Tómas is moaning and this brings our attention back to that unworthy subject. Donal has also been somewhat diverted in listening to Septimus, but soon enough re-focuses his attention to the matter at hand.

"Well, then, as you pointed out so clearly, this is your land. Where would you like him hanged?"

"Could you kindly do it up on the top from that oak tree yonder? It would be most kind of all of you. It's nice and clear there and it will be ever so much easier to lay out and measure in such a place. And, thank you for asking."

Nicholas remembers the lame horse.

"Septimus, if I may call you by your Christian name, there is Tómas' horse two valleys over to the north. He has gone a bit lame but he could be of service to you for taking the body away."

With Donal in the lead the four of them and Nimue now make their way up the side of the ravine. Tómas blubbers and finds himself getting a few prods along the way. Septimus is directly behind Tómas with Nicholas behind him.

"That would be most handy. I'll go and fetch him after you're done with this one. My, from this view he is quite fat. Quite fat indeed. Can't understand why people let themselves go so!"

At the top the men allow Tómas to sink to the ground. Without a word he is pushed face-down, his hands are tied and then he is helped to his feet. A rope is tossed over a limb of the oak tree and a noose is tied and put around his neck.

"Have you anything final to say, Tómas MacCarthy?"

182

"I don't think so. What good would it do?"

"None. Up you go then."

Tómas is hoisted up backward on Donal's horse. Donal smacks the horse across the flank, the horse jumps forward and neighs at such strange goings-on. It is over.

The body of Tómas MacCarthy Reagh hangs from the tree, eyes bulging and tongue now hanging out. There are much prettier things to look at in this peaceful valley by the sea, but they stare at him for a few moments.

"That's over. Thank you, Septimus, for the use of your tree and for taking care of the rest. Would you like a ride back to his horse?"

"You're very welcome, Donal, and thanks for the offer, but it's a fine day and I must get the measurements done before he stiffens all up, you know what I mean?"

"I think so, Septimus."

"I'll work my way over to the horse later."

"Fair play to Septimus Boggs, then. 'Til we meet again."

"Good bye to you both and take good care of that dog Nimue. She is a wonderful little girl."

"I shall take good care of her, Septimus. Be assured. And, I have learned a good deal today about the Irish mind."

"You'd be the first one who has, Nicholas Browne. Good day to you," says Septimus Boggs.

Donal and Nicholas return to the bottom of the ravine and re-mount their horses and ride out the far end toward home.

"I will be riding north, Nonthus. I must say the past few days have been most enlightening."

"And, for me as well, Nicholas Browne. Will you and Nimue be all right the rest of the way? You seem a bit knackered."

"I'll make it. The lung rot gets me down once in a while. Sheila knows what to do."

"But do you? You cannot keep fighting against me or it will kill you and Jack Willis as well."

"I don't care to think about it. For now I will just see my wife, find the children and sleep for a week."

"That sounds the thing to do, Nicholas Browne. Farewell to you. Kiss your wife Sheila for me!"

"I'll do nothing of the sort for you, Nonthus, but I surely will for myself. Farewell. I'm sure we'll meet over swords again."

"I hope not, Nicholas. I truly hope not."

Chapter Eighteen

Bawn is Killed; The Rush to London to Settle His Holdings

> *"On the 16th day of March, 1599, in a*
> *solemn assembly of grave counsellors and*
> *learned lawyers the claims to the inheritance*
> *of the late Earl were considered, and following*
> *the track broadly beaten by Donal and his*
> *bonies, these venerable men swept legally*
> *before them all pretensions..."*
> Daniel MacCarthy Glas

Now that the O'Sullivans and the McCarthys are getting on so well, being closely allied as they are by marriage and by the strengthening of the septs' military positions, Bawn is only too happy to accept the opportunity for a week-end outing. Owen is offering Bawn a package that includes everything one needs for hunting the stag, which incidentally, is the heraldic centerpiece of the McCarthy clan. Free room and board, Owen's ships make his cellar good and Owen will furnish the rest of the hunting party. It is the best offer on the Beara Peninsula and Bawn grabs it lustily. Unfortunately, Donal is off hunting this Tómas McCarthy at the time and cannot join in the fun.

The hunting party gathers at Dunboy Castle at the western end of the peninsula and there are eight in the group, not including the twelve lads who will help in any and all ways. There is still a hazy mist hanging over the land as the horses are being readied and the dogs are being sorted out and leashed in the courtyard. They will go eastward from Black Ball Head past Bear Island and then to the foothills of the Caha Mountains and up inside the ridges to the gap, the reason being the very best. There have been some very large stags reportedly seen up there. Seven foot wingspan, according to some.

Everyone is ready, the pack horses are being loaded and the last drinks taken to fortify themselves against the cold.

"Here, Owen, try a drop of this Jerez."

"Thank you, chief. We should reach the Caha Mountains by half day."

"We have a grand morning for a ride up the side. From what you say, your scouts have sighted a fine beast for us."

The troop form a line and start out along the narrow road, the dogs nervously jerking at their leashes and their handlers quietly coaxing them back. In four hours time they reach the trail and start the sharp climb up the mountainside. There, above them 300 feet, the red deer are watching the procession. Behind them, standing calmly on a crag, is a magnificent red stag. He is looking from deer to men, back to the deer and again to the party below. As the party goes further up, the herd starts slowly down.

The party climbs slowly up the incline toward the summit and the stag. As they reach the top, the first of the scouts returns to Owen and Bawn.

"Lord Owen, if you look downward to the high lake below the tree line on the left you will likely see a grand stag."

Owen and Bawn are quickly rewarded - a look at the promontory and they sight the beast. They stop and admire him before trying to determine how to get to him.

"He's a great old fellow, isn't he Bawn?"

"He's absolutely magnificent. How can we get around him? I think the clever gentleman already knows we're here. He's making a game of it, is what he's doing."

"Oh, he's on to us all right. One that old has been in human company before, I'll wager!"

"We could start back down and come across the other side past the lake. It will take us a few hours but it will be well worth it."

"I'd say a better chance would be to go over the peak and down the other side. He'll at least have lost sight of us then," says Owen.

"That's it then. I'll lead up to the next crag and we'll have another look."

"I'll be right behind you, Bawn. Mind your way amongst the loose stone."

"My horse is steady."

The party starts up the trail and Bawn stops at the peak,

186

sidling his horse to the edge where he is able to have a better look down into the valley. The view is breathtaking with the sea behind them and the mountains all around.

Owen O'Sullivan Beare and Bantry rides to Bawn's right side and stops.

"Have you spotted him again?"

"He's very brave. He's still standing on that out-cropping. He really is making a game of it, isn't he? I don't recall ever having seen one so splendid as he."

Suddenly Owen's horse skitters forward and into the side of Bawn's horse. The left foreleg of Bawn's horse loses its purchase on the rocks and the horse and Bawn go tumbling down the steep, 100 foot defile to the ledge directly below them, rolling forward and over to another 100 foot drop.

The stag, the ever-watching stag, tosses his head back and snorts in derision and prances away as the red deer scatter.

Owen and his men quickly dismount and scrabble down the rounded side of the precipice as fast and as best they can. O'Sullivan is the first to reach Bawn, who is lying on his back, eyes open. The horse is dead.

"Don't touch him men. He's badly broken."

Bawn is still semi-conscious and he looks into Owen's eyes.

"I seem to have fallen from my horse....again..."

"Oh, Christ all Mighty! What have we done?"

"...and I never found that sodding gold," Bawn says as he closes his eyes and dies.

To tell the truth, what they had done, whether it was accidental or intentional, was to upset the whole of Munster and place it in peril from without and within. Bawn and Donal had teamed to put the Crown's very orders at risk and had defied the best of her soldiers. With the Lord Clancar dead, there would be a great rush by pretenders and heirs to grab what they could and run with it for as long and as far as possible. Donal was the heir apparent since Tadgh, his half-brother and son of Honoria and Bawn, had been taken to France by William Barry in a deceptive plot traceable to Florence. And, you already know about the Barry Boys and their faulted addiction to poisoning people. Watch this space. More to follow. What the hell, Tadgh had never been interested in much other than the simple

187

and pure title of Clancar anyhow.

That, too, is what is so strange about the Barry clan and Florence. Here is William Barry colluding with him in the most diabolical of plots against the MacCarthy Mor, involving all sorts of clever major ploys including the marrying of Ellen. He is treating anyone who stands in his way with the most monstrous perfidy and callousness. And, like him or not, David Barry hates the "counterfeit Englishman," as Donal calls Florence, beyond the bounderies of sanity.

Part of that comes from a rather solemn occasion a few years back when David was down at Timoleague Abbey putting in some flowers and tidying up the graveyard whilst casually digging up Florence's ancestors and tossing them into Courtmacsherry Bay. Right about then, Florence, who had informers everywhere mind you, showed up with about one hundred well-armed folk.

"What in name of God do you think you are doing?" he asked David.

"What in the name of God does it look like I'm doing? I am digging up the bones of your illegally interred ancestors and replacing them with mine. Mine belong in the nave. Yours do not."

"Just stop while I am talking to you! In fact, stop what you are doing instantly or you shall be very sorry!"

David stops digging and tossing and hurls a large femur bone, vintage 1446, at Florence's well groomed head.

"Here, now! That is just about enough!"

"Enough? Enough? Next time I won't miss!" says David, with gall flying out in all directions.

This is where you find the intensity of loyalty that makes fighting on sides worthwhile. What I mean is, David's men are already filing out from the Abbey with quickened steps. They know the mass is over. In a sleepy, one-eyed town like Timoleague, one can only cope with so much excitement.

"If you don't cease immediately I shall be compelled to force you to stop and take your leave!"

"You and what army?" sneers David.

"This one," states Florence, turning in his saddle and pointing with his beautiful four foot long Toledo steel sword to the marvelously trained horsemen behind him who are shifting

their own swords from scabbard to hand and grinning lascivi-
ously in anticipation of finally getting to kill some people.

David only then realizes that he has been all but deserted. He clears his throat quite audibly.

"Since you, ahem, feel so, ahem, strongly about it, I shall
take my shovel and go home."

Which he did. But he never once forgot the humiliation
he suffered and vowed then and there to poison that sanctimo-
nious phoney some day soon.

And, speaking of bodies, old Bawn's, dead at the ripe old
age of 67 from falling off a mountain, is lying in state at Castle
Lough and everyone is there. The O'Sullivans, the Fitzgeralds
to please Honoria, the Brownes, the O'Driscolls, the O'Dalys,
the O'Donovans, the O'Leynes, the honoured guards. Such a
gathering! And the Barrys. Let's not forget the Barrys. Just
everyone, but especially, especially, the damnable Florence and
Ellen. Ellen is quite shaken; Florence is acting the patrician
about to at last snatch the over-due prize. The title of Mor.

There is Donal, Kate, Frank and Cormac talking to Sheila
and Nicholas.

"Ellen looks very distressed by father's death. She is
taking it very hard but dares not show too much."

Frank is taking it hard, too, but he doesn't know what he
is to do. He is shifting from one foot to the other, nervously
waiting to ask Donal.

"What do we have to do, Donal. I don't like funerals.
Everyone knows I don't like funerals."

"I don't either, brother Frank. And, look at Florence.
Wheedling his way into favour wherever he is."

Kate quite agrees. She is not among Florence's admirers.

"It's galling to see that pretender strutting himself here."

"What do you think will be his next move, Donal?" asks
Cormac.

"No one is talking about it yet, but everyone here knows
there will be a mad rush to London for the settlement of father's
affairs. God knows they are in a horrible state."

"That means you, too, Donal?" asks Kate.

"I'm afraid it does, dear Kate. Especially me. Florence
will be fairly storming Westminster to get everything he can of
Ellen's share."

Nicholas is looking at Donal's face most intently, reading him.

"...and everyone else's share. He'll try to claim the title of McCarthy Mor and before you know it he'll be back in Molahiffe."

"Could he do that, Donal?"

"He could, and he will try."

Cormac thinks he knows the answer, but asks the question anyhow.

"What's to be done?"

"I'm away on the first ship to England out of Bantry. I'm sure the others will be doing the same. Nicholas, will I see you there?"

"I'll be there as soon as I can get away from Molahiffe."

In a while, Donal is standing aside with just Kate, collecting his thoughts and sorting through his plans. Florence approaches him.

"It seems a great pity, does it not, Donal, that it takes the death of our dear father to bring the family together?"

"Our father? How dare you even infer that you are a part of this family?"

"Don't be so crude, Donal. I am a member of the family, like it or not. It is you who is by birth out of place here."

"You well know father considered me his heir!"

"He may have done, Donal, but he is no longer with us. Others do not see it in the same way. I shall be Mor. You only need wait to see it happen."

Donal loses it and grabs Florence by the ruff at his throat.

"If this were any other day I would slit your throat here and now. Beware, brother. Stay away from me."

Everyone in the great hall is turning away from this scene. They are seriously pretending that they cannot see Donal putting his hands on Florence. Actually, that doesn't seem a bad idea. They are already abundantly aware of the issues and the hatred that exists between the two. We mustn't get involved, they are thinking.

Whatever the ensuing problems were at the death of Bawn, the royal court has sorted them out and Bawn's cousin, Queen Elizabeth is giving, well, no, she isn't 'giving,' she is 'hosting' a ball because she is tighter than a ram's bung in fly

190

time. It is one of the big events of the year and Lord Essex, her present paramour, is standing proudly beside her. All of the men who have dashed to London to place claims against the dead man's estate, and there are many, are present and looking about to see who is with whom and what they have been doing or are likely to do.

All of these people are dressed to the nines and some of the ladies of the court are being self-dazzled by the two Irish giants, Donal and Florence. One in particular, a handsome woman in a gray wig, Lady Ap Huw, is greatly aroused by the sight of the young and quietly charming Donal. Florence has been cornered by the lady, who, in case you didn't already know, has been his long-time-away-from-home lover.

"Florence, dear, who is that charming young man speaking to Nicholas Browne?"

"That 'charming young man' is Donal McCarthy, Lady Ap Huw. He is the base son of why we are all here."

"Do I detect a note of jealousy, Florence?"

"No jealousy, my Lady. Merely a touch of disgust. He is but a monkey in velvet."

"Why even disgust, Florence? My sources say you and your Lady Ellen did quite nicely by the adjudicators."

"Yes, that is partly true. Well enough for Lady Ellen, but far too much for Donal. There is more to be gained."

"The 'more' you speak of is 'Mor' as in McCarthy Mor, I take it?"

"As part of the larger goal, yes."

"So you will be staying on as a guest of the Queen, so to speak, Florence?"

"As resident of the Tower, dear Lady Ap Huw. A privileged guest held here under the false charges of spying."

"How very exciting for you. Then I will still be seeing you?"

"You will indeed!"

"Then you must introduce me to your brother-in-law immediately. He is devastating, Florence, my love."

Lady Ap Huw is now rubbing her thrusted bosom against the left arm of Florence, warming up for the fray to follow.

"You want me to introduce you to that beast?"

191

"If you do not I shall have to seduce him without introduction."

"I believe you would."

"Rest assured I would, darling. There are times to come
when you and I can enjoy each others charms, but I cannot
allow this red stag to bound off into the forests of Ireland before
the rutting season is over!"

Florence sees he has been trumped and agrees to the
introduction. He leads Lady Ap Huw to where Donal and
Nicholas are chatting with several young ladies who part a path
as the Court's Senior Seducer is escorted toward her target.

"Donal, Nicholas, I wish to present Lady Ap Huw, a very
dear friend and confident of the Queen. Lady Ap Huw, this is
Donal McCarthy, son of the late Lord Clancar."

Donal gives her a huge and smooth smile with a tilt of
the head and a nod before the best bow in Britain. He takes her
hand lightly.

"Lady Ap Huw. This is a very great pleasure."

"Florence has been telling me about you. Welcome here."

"May I introduce to you Nicholas Francis Browne, son of
the late Valentine Browne?"

Nicholas bows. It is not even in the contest with Donal's
in terms of elegance.

"A great pleasure, Lady Ap Huw."

"Yes, of course," says Lady Ap Huw without the slightest
bit of interest. Her eyes are riveted upon the prey, Donal.

Florence is getting the cue to disappear.

"I apologise, Lady Ap Huw, but I must steal Nicholas
away for a moment."

"Of course, Florence. Dally as long as you wish."

"Donal, would you care for Lady Ap Huw?" asks Florence.

"I will, indeed, care for Lady Ap Huw. Would you
honour me with a dance, my Lady?"

"Thank you, Donal I would be delighted."

Now you know that Donal is a swell dancer, but Lady Ap
Huw does not. Consequently, she really is delighted when they
move effortlessly to the floor and join in the pavanne. Lady Ap
Huw leans seductively away from him.

"I understand that you will be leaving us to return to

192

your own country."

"Yes, my Lady, I will be leaving London very shortly, more's the pity."

"How charming of you to say so. Lord Northome advises that you are pardoned for your previous transgressions."

"I am pardoned for alleged transgressions, yes. I am happy to be starting my life anew."

"How interesting a challenge for you, dear boy."

"I enjoy a challenge."

There is a pause in his speech.

"Is there some place we could become better acquainted?" asks Donal.

"You are very quick to the point, my Lord Donal. Yes, there is. Do you know the west corridor leading to the dining hall?"

"I'm sure I could find it, my Lady."

"There is a room I keep. I will go there now and you follow me in a few minutes.

"To be sure, Lady Apu Huw. MacCarthy will be there."

"Don't make me wait, dearest!"

"Never, my Lady!"

Lady Ap Huw hustles, yes, that is the word, hustles toward the sacred room while Donal starts down the stairs to rejoin Florence and Nicholas.

"I have an urgent message for you from Lady Ap Huw, Florence. And yet another one for you, Nicholas."

"For me, Donal? What is it?"

"Excuse me, Nicholas."

Donal whispers in Florence's wiggy ear. Florence draws back in surprise and pleasure.

"Yes, you lucky scoundrel!"

Florence rushes off with an almost inaudible, 'by your leave.' You had to be there.

"That was hastily organized," says Nicholas.

"As I said, Nicholas, it was urgent. For me, in any case."

"There is a message from Lady Ap Huw for me as well? A message not so urgent?"

"And, not directly from Lady Ap Huw, I fear. More as a result of my having met her. But it is far more urgent."

"What in the name of God are you going on about. Either I have a message or I don't."

Donal laughs and leans to whisper in Nicholas's ear.

Nicholas jumps back in surprise.

"Holy Mother of Jesus, Donal. You've done it this time. We'd best be gone!"

Down the corridor and well known to Florence is the entrance to Lady Ap Huw's little hide-away. He knocks and puts his ear to the chamber door, listening as he speaks in a low voice.

"It's me, Lady Ap Huw."

The door opens quietly and Lady Ap Huw peeks out. She is nearly stunned.

"Florence! What are you doing here?" she asks.

"I was given the message you sent with Donal for an assignation!"

"You're mad, Florence! I told him to meet me here!"

"The rogue! He has betrayed us!"

"He shall pay for this some day. No one, absolutely no, one crosses me, my pet!"

"You are upset, my Lady. Perhaps I should leave."

"You'll do no such thing. Waste not, want not!"

Lady Ap Huw takes his hand and draws him quickly inside.

Like his father before him, Donal makes his escape from the royal court and one of the Queen's ladies. Nicholas Browne, though nearly shattered by the rulings, is determined to hang on to Molahiffe as best he can. He is returning, but unable to make any promises to Sheila about what the future will drop upon them. He still has a bit of money and some legal holdings he will try to expand and profit from. And, of course, he has the safety net of myriad relatives in England he can rely upon.

The Queen has grown weary of nothing but reports of mischief and wrong doings on the part of the Irish Lords. Now that Clancar is gone she is determined to complete the break-up the last of the warring Munster land barons. She will break them in any way she can and she just might have the key with Florence still under her control in the Tower. First, however, there is something she must do which is even more unpleasant. She must listen. A private meeting is being held with only her lover Essex, Florence, and Lady Ap Huw. The latter is wailing as the Queen paces up and down the floor, one hand to her face, the other waving about.

"...and what is more, MacCarthy and Browne have left for Ireland without taking leave of your Majesty," the angry Ap Huw states.

"Is there no one among you who can give us relief from the incessant iritation caused by these squabbling Irish?"

"Your Grace, I was about to..." starts Ap Huw again.

"Don't interrrupt me with your lover's quarrels. I wish to hear no more about our cousins there!"

Florence has been waiting for this.

"Your Majesty, if I may be so bold as to..."

"You have something to offer, Lord MacCarthy?"

"May I propose that I be the one to quiet Munster?"

"And, just how would you do that, my Lord MacCarthy?"

"With your permission I will assemble an Irish army from my lands there and rid the world of that band of outlaws. I pledge you 2,000 well-armed and battle ready soldiers."

"You would do that to your own kin?"

"Of course, if your Majesty commands!"

"Then you shall do so. You have my permission to leave. You will also collect the £500 that pseudo-loyalist David Barry owes my treasury when you arrive there and use it to arm your men. What with the warring Irish Lords and the Spanish poised for invasion, I am left with no peace."

She turns full face to Essex who is listening with great interest and concern.

"Lord Essex, you are to immediately prepare your armies for Ireland. You shall have all the soldiers and horse needed. I trust that along with Florence's 2,000 you will rid the north of O'Neill and his fellow Catholic Army leaders, O'Donnell, McGuire and O'Connell. Then sweep southward and lay waste to all those who are in rebellion there."

Florence looks at Lady Ap Huw and smiles.

"It will be done," says Florence.

Essex simply stands there. A perplexed face, if ever there is one to be seen.

"I have done it," the Queen says to herself as she smiles for the first time in days. "I will make that Florence pay me yet for his marriage."

Chapter Nineteen

Donal Rushes Home to Seek Help From Lord Hugh O'Neill and Battles Duhallow for the Title of MacCarthy Mor

Ceycll is not ignorant of the state of
Munster! He knows that the Earl of Desmond,
Tyrell, Dermod O'Connor, Burke, Pierce
Lacey, and other minor chieftans, each with
several hundreds of hired soldiers, occupy
the province; that Donal, with O'Neill's,
authority and with many of O'Neill's forces,
keep the gentlemen of Desmond in subjection."
Sir Thomas Norreys

You must have gathered by this time that our Donal is going to fairly wing it back to Bantry town, a place which would disoblige most persons. Not to worry, he isn't staying there long enough to find out as it is market day in the square and the Bay mussels have gone off. He is smacking at the fat rump of his borrowed horse to get to Castle Lough. Which he does, much to the joy of sweet Kate who thinks that perhaps, just this once, he can stay at the castle and enjoy a few days of rest and recuperation.

The pleasure of his return is grand, to be sure, but he is not long in bed or at board, for his future depends upon his meeting with the Bengal of the North, O'Neill. He is quick to summon his old mate, Pat Spleen, and they set out for an audience with the only man in all Ireland who can supply the support he will need in order to claim and hold the title of Mor.

Now, he could have had the title out-right, but wouldn't you know, the White Rod that signifies his ascendency is being withheld by the keeper of the Rod. You can just imagine who is behind that hideous bit of perfidy! It is that Florence MacCarthy, up to his naughty tricks. Anyhow, as the saying goes, when in doubt, go with the power. And, that is definitely, in this country anyhow, Hugh O'Neill and that is what Donal is

197

doing by going to Holy Cross in Tipperary. Nothing less will do for Donal and Pat Spleen than to ride right through half the Catholic Army gathered around in the encampment and up to the main man's tent.

Aha! What have we here? It is the flag and staff banners of the Pope flying alongside those of O'Neill! Is this a good sign? Not necessarily, but one never knows what our Christian leaders might do by intent or whimsy. It does mean that Hugh has a papal emissary present and that there is strong backing for his war.

One thing is certain, nothing is going to stand in the way of Donal achieving an audience with O'Neill and right now he is telling the sentry stationed at the tent flap that is what he wants. A bit cheeky at times, is Donal, but much must be said for his mission herewith. Keep in mind that although this is a military camp and the avowed purpose at Holy Cross is to see who is willing to put up men and arms to defeat the English once and for all, the sanctity of the Church is closing fast in second place.

Out comes the sentry and in go Donal and alongside, Pat Spleen.

The two are standing bareheaded before the massive face and chest of O'Neill, whose old fashioned link chain armour seems a bit constricting. He is staring down his nose at them as is his fellow crusader and chief of staff, the impatient O'Donnell, hand to face and leaning on the arm of his carved chair in the direction of O'Neill.

There are more here than Donal expected to see at one gathering so early in a campaign. To the left is the distinguished figure and handsome face of James Fitzgerald, Earl of Desmond, who is known as the Sugaun, or Straw Earl. He is actually smiling at them in a most friendly way, which helps.

Another who is smiling is Duhallow, a sub chief of the MacCarthy Reagh clan and a massively impressive warrior is he, being covered everywhere from head to toe with muscles. He is battle scarred and battle ready, with both hands upon the down-struck sword before him. All are curious. All are silent.

"You have ridden far to see me, Donal MacCarthy. May God be with you and welcome you here. What is so urgent as to interrupt a council of war?"

"Your summons to all chiefs, my Lord O'Neill. I am here to join you, if you will have me. With my father dead my country needs more protection than I can provide without alliances. The English intruders are fairly surging into the land."

"So I know. Those planters will be put to flight soon enough. What can you offer me to assist the Catholic cause with our Southern Armies?"

"I have but 50 sword and horse since returning with my inheritance of Clancar's land and a pardon from the Queen. I pledge you 500 when I return to Castle Lough."

"A rich pledge, indeed. Meet my commander of the Southern forces for the Pope and our Church. He is, as you know him, James Fitzthomas Fitzgerald, 16th Earl of Desmond."

"Yes, my Lord. We have met through my step-mother, Honoria MacCarthy nee Fitzgerald."

So there are some rather meaningless pleasantries which must be exchanged. Here is the fate of Ireland hanging in the balance and they stand there nodding and smiling and asking how are the kids, etc. O'Neill, thank God, gets them out of the social mode.

"What is it you require, MacCarthy? What is it you want in return for your promise of 500 soldiers for Christ and where do you expect to find them?"

"It is my desire to be known as the Mor and further known to be so titled with your endorsement, my Lord."

"I know nothing of your achievements. You will have to persuade me you are a leader and one worthy of your father's title. To lead a band of outlaws as Robin Hood is one thing, to lead an army is another."

"Begging your pardon, Lord Hugh. I will vouch for Donal's abilities as a soldier and strategist. He is, in my mind, the most qualified of all men to come forward to serve with you," says Sugaun.

"Will you give me what I ask for so I may give you the men I pledged?"

O'Neill is somewhat offended by the brass of this upstart, Nonthus.

"I am told that this young man behind me, Duhallow, is also in line for the Mor, he being a nephew of your father. And, there is Florence MacCarthy Reagh. Since he cannot be here at this time I shall choose between you and Duhallow, but only after single combat."

"My Lord, I know Duhallow well. We served together as field soldiers. He is a good and capable leader, but I am in direct lineage and he is not. I stand to lose everything by single combat."

"You may stand wherever you like, MacCarthy. He already has more than 500 men ready to fight for God and us. Whichever of you two is left standing is the Mor and I shall still have the men of the loser."

The eyebrows of Sugaun raise in recognition of fact.

"A point well made, Lord Hugh. I rather fancy a bit of the blood of proof."

Pat Spleen sends a warning look to Donal, but there really isn't much a fellow can do when faced with yes or no.

"Very well. If there is no other way, then you shall have it," states Donal.

He only pauses a second, then raises his hand to Duhallow.

"My lords, I challenge you, Duhallow, to single combat at the ford on the river just below. Tomorrow at noon, should we say?"

Duhallow's smile is still frozen on his face.

"Any time you say, Donal, though I dislike killing anyone so early in the day."

"I need some rest, Duhallow. Surely you can appreciate that."

"Then, by all means, noon it will be."

After a restless night under an awning pitched beside the camp, Pat is busy sharpening Donal's sword and sits humming an ancient Scottish death chorus. Or is it Hebridian? Not to worry. It isn't very good humming in the first place. They watch as the men of the encampment move to the riverside to get good seats for they are certain this will be quite a show. Most look at Donal and Pat and shake their heads. Then the Chiefs and Sugaun move to the embankment to enjoy the spectacle.

"Are you quite ready, Donal? We could perhaps peg a few more minutes if you are not."

"No, Pat, I'm ready. I am touched, however, by your

concern."

Both Donal and Duhallow are attired in battle dress for this kind of work. Wearing a mantle and carrying a small shield and his sword, Donal moves forward. Duhallow, on cue, emerges from his circle of clansmen and supporters. He sees Donal watching him with hooded eye and takes the opportunity to take a few flourishing practice slashes. You can actually hear them, with his great Claymore sword.

Pat is still making a few last minute passes over Donal's sword with a field stone and then he hands it over. Donal approaches Duhallow along the level area of the river's ford. There, with the sun behind them, is the horde of spectators, already nipping at the mead. They allow the combatants room for the work to be done.

Duhallow steps forward to meet him and still has that irritating smile on his broad face.

"How's she cuttin', Donal?" he asks in a friendly tone.

"I have never understood that silly Cork expression. Are you ready?"

"I'm ready and fit, boyo. 'Tis a fine day for a battle altogether!"

"Are you sure you want to go through with this, Duhallow?"

Duhallow stops and gives Donal a relieved but quizzical look.

"I've given some thought to that, Donal. Doesn't make a lot of sense, does it, being so hot and all?"

"It makes no sense at all. There has to be a better way."

"Yet, we cannot disappoint the crowd here. There's been some fierce betting going on and they all have such high hopes for some blood."

"It's true, I know, but it is still a matter between our-selves."

"Donal, would you believe that just as you were saying that, a pure thought has entered my head of a sudden?"

"What's that, then, Duhallow?"

The crowd is getting edgy and restless and so are the Lords. Suguan calls out to them in a clear and firm voice.

"What is the delay, gentlemen? We have come here to witness a battle, not a debate!"

"We are making certain of the rules, My Lord James," calls back Donal.

"There are no rules! Get on with it!"

"What is this grand idea, Duhallow? It better be a good one or we'll both be dead and then what have we got?"

"What say you to a grand mill instead of armed combat?"

"You mean a wrestling, gouging and kicking match? We could be hurt!"

It takes no time at all for Duhallow to reply, "Would you rather have my sword in your head? The Great O'Neill said single combat. He didn't say what kind!"

"You are absolutely correct. Let's drop our weapons."

Which they do, turning to stand looking at O'Neill and company.

"What is it now? Have you lost your courage?" asks Sugaun.

"We have not, my Lord, but since this is single combat we have decided that the last man to rise loses. It will be a mill and not an armed conflict. That way my Lord O'Neill will still have two commanders. With my Lord's acceptance, the one standing will be Mor," answers Donal.

"It makes some sense at that. Get to it, then!"

Sugaun's hand goes to his mouth in horror.

"But Hugh! It is so brutal!"

"You Desmonds are all alike! Now, will you get to it before it gets dark?"

"We shall, my Lords," says Donal and turning back to Duhallow asks, "Are you ready, Duhallow...winner takes all?"

"Winner takes all, Donal!"

As the Sugaun Earl has said, it is brutal. Viciously brutal, with no mercy shown by either contestant. Evenly matched in size and strength, they circle, they lunge, they lash at each other and whip their legs and arms.

Biff! Bam! Ugh and Ooofff!

There is a good deal of head butting, eye gouging, finger breaking, thumb bending, body slams and attempts to neuter and disfigure. It goes on like this for several minutes actually and the crowd is getting along quite well with this fare, sloshing the mead, tossing back the brandy and hooting at near misses.

202

The two are in the water over the ford and out of it back on the land.

Finally, Donal bests Duhallow and the latter goes face down in the water and does not get up. Donal stands over him, panting and heaving. Duhallow rolls over and tries to rise but cannot. He raises his head, signalling with a waving movement of his arm that he has had enough. Donal bends and with a weary heave, hoists Duhallow up beside him as a sign of a worthy opponent. Duhallow, bleeding from every pore, reaches to hold up Donal's arm in victory. The crowd goes wild.

O'Neill and the other Chiefs are standing and clanking their swords in approval.

"An amusing time, gentlemen. Donal MacCarthy, I hereby declare you the winner and as agreed, the new MacCarthy Mor."

Donal, turning away from O'Neill's salute calls to Pat.

"Pat! Bring us a few buckets of that mead. I think we have earned a reward. A great battle, Duhallow!"

Duhallow's eyes are somewhat fogged, it seems.

"If it's all the same to you, Donal, could you let me fall back into the water? I feel a bit giddy!"

So, splash, down goes Duhallow in a heap. Donal turns back to the river and takes what remains of his mantel off and walks into the water, sinking into it to cool and wash. Pat stands on the bank, shaking his head and gathering up Donal's battle gear.

"Christ's knees! He said he was going to be a commander and now he is one!"

By now Duhallow is sitting on his haunches, recovering.

"But, Pat Spleen, there is still a Fitzgerald standing over him!"

"You're right, sir. You are absolutely right!"

On the morning following the single combat only a small gathering of chiefs have returned to the tent for a conference. They are O'Neill, O'Donnell, and Sugaun, facing Donal and Pat.

"Chief O'Donnell and I have only a few comments before we leave to return north. Earl James will be going south to reassemble his army. I want you and those 500 men promised to join him at his encampment in a fortnight."

"I will be near Buttevant in County Cork. I am to make

203

the advance from there. Find me and we shall discuss your command and your immediate role. I warn you, it will be a test of my faith in your leadership."

"I shall not disappoint you. I will leave tomorrow to gather the men and join you as you command."

Pat is sent ahead to bring out the promised men.

Kate is in the kitchen supervising the preparation of dinner. There is much to-ing and fro-ing from the cooks, the scullery maids, the gardeners bringing in fresh vegetables and the servers preparing the tableware. Pots are boiling, roasts are being basted and slowly turned by their tenders over the open fire.

Donal comes in, cautioning those who see him to be quiet. The devil in his eye, he comes up behind Kate and tweaks her firm bum, puts his arms around her and kisses her hair and neck.

No, she doesn't call another's name.

She cuddles into him, turns and kisses him passionately.

So, back in Castle Lough is Donal, drawing great sympathy from his wife and with added kisses of affection and devotion for his wounds and for the joy of his being about as alive as could be expected after his mill with Duhallow.

Much of the consoling takes place after the dinner, and quickly after it, considering the amount of time Donal has to tarry at the castle. It is located in the bedchamber. Much of the ooohing and aaahing has nothing to do with his injuries. Oh, no! Indeed it doesn't!

Pat Spleen quickly gathers the men needed and returns in three days to announce the success, based largely, he says, on the increasing number of men they had gathered to Donal before Bawn died. For better or worse, Donal's half- brothers, Frank and Cormac, are among those who are in this rag-tag force of 500 plus men.

Riding at the head of this column, they approach Buttevant on course to join the Southern Army. Suddenly, coming toward them, they see the lone figure, finely dressed in leathers and holding out an arm with a hooded falcon perched upon it.

Wouldn't you know it would be Sugaun? Unconcerned as ever, casual and looking good. There is this war going on and there is the 16th Earl of Desmond, commander of all Southern forces, out jogging along on his horsie and falconing! My God, some people are just so irresponsible, but then he is a Fitzgerald, isn't he? Well, seeing Donal, he kicks his horse into a canter toward them and reins in a couple of meters short.

"You're a few days early, Donal. I was just out for a bit of hunting. Care to join me?"

"Thank you, my Lord, but I think it wiser to go to your camp and settle my men while we wait for the foot soldiers to catch up."

"As you please, of course, my boy. By the way, I've sent William Burke and his brother Liam with their bonnachts to take Molahiffe. They should be there and have the seige well underway by now."

You can also well imagine what this information does to Donal's already troubled mind. He is, most certainly, outraged.

"You have sent Liam and William Burke to take a castle that belongs to me? It is my prize to seize, sir!"

"That funny little fortified heap of rocks? I thought you had no interest in it any longer now that you are Mor!"

"Forgive the outburst, Earl James. That makes me especially interested in it as it was ours for two hundred years."

He shakes his head and turns first to Pat and then back to Sugaun.

"My Lord James, would you have any objection to my going there to aide the Burkes?"

Lord James casually removes the hood from the falcon's head. He blows gently on the beautiful bird and replaces the leather. He cocks his head and looks most innocently at Donal.

"Suit yourself, young sir. I shall arrange for the care of your foot soldiers when they arrive. You take your horsemen and go. The Burkes could probably use some help from you. That impudent Browne is most stubborn."

"He is indeed, my Lord. Thank you for permission and I shall return to you when this is finished. Browne must be rooted out, though he is less offensive than most planters."

"You would, of course, say that. He is your brother-in-law, is he not? Never mind. Go to Molahiffe and rout him."

"I shall do my level best, my Lord!"

As Donal turns away the Earl of Desmond, James

Fitzthomas Fitzgerald, has once more taken the hood from the falcon's lovely head.

"Seek!" says Sugaun, and the bird of prey lifts off.

Chapter Twenty

Florence Arrives in Ireland, the Daanan Hoard, Ethné, and the Siege of Molahiffe

Molahiffe was defended by thirty royalist
soldiers, placed there by Nicholas Browne.
Three hundred foot, led by William Burke,
Thomas FitsGerald and some horse of the
MacCarthys, who dwelt on the River Mang,
were sent to assail this stronghold.
Camden

While Donal is whipping his horse to get to Molahiffe with his 80 mounted soldiers, O'Neill is still at Holy Cross with his fellow clan chiefs, O'Donnell and Tyrell, and his personal Priest, Father Bartholome. You will never be able to guess who else is there by now.

It is Florence MacCarthy Reagh who stayed on in London only long enough to ensure he had gathered up all the spoils that were spilt at the death of Bawn.

As you will certainly recall, Florence has been freed from the Tower and commissioned to quiet Munster and get everything in the south settled to accounts with the roving armies there. And, to put shut to David Barry. It is Essex who is to swing his axe of 16,000 men and 3,500 horse at those folks Florence is now sitting to table with. So, just what in the name of gravy is he doing here? If you haven't already seen through this ploy, watch and you will. The Pope's representative has the floor, but only momentarily.

"...and I replied to the Pope, 'Cross? Cross? You never wrote, you never sent your emissary...'"

"Well said, father!" says O'Neill. "Have you ever had audience with the Pope, Florence?"

"Never so fortunate, my Lord O'Neill. My cousin, Don Dermutio, is in Spain and visits the Vatican quite regularly."

"I had not known of your close connections with our sister, Spain."

"How useful. The Lord works in mysterious ways, Florence," says Father Bartholome.

"Indeed! He has brought Florence here to us. But, to what purpose? Surely not just to take dinner and drink at our table," says O'Donnell.

"Certainly not, Lord O'Donnell. It is the Queen of England who has made it possible for me to be with you to-night. She believes me to be in the south dealing roughly with that wretched brother-in-law of mine, Donal Nonthus. He really must believe he is the Robin Hood of Munster, riding about the way he does."

This sort of slagging gets a laugh from some and a look of disdain from others for they truly do understand this fellow who just kicked the porridge out of Duhallow.

"Maybe so," says Tyrell, "but he is popular in Munster. I hear he commands a good sized army now."

"I wonder if that army can stand to my 2,000," muses Florence.

Florence is sipping his wine and his eyes meet those of O'Neill across the table. A small smile of understanding passes between them.

There is no such understanding on the part of Donal as he rides hard for the northwest. Donal, Pat, and his fellow horsemen draw near Molahiffe at a good clip and we can hear the booming of the seige cannons and the firing of fusils. Between the sounds of guns and shouts we hear a single piper skirling encouragement to McWilliam Burke's bonnachts.

Coming in from the south as they are, Donal, Pat and their men can see the battle is intense and the besieged are giving back all that they are being given. The casualties are heavy among Burke's troops and there are bodies dropping with heartbreaking regularity.

"Christ's crucibles, Donal. They are taking a frightful kicking against the walls. What will you do when we join them?" asks Pat.

"We will take it as another battle, Pat. There's no need to give McWilliam the satisfaction of seeing us upset and anxious."

"Right you are. Look to the left of the bailey gate. There is that prat William carrying on like insane."

It is now near noontime and the cursing and roaring that

is so evident is coming from William himself as he sees that the castle will hold for another day. As he draws away from his command position, William sees Donal. He is not a quiet person to begin with, nor is he shy, and he is still roaring at the top of his lungs. Some persons of Scottish background can keep on doing that for days at a time and that is why they like bagpipes. They are kin, in a manner of speaking.

"MacCarthy! I'm glad you've come. How did you know we were here? Never mind, just tell me how to root that Englishman Nicholas Browne out of there. It's only the second day and he's killing my men by the dozen!"

"That would be Nicholas, all right. I've been after him for ten years. What will you do now, William?"

"We're going to batter down the gates. You'll hear it when we do. Then we'll finish this off."

"Good! I'll keep my men in reserve for then if they are needed. It looks a slaughterhouse out here."

The sound coming to Donal and company now is that of the great wooden wheels cut from a huge log which is being prepared for the ram. It is screeking like fingernails on slate. It is grinding forward and before the war machine is brought into position, a crude testudo is being built and fastened over it to protect horse and soldier who will man it. Under the protection of the canopy, the log is now being pulled and hauled by two horses on either side to a position directly in front of the gate. It is now getting uglier by the minute and William Burke is growing impatient with the horrible grating sound and screams for someone to oil the bloody wheels.

Which is immediately done, not by the men attending the ram, but from the ramparts adjoining the gate. Pot after pot of oil is being poured over the edge and onto the ground surrounding the siegers. From behind the men on the ramparts we see sudden flames as torches are lighted. They are dancing about up there doing a mad Tarantino with the best of them. Now the torches are being thrown down to light the oil and the testudo. Burke's men are snatching them as fast as they land and hurling them to the side.

"I'd have to say they are getting close to using the ram, Donal," says Pat.

Frank is getting excited, as he always does near open

flames.

"Could I go watch, please, Donal? I like them fires and things like that, you know," he says while knocking back a liter of mead.

"Calm down, Frank," replies Cormac. "Yer as bad as yer father!" copying what everyone else says.

"He's your father too, isn't he, Cormac?"

"Oh, yeah, right. He is at that," replies Cormac, more interested in the goings on than Frank's questions. He turns back to Donal and Pat.

"What will we do when the gates go down?" he asks.

"We will go to the lower reaches beneath the keep and look for the gold, Cormac."

Frank is by no means a man to be put aside by inattention.

"But, if we find the gold, Donal, what do we do with it?"

"Frank, you are as dense as that log they are thumping at the gates!" says Cormac.

"Why, we'll take the gold and keep it for ourselves, of course, Frank."

"Then I shall be as rich as rich can be, won't I, Donal?"

"You will, indeed, be rich, Frank."

"Oh, won't that be grand. Let us now go to dig up the gold."

"Balls on a goose, Frank! Will you fookin' wait 'til yer man here gives the signal?"

Donal grins to himself and is thinking that perhaps this wasn't such a good idea to bring these two along. Aw, well, too late to send them home now.

"Good thinking, Cormac. When I shout, we go through the gates on this side of the ram and make to the base of the keep. There is a small tunnel door flat to the ground beside the west side, as I recall."

Up on the walls, Nicholas Browne and his captain, Jack Willis, are bloodsoaked and weary, but continue to drive their men and shout encouragement. Though they are near complete exhaustion they are not giving up, even when it is made clear that they are running out of everything.

"Come on, men! Don't give in now!" shouts Nicholas. We've held this castle for years. Don't let them take it now!"

Jack Willis is at his wits ends, flying here and there and everywhere in defense. He shouts back to Nicholas.

"We're out of ammunition and arrows. We have nothing left but our swords. What use are they against a battering ram?"

"Find something to hurl at them. The castle walls themselves if you must!"

Jack's head is not made of mutton.

"Quickly, men! Those flagstones underfoot. Prise them up with your swords and heave them down!"

That is exactly what they do. Levering the flat stones up, they work them to the edge and over onto the men besieging Castle Molahiffe. Those on the receiving end, the men of Burke are depressed by this action and dislike furthering the attack. McWilliam and Liam are still shouting instructions and orders and things of that nature.

"Put your shields over your heads, you bleedin' eejits!" they say.

Just about now there is a great shout from the men themselves as the gates give way to the ram. They are pouring through the gate. Donal also shouts the order to move forward and it is followed out by Pat, Frank, and Cormac. The four keep themselves detached from the others and make their way to the tunnel door and are quickly entering a sub-chamber. Inside, the light from their torches shows nothing but refuse. Donal pushes at Frank and Cormac.

"You two start over there and check the next chamber. Pat, you must stop anything that comes this way!"

Up above them, Jack Willis and Nicholas can only watch as the men continue to dig up the flagstones. Suddenly some of Burke's bonnachts appear and the close, hand to hand, sword and axe to head sort of combat is taking place. The Scots just love this sort of encounter and they are shouting and hollering, those damned pipes are skirling insanely once again and God only knows what else. Victory is close at hand and both Nicholas and Jack are rendered unconscious in the wild fray.

No one knows what earthly good it does, but Liam and William are still roaring away when an especially piercing screechy scream is heard from one of the men. In the shallow depression made by removing the flagstones the churning feet

211

of the raiders has uncovered gold.

Yes! It is the Daanan Gold!

Donal, far below, is alone as the others have spread to do his bidding. Suddenly, there is a light from the corner of the chamber. It reveals a little girl, clad in a white shift. It is Ethné.

"This cannot be! I buried you and your father!"

"Honestly, Donal! You can be so thick! Of course it is me!"

"But, but, but...Ethné! I cannot believe it!"

"There is nothing to believe or not believe. Be quick. There is little time to save Nicholas and get the gold."

"Save Nicholas?"

"Don't be such a kerne! Go to the battlements. The way is clear and the gold is there. For goodness sakes, hurry! Must I do everything around here?"

Most of us would be in shock, right? How often do you encounter a talking vision? Some persons go years without observing such an apparition. Others frequently have such an experience, most especially in dark places in Ireland. They are called pubs.

Not to put too fine a point on it, Donal is going up the walls before and is now shouting to Pat and his brothers to follow him as he bounds up the stairs into the keep and out the upper door. They are moving at astonishing speed for not knowing what Donal is so excited about. Could it be fear or the anticipation of mortal combat? No. They are following orders.

It is a scene of absolute mayhem, a pandemonium in D Major. The gold has been found and the men of Burke have gone out of control. So have Liam and William, truth be told. All are scooping up the old chains, pendants of gold, earrings, breast plates and every other kind of gold adornment imaginable. Donal and his troop of breath-gasping men stare in disbelief at first. Then they stare at each other. Woe, oh woe is me! They are too late! That may be what you think, but that isn't exactly the way in which Donal sees the situation. He is miles ahead on this road.

"It's no use now. They'll kill us before we can move against them. Just let it be. Find Nicholas Browne and Jack Willis. Hurry!"

Frank is already wandering around to see who got the

most gold as he is very much taken by that sort of thing. Adornments quite fascinate him. Now he espies the unconscious Nicholas and Jack. Lying along the inner wall in their present state, they are quite unrecognisable to William and his crowd. With all the gold and excitement available to them, there is no interest in two more dirt encrusted bodies clumped there. No interest at all.

Frank knows what he is about and is hoisting Nicholas onto his shoulder. Cormac, not to be outdone, tries to do the same to Jack but is pushed away as the captain tries to stand and to walk. He collapses and Pat Spleen helps him back to his feet and supports him as they all make their way down the stairs. The Burke men are delirious with joy and are carrying off the gold. Liam Burke has regained his attitude of command and is directing the looting.

Donal goes to the side of McWilliam Burke and shouts, "That is the Fieries hoard you've uncovered, William. I think you know it goes to my clan."

William is suddenly feeling extraordinarily superior, an attitude related to many with sudden and undeserved wealth and power.

"It goes to the conqueror of this castle, bastard! It's the spoils and loot of battle and I'm the winner, by God!"

"You are for the moment, William. But just remember this. I claim it."

"Claim all you want, MacCarthy. It's mine and it will stay mine, unless you care to try for it now!"

"No, William. You win. We are, after all, in the same army. I know where you will be every day henceforth."

McWilliam is smiling sweetly at Donal and mocking him. He's gone a bit crazy. More exhibitionism of the sudden wealth and all that. Makes him go overboard in the acting business and he is showing himself to be quite unbalanced at the moment.

"Oh, you frighten me so, Donal! Why don't you go after it now?"

"I'm neither so stupid nor am I so crazy as to do that. I'll be around you until this campaign is over and you've gone back north to Connaught."

That's about all one can say when you are outnumbered

213

and in the proverbial wrong place at the wrong time. He and his men plus Nicholas and Jack are as dead as last week's mackeral if he goes for it now. So he doesn't. Simple as that. He can work out something later. Or so he thinks, and that is not rationalizing, it is just good common sense and logic inspired by the fact that he hasn't a single death wish in this whole wide world.

So, why not get a night's rest and see what the morrow brings? He finds the campfire of his men and makes certain that they are as secure as needs be in this unattractive place. Nicholas and Jack are wrapped up in blankets and are lying beside the fire. He passes a few words to the guard on duty, to Pat who sits having a bite to eat, and rolls himself up to get a good night's sleep, which is never a bad idea.

The next morning is one of those kinds of mornings that, with the mist hanging in the air, never seems to quite warm up. What is warming up, however, are the drunken soldiers of Burke's army. They have been having at the castle's wine cellar since they found it and are potted to the tops of their heather sprigs. They are industrious, however, in this respect. They are loading the gold and anything that isn't tied down or burned up into their carts to haul them off to be sorted and counted later. So, of course, they are paying no heed to those huddled around the campfire. That suits Donal's party just fine, for there is much to be done.

Nicholas, coughing and heaving but otherwise cleaned up, is sitting drinking something from a flask beside the morning fire. Donal comes to him and puts a friendly hand upon his shoulder.

"Are you able to ride?"

"I am. It's these bloody lungs acting up. I cannot be sure whether I should thank you or curse you for saving me."

"Think of Sheila, away and safely waiting for you. Go back to England, Nicholas. This is no place here for you now."

"You're right, Donal. Think of it. Living under all that gold. We should have pulled the place down ourselves."

With the horses ready they are now mounting, preparing to get out of there and for Nicholas to try to rejoin his wife. Jack Willis speaks up for the first time.

"I'll be back to join your troop after I have settled Sir

214

Nicholas. That is if you will have me."

"Any time you can make it we will welcome you. Fare-well to both of you. Safe journey!"

The mounting of their horses is a painful exercise for Nicholas and Jack but at last they ride away at a comfortable pace. Donal watches them leave and then turns back to his men.

"Come lads, there is nothing more we can do here. We must be getting back to Sugaun's camp."

Sugaun, of course, is James Fitzthomas Fitzgerald, 16th Earl of Desmond and Donal's commander, and he of the falcon.

Well, now! That was just about enough disappointment for that week, one would have to say. But, no, it is not over yet. They must and are going to have to go fight a war no one was much interested in fighting. However, when one is paid to fight wars nothing will do but to fight wars So progress they do to the edge of the Sugaun's encampment. A word of caution is felt necessary.

"Not one word about the gold to Sugaun or anyone else! When Burke and his men finally get back here let him tell him themselves. Remember, not a word!"

The Sugaun Earl is not impressed with the fall of Molahiffe Castle and there are few reasons why he should be. One less English planter is how he looks at it. The fact that the Burkes lost so many men is disconcerting, but the war goes on. Donal can never fully adjust to the way the Sugaun has of telling him of the latest events. It has something to do with the Fitzgerald state of mind.

Donal comes into the GHQ and there is Sugaun playing solitaire whilst his bodyman is cleaning the birdie doo from his doublet. Casual as that, mind you. After Donal completes his story he asks a perfectly simple question.

"How fares my Lord O'Neill?"

"Your cousin Florence has confounded everyone."

Just like that. Now, one would be startled enough by just the name, 'Florence', but to muddy it with words like 'con-founded everyone' will surely make the hackles on the back of your neck or wherever they are stand up and your face turn red. I mean this Sugaun is somewhere out there circling Venus.

"Florence! Where?" is the best Donal can do on the spur

215

of the moment.

"He is sent by the Queen to put down the troubles here. You and David Barry in particular. Instead, he has ridden directly to O'Neill and has offered to serve the Southern Army along with us."

"That scoundrel!"

Donal is not much for pauses as his mind is so quick and before you could take another breath he is reciting his thoughts.

"He would never do that without gaining a huge concession in return."

"That concerns me not at all. Oh, yes. I nearly forgot. We've been so busy here!"

"What is it, Lord James?"

"Oh! Bother! Lord Essex and his army have landed near Dublin. He was supposed to attack O'Neill in the north, but instead is heading south toward Munster and us. He has 2,300 men and 350 horse fairly flying toward Cahir to retake the Butler castle there. Aren't you through with that doublet yet, Declan?"

Donal is in need of a chair.

"We cannot allow that to happen. That kind of penetration must be turned away immediately. There is nothing between him and Cork and the rest of the south but us!"

"Yes. We should have some sort of plan. You are very good at that, aren't you, Donal? Yes. You are. I am putting you in command of that operation."

Now Donal does find a chair.

"I will first send Pat Spleen to Cahir to reconnoitre."

"Do whatever you must."

Sugaun turns to Declan who is waiting to help him into the doublet.

"Ah, there. That's much better. Falcons are such fun but they can be so messy."

"I beg your leave, my Lord. I must inform my brothers and send parties forward to intercept Essex and learn what they can. Do I have a free hand, Lord James?"

"With the exception of choosing your second in command. That will be Peter de Lacey. A most suitable gentleman who can parley in three languages. You are excused and let me ask for your plan as soon as you can possibly put one together.

Plans are so necessary these days."

"Do I need a lieutenant who speaks three languages? I understand this Lacey is susceptible to turning coat in crisis."

"Never! Never, never, never! He is as solid as the rocks. And, I can hardly imagine these Burkes or your brothers, Francis and Cormac isn't it, parlaying with an invader, can you? You will have a plan for me soon, won't you , Donal?"

Donal is smiling at the thought he has been given by Sugaun, that being Frank or Cormac trying to talk to a Spanish Commander.

"I will, my Lord."

He turns to Pat Spleen.

"Take two of your best men and go to Cahir to find what is now there and then return at the gallop and report to me."

"I will be back within a day."

"Make certain you do. Engage no one."

The next morning Donal calls a council of war. William and Liam Burke have arrived and Owenie O'Moore, Liam O'Driscoll, Diarmuid O'Connor Sligo, Walter Tyrell Ulster and Thomas Plunkett Leinster are present with their lieutenants. Suguan enters the tent with Peter de Lacey. Cormac and Frank are standing beside Donal. "This is one hell of a group, if you ask me, thinks Donal. "There is something sinister about half of them and the other half look a bit simple; which to my mind is not a good omen." Again, hmmm, hmmm, and hmmm.

"Gentlemen, we will go to intercept Lord Essex at the Royalist Butler's castle at Cahir. From there we will attempt to create an entrapment for Essex. For those of you who have not yet met him, this is my second in command, Peter de Lacey."

"Gentlemen, I am honoured to serve with you," says Peter.

There is a murmering of begrudged welcomes. Donal resumes.

"We shall leave for Cahir in the morning. When Pat returns we will know better where to ambush Lord Essex. Liam, William, prepare your men for battle. Make rations for the journey and make sure the armourers have your weapons in first order."

"Christ guide you, Donal. My brother Liam and me is rich men. You don't think you can command me, do you?"

"Perhaps not myself, William, but surely O'Neill, O'Donnell, and Sugaun can."

William's hand goes to his mouth. The sudden picture of O'Neill is enough.

"I'm off to see to my men, then."

"You are a good soldier, William, to be thinking of them at this time!"

Chapter Twenty One

Lord Essex and the Queen's Army Arrives; Donal Traps Him in the Pass of Plumes

*As for Lord Essex, Sir William Warren said,
"His greatness was such he was called the
Earl of Excess...or if the wealth of England
and Spain had been put into his hands he
would have consumed it winning towers in
the air, promising much and performing
nothing."*

Daniel MacCarthy Glas

Pat Spleen is back from his foray to Cahir. He is just so good at that sort of thing; riding up and down the mountains and spying and all. But, then, he comes by it naturally, what with all those horrid McDonalds and Campbells and their ilk at home in Scotland. One must learn or it is unsafe. Donal has taken him to a nice quiet place in which they can have a chat about the enemy and war and such.

"What can you tell me, Pat?"

"Cahir has been taken by Essex's advance forces. The Butlers are back in the castle. That place is in the hands of the oddest creature in God's green Ireland, and he is holding the bridge!"

"Does this creature have a name?"

"His name is Fisher Winkle, Donal. He's short and so broad of chest that you cannot miss him. We could see him from our position above the bridge. His arms are the size and length of a bull yoke!"

"How many men does he have?"

"He has ten men and they all look alike, like brothers, sort of. And, they're a fierce bunch you'd have to get through or quit. There is no quick way to win the castle other than across that bridge."

"What else?"

"We took a castle woodcutter above in the forest when he was less cautious than he should have been."

"A wood-cutter? What a strange source for information."

"He was most talkative when he saw our swords."

"And? What did he talk about?"

"He said there were 100 men already there and more on the way."

"Did he know if Essex would come this far south?"

Pat takes a deep breath and begins.

"The wood-cutter said a Butler commander had told a scullery maid that Essex was taking 2,500 men to Askeaton in the west. He will reinforce that stronghold and that he will return from there to Dublin before he relieves Mountjoy in the north against O'Neill."

"Askeaton has fallen to the English?"

"A month or more ago. Since we came south, at least."

"That is astonishing, Pat. That is fantastically good news if it is true, that Essex is not yet here himself. We can do O'Neill good if we cut Essex and his others in half after they turn north. Do we rely on what a scullery maid has told a woodcutter?"

"I would have to say, Donal, that in my limited experience with scullery maids that it would be highly reliable. They always know where the new master is!"

"You're right, Pat. Will you call our own commanders in and come back with them. I cannot give you leave to rest as yet, Pat. I'm sorry."

"I'll bring them to you as soon as possible."

So the whole group of commanders is rounded up once more and Sugaun is accompanying Donal to present the plans for entrapment and destruction of Lord Essex's army.

"All of the commanders are present and waiting, Donal. Let's hear your plan."

"Yes, Lord James," replies Donal and goes quickly to his strategy. "Gentlemen, this is what we will do. From what Pat has told us we must pass by Cahir. Instead we will take our forces to intercept Essex at Rower Bog to the north and east."

"That is my country and I know it well," calls out Owenie O'Moore.

"Good. Then you will feel much at home there. The first troops will be commanded by McWilliam Burke at Hill Pass. The second will be Diarmuid O'Connor Sligo at ground level below McWilliam. In the third position will be Tyrell and

Plunkett with your mercenary forces."

He pauses and looks directly at Tyrell and Plunkett.

"You will attack first, but only after the main force of Essex has passed O'Connor Sligo and Burke's position. Is that clear so far?"

They all nod in agreement.

"We will go over this again, to be sure," states DeLacey.

"Good! Then, when Essex is engaged with Tyrell and Plunkett, I want Sligo and Burke to attack from the rear divisions, and Cormac, O'Driscoll and myself will finish off the stragglers as Essex passes. With Owenie's help in positioning, we should have a complete victory. All movements of your troops before encountering Essex and his men must be covered through the forest and glen or at night."

So, of course, that is what happened. Even the Burkes understand the need for secret movements and all manner of hiding and reappearance in proper places. Never-the-less, there is a good deal of scurrying and dashing and confusion as they do as they were ordered. The men are positioned at the designated locations along the pass. All is quiet as Essex and his men are marching in columns through Rower Bog and into saddle of the pass.

Suddenly there is gunfire and Essex is prematurely under attack. Shocked, Donal realizes he is being betrayed. The wholly Irish division of Essex's force now passes through the narrow Rower Bog to O'Connor's level ground. O'Connor thinks Tyrell and Plunkett have allowed the division through and attacks Essex. Burke is forced to support him. The enemy is running, but is suffering few losses and they are now free of the passes and Tyrell and Plunkett have not fired a shot nor raised a pike against them. Donal and de Lacey are watching from their observation point above the action and to the south.

"What in the name of God is happening, de Lacey?"

"My guess is that you have been done by Tyrell and Plunkett. They did not attack as they were ordered, but instead let the Essex men get all the way through the first pass."

"Organize the pursuit, but first get those two to me. I shall hang them both!"

"I shall bring them myself," says DeLacey.

This de Lacey is very good. It takes him no time at all to

round up the two suspected of being traitors and has hustled them back to Donal who is chewing his lip and getting angrier by the minute. He is really very unsettled as fits the occasion for one who has had his enemy ready to be destroyed and then sees them escaping to the north. Tyrell and Plunkett are standing defiantly before Donal and this doesn't do much to ease his tension. "Explain your action, Tyrell!"

"DeLacey here told us to hold our fire until the Essex men had entered Burke and O'Connor's area."

"That is an outright lie. I told you nothing of the kind."

"I have no time for this. Hang them!" says Donal with great conviction and finality.

You have just one guess as to who shows up. No falcon this time, but it is the same rather tiresome gentleman, the 16th Earl of Desmond, Sugaun. He arrives just as the nooses are being prepared for the final run.

"What in God's name are you doing, Donal?"

"Sir, these men are traitors to all our cause. They have corrupted our plans to ambush Essex and the battle is lost. I will hang them."

"I will have no hanging of these men!"

"If they are let off and left to live, what discipline will there ever be again against such treachery?"

"That will be a matter for me to decide, commander MacCarthy! Now loosen them or you will be instantly relieved of your command. They could still be of use to us. I shall have no officer of mine set himself so high as to take vengence to himself."

This is something that Donal has never looked at as he is dead certain that he has heard somewhere of the practice, "an eye for an eye, a tooth for a tooth" and the like. It is a great temptation to continue with the hanging and perhaps string Sugaun upon the gibbet as well. He gives an order to de Lacey.

"Untie them, Peter....and keep them out of my sight! Turn them over to Lord James. It would seem he has better plans for them than I can imagine."

He is steaming and he begs his leave to pursue the escaping Essex men. He rides fast for the valley floor as the other commanders are kicking their heels into their horses and chopping great clops of earth from the hillsides as they gallop to the top. They are gaining sight of the enemy. Behind them comes the thundering 500 horse and foot, the best of Donal's kernes and gallowglass, led by a salivating de Lacey, lusting, lusting, lusting for contact. Still ahead of them the Irish Division soldiers are throwing down their plumed helmets and legging it into the forested hillside.

De Lacey is joining up with Donal once more. Donal shouts to him.

"Look there, de Lacey. The Irish Division is deserting!"

"Perhaps they realize their next meal lies over the hill!"

"And that leaves the English divisions to us."

Nobody believes this next bit. Just as they are pulling an attack force together there is an officer approaching on a lathering horse. It is Plunkett! Most unusual and quite unexpected. Donal is still seething at what has already happened with him around.

"What in the name of God do you want, Plunkett? Are you here to betray us once more? You have already lost us too many men and hours."

"I swear I did nothing wrong. It was de Lacey who himself gave me the orders! I am only here to serve against the English!"

De Lacey surges forward.

"That is a lie and a very bad one, Plunkett. Your service in the Pale has already made you a traitor."

"And, you think I would come here if I wasn't telling the truth? I could be back with Sugaun in safety and comfort, but I chose to come here to fight instead!"

"You are a liar. You didn't finish the job you were paid to do and you know the English will kill you one way or the other!"

By this time their horses are rubbing against one another, jostling and jolting into the other's sides and snorting and churning up the earth quite nicely.

Plunkett is the first to draw his sword, but in seeing him start to do so, de Lacey digs his horse into him and knocks him to the ground. DeLacy swings his off leg over the top of his horse and pounces like a steel tiger to the ground, facing off against the fast recovering Plunkett.

Swoosh! Clank, clank, whack.

De Lacey spins under a slashing sword swing and opens Plunkett's lower gut effectively. He then polishes him off with a couple of absolutely grand moves and Plunkett's death is presently here.

It happens so fast that Donal is powerless to intercede. Heh, heh!

"Where in the name of God did you learn that kind of swordsmanship, de Lacey? It was quite incredible, really!"

"From Jacques Franceschi, Lord Donal. Your brother-in-law Florence's sword master and adviser. The one who cleverly suggested he marry Lady Ellen. He is one of Stanley's conspirators."

"Why didn't you tell me?"

"Tell you what, sir? Tell you that and lose the chance to serve you? Not in this lifetime, Donal MacCarthy Mor!"

"Thank you, Peter. And, well done!"

"You are most welcome...but sir, if we do not hurry the men will be past us."

"Right, Peter. Lead on."

As the leaders and the 500 crest the hillside about sixty of the foot kernes are stripping to the buff in preparation for contact and combat. They really are naked as you can get. It is not a pretty sight. It is effective in combat, if not elsewhere. The English, complaining as always about fairness, say they cannot get ahold of anything. Well! That is just too bad for them, for with all their silly armour and heavy things strapped about them they are easy targets for the attackers, who pull them from their horses or more simply, pull them down for those following to finish off. Nowadays one would call them shock troops. I must ask you; what could be more shocking than to be attacked by a screaming, long haired naked man with an axe dripping blood who is tugging at your trews? Anyhow, the naked lads inflict quite a heavy casualty count upon the English, distracting as they are.

Wouldn't you know it? Just when the battle is getting interesting along comes Cormac ever so rapidly and he has obviously got something to say to Donal as he is shouting from 326 meters away, completely unheard, of course. As he roars nearer, Donal reins in and stops.

"What is it, Cormac?"

224

"It's that cursed Richard Burke of Clanricard. He is coming over the horizon at full speed to join Essex. We saw his banner and he is fair humping it. I think he knows we're here, all right."

Donal turns himself in the saddle and his eyes level on William McBurke.

"I don't normally put blood against blood, William, but Richard Burke is here to destroy us."

"Not to worry, sir. All in a day's work. Don't mind doing him at all. He'd be hounding me for gold should he make it through. No share for that heathen, sir, if you don't mind my saying so."

"Good man yourself, William. You're beginning to show good judgement at that. Take the far side of Clanrickard's column and we shall attack them from here.

"As good as done, Donal. I'll meet you in the middle of Clanrickard's horse. We shall roll them up quite nicely, I'd have to say."

As the attackers plow onward into the valley and in between the two armies, the devastating onslaught is begun against Burke from both sides. His men and those of Essex's who have fallen back to join them are fighting fiercely and holding off both McWilliam and Donal's men. Suddenly, de Lacey rushes forward with four of his best kerne archers, unleashing arrow after arrow. One of iron-tipped slices between the eyes of Henry Norris, one of Clanrickard's commanders. He falls dead from his horse and the flag-bearer is the first to turn and spur his horse out. Seeing him down, the men roll like a wave before McWilliam's screaming demons. Essex knows this is a very good time to do a bunk and he is gone out the end of the valley, quickly followed by the fleeing survivors of the short battle.

"Have our men fall back and take them back to Sugaun's camp, Pat. De Lacey and I will take a few horsemen to see how Essex has really fared. I fear we have again done him little harm."

"I think the same, Donal. I will wait for you there at the camp," says Pat.

As Donal and de Lacey leave they are joined by Owenie O'Moore who is just now coming up from the valley with his

225

exhausted horsemen.

"They are fast escaping, sir. I've followed them but could do nothing to catch them or to attack them," says Owenie.

"I know you did your best, Owenie. We lost the advantage at Rower Bog because of those traitors. We've probably lost the war, too."

"We aren't done yet. Here is a souvenir or two of your visit with Essex."

Owenie hands Donal a dozen scarlet plumes which have fallen from the English helmets.

"These might amuse your flame-haired wife. By your leave, Chief Donal, farewell. Give my regards to Kate and don't ever give up. We should call this place 'Bearna na Glechthi' in honour of the day the plumes fell here."

Donal is scraping his army back together and leaving for the camp. When he reaches there he wastes no time in getting to Sugaun who is waiting nervously to speak with him. He is brought before the commander of the Southern Armies immediately.

"I trust my Lord is satisfied with the humiliation we suffered. I've never lost a battle before," he says.

"You lost no battle. Victory was taken from you. There may have been traitors or someone may well have made a fatal mistake."

"For whatever reasons, we lost and Essex got away. Am I to be removed from the command, my Lord?"

"Yes, I'm sorry to say you are, but not for the reasons you suggest. There is yet more folly."

"May I ask Lord James what that could possibly be?"

"Florence has convinced O'Neill that he must reduce you to a common soldier."

"And, he expects me to continue to serve?"

"That is the way it appears to me. What is more, when O'Neill saw the number of Florence's army he withdrew his backing for your claim as MacCarthy Mor and has awarded it to him."

"He cannot do that. He has no right to award or take away anything through force."

"Exactly what I would have thought and said, Donal, but the fact remains he is the most powerful man in all Ireland and

226

that is what he has done."

"That is wrong, my Lord! I fought Duhallow for the right to carry the title and it is mine!"

"Donal, your command has been removed and you will serve under Florence in our battles against the English."

"I will not be so humiliated. Nor will I serve any longer with the Southern Army!"

"Is this then your final decision? Are you quite certain this is what you want to do? If it is a threat, spit it all out."

"Not a threat, my Lord. I will take what men will serve with me and return to Castle Lough."

Thankfully, one seldom runs into anyone like Donal who has a monopoly on bad luck and evil results plotted against him. First, he's a bastard, right? Then he gets tossed into Cork gaol for being on the wrong side in the Geraldine Rebellion, he gets betrayed by David Barry at Dublin Castle, escapes in a cute whore's best frock, has these illusions about seeing this little girl, his father loses Castle Molahiffe, then dies on him, his beloved dog, Kaigengaire is murdered, he gets the title of Mor only after being half killed by Duhallow, he loses the treasure to those asinine Burkes, rescues Nicholas Browne, for God's sake, when he's an English enemy, leads a sad little army against Essex, becomes betrayed and finally loses the title to his hateful brother-in-law Florence. What more can happen to this well-meaning lad from Kerry?

The answer is quite simple. It is, "plenty."

He bloody well deserves a long rest at home with his beautiful wife making babies and tending to the rusting hinges at Castle Lough. Can he do this? Not on your Nelly! Listen.

"Donal, now that you are home again, what are your plans?"

"Not nearly so grand nor so good as yours, Kate."

"We have no money, you've refused to serve in Florenc's army and he has the title. What will become of us?"

"When this war is done Florence's next move will be to take the lands that go with his title. I am now powerless. To fight back I must retrieve the gold from the Burkes or we shall have nothing."

"But how?"

"I will find a way. First I must go and see what the

227

English army has to offer in trade for me."

See what I mean? This poor chap cannot even get his wheels greased or his oil changed and he's out chasing again. There are some who would say he is quite simple to be so persistent when the sensible thing to do is to relax in his hose and let the world spin. However, that is not the case with the irrepressible David Barry who shows up at the gates, flamboyantly dressed as always and mounted on some huge white thing, asking admission to speak to Donal. Not surprisingly, it is granted.

"Well, then, Donal. What is this Pat Spleen tells me now about your wish to look over Mountjoy's position at Kinsale? Have you finally come to your senses about allying yourself to the Crown?"

"And greetings to you, too, David. Your assumption is correct. Why must you ask?"

"It seems our mutual enemy is intent upon killing us and worse, taking money the Queen insists I owe her. She is becoming such a stingy old harridan, Donal, that I hardly can speak her name!"

"And so while I am turning toward her you are now turning away?"

"Not so, Donal. I am merely seeking the goodness of your protection and perhaps returning a favour or two in the proceedings which will surely follow."

"I see. Then perhaps for the saftey of both of us, you would be agreeable to escorting me there under your pardon of passage in that country?"

"Oh, yes, my dear. I am always most ready to go to Kinsale. It is such an exciting place..."

"...and one filled with spies and strumpets...."

"....and beautiful young soldiers a long way from home!"

"Exactly what I was about to say. When will you be ready to travel? You appear ready for Court, if I may say so."

"You are indeed a keen observer and more kind than I thought possible. One does like to make a good impression."

"Oh, you do, you certainly do make an impression, all right!"

"In that case I will state that I am quite as prepared as I need be now, Donal. Kiss Kate and we will be on our way."

Pat looks at Donal and Donal looks at Pat. They shake their heads slowly and make ready to depart. First, he must do as suggested by David Barry and make things good with his wife, Kate of his dreams.

And, oh, does he ever! In the deserted kitchen! On the kitchen table! And the chopping block! When she finally reaches the floor with her feet, her mouth is wide open. As are her eyes. Those gorgeous green eyes are totally dilated! And her bodice! Half are in and half are out. She would gasp if she could but catch her breath. Jack, the lad? Comparãre? Not by half!

Chapter Twenty-Two

Donal Meets Randall Hurly and Makes a Deal with Governor Carewe

> *"Gold is the great love of leprechauns and
> when not tinkering or tailoring to earn it
> from the other faeries, they go hunting for
> buried treasure. They do not always dig
> it up though; once they find the location of
> buried treasure they are often happy just
> to know where it is...Some philosophers
> have speculated that gold is somehow the
> cause of the leprechauns' extreme longevity
> and that is why they prize it so much."*
>   Niall Macnamara
>   *Leprechaun Companion*

Donal, Pat, and David are plopping along the lane in the parish of Dunderrow near to Kinsale in the southwest of Cork when they come to a crossroad and there they encounter a very small man on a very big destrie. He is riding at full gallop toward some black cattle which are attempting to get through a narrow gate in a hedgerow before this fierce creature coming at them can smack them with a rather large pole he is somehow managing to brandish and still stay upright. It is an awe-inspiring sight.

This be Randall Hurly.

He wheels to confront the interlopers, but unbalanced by the oak staff, slides off and bounces to the ground instead and his horse deserts him. He is undaunted.

"Who in the hell are you?" asks this fellow.

"The same to you, sir!" says Donal.

"I am Randall Hurly of Rincurrran. That's H.U.R.L.Y."

"We mean no harm. We seek directions to the English camp. I'm Donal MacCarthy."

"And, sir, I am David Barry of Barryroe."

"MacCarthy! MacCarthy, is it? A two-faced bunch if ever I met one. You needn't have finally told me as I would have guessed it."

"Cleverly spotted, Mr. Hurly," says David with a grin.

"Ah, well, it takes all sorts to make a MacCarthy. I know for certain, as I am a student of mankind. A man your size should be out fighting wars and attending to widows and the like."

"Look here, Hurly. We asked directions to the English camp, not advice on the obvious. We seek Lord Mountjoy."

"If you'd just said that to start with, I'd have told you. He's at O'Donovan's Mill."

"Will you take us there, Mr. Hurly?"

"You have frightened off my horse in your thwarted attempts to kill me. You expect me to run behind yours giving you directions while they farts all over me and worse?"

"Give me your hand, Randall Hurly. You will ride up behind me as my guest."

Donal easily pulls the wee fellow up on his horse.

"Sure it is that I could stab you to death in the back if I but had a dagger on my person."

"I'm sure the Kinsale Hurlys are honourable men. Sit still, please. Your vastness is upsetting my horse."

"We shall begin to the camp by taking one of those roads ahead."

Donal turns his head to look down at the fellow behind him.

"Which road would that be, then, Hurly. Are you not from Kinsale and if not why do you say you are?"

"I'm a right proper Kinsale man, I am. It should be the road to the right, I think."

"That would be the one to the south, is it?"

"It would."

"Will it be quite comfortable for you to leave your cattle as they are?"

"They are not my bleedin' cattle!"

"Not your cattle? Then what were you doing..ah...ah.. 'herding' them?"

"I am challenged by many things, MacCarthy."

"Oh, I see. The road to the right, then?"

232

"Suit yourself. I've already said that."

David is laughing at the cheek of this little fellow. Pat is not allowed to. They proceed along their merry way with Randall Hurly chattering and insulting all and any. They soon reach the heights of Ballyregan and see the English camp to the east.

"My God, they certainly have the town covered," says Pat.

They ride on toward the point at a small bridge where a sentry is inspecting the frogs. They go through the usual "Halt-Who-Goes-There-Friend-or-Foe without much interest or enthusiasm on the part of the sentry, especially when Randall speaks out.

"Mr. Randall Hurly and his friends. We are going to call upon General Mountjoy."

"Pass on, Mr. Hurly."

Going by the encampment, the party of four rides down toward the little wharf at Browne's Mill on Oysterhaven Creek where a small English supply ship is being unloaded. There Donal recognizes one of Burke's lieutenants from the Pass of the Plumes speaking to a fat man covered with white dust. He reins in and comes to a stop beside them. Randall Hurly looks at the subject of their attention and speaks.

"This is O'Donovan, the millkeeper."

"I suppose that you are a Queen's man, O'Donovan?"

"God Save Her Highness!"

"You seem very friendly with this officer, O'Donovan," says Donal.

"His master, McWilliam Burke saved my son's life at Rower Bog. I owed him a favour or two, it's certain."

Donal looks sharply at the Burke's man.

"Were you also at Molahiffe?"

"Yes, sir. A great coup for all of us. A boost for all the Clan William.

"You mean the gold, of course?"

"Gold, sir? I was speaking of our victory over the Englishman, Nicholas Browne."

" A victory over the English in whose camp you now stand?"

"It was a victory in another place at another time, sir. We

233

are soldiers and we must live, too, you know?"

Donal looks quickly to O'Donovan's broad face. He has been caught out by the mention of the gold and has a rather guilty tinge about him. But, Donal knows that the O'Donovans always look guilty about something they have done or sinned in trying to do, so he is just glancing around the place wondering where this bunch might have hidden the gold. The mill is vast and there are hundreds of places where the treasure could be kept. His concentration on the matter is broken by the voice of Randall.

"Where is my wife?"

Donal is much surprised that this wee fellow would or could keep a wife, but O'Donovan's question beats his.

"Your wife?"

"She's always here spending her time with the soldiers when she should be home spending time with me."

"Oh! That one. She's inside."

"Well, get her out! She's coming home with me."

"Get her yourself, Randall. I'm not going in there while she's entertaining them English officers with her clever songs and such."

At this affront Randall goes a trifle mad. He snatches Barry's short sword from the saddle scabbard and rushes madly toward the house where his wife is 'singing.' He is swearing a streak and cursing a good bit with the steam fairly rising from his fiery head in overheated hyper-ventilation.

"My God, sirs! He'll get us all hung!" says O'Donovan most wisely.

In a flash, Donal takes after Hurly, bringing him down in a tackle. Randall falls before the door and in one sweeping motion Donal picks up the dazed Hurly and places him nearly upright while recovering his own stance. A startled shriek comes from inside and the door is quickly thrown open and out steps the Commander of Her Majesty's Forces, Lord Mountjoy. Behind him is George Carewe, the Deputy Governor of Cork and parts of Munster and a strange piece of work, to be sure. Here also stands the Governor, Carewe, an unsentenced but convicted murderer consorting with the top brass in Her Majesty's army. This does not bode well for our missionary, Donal. It is especially true as both of the English gentlemen are standing with swords drawn, ready to take a swing at anything and everything which is likely to interrupt their little téte-à-téte with the two ladies who now come to the door whilst hastily rearranging items of clothing surrounding both the upper and lower portions of their bodies.

The first to step forward, sort of dazed-like, is Meg Hurly, a beautiful, tall, brown-eyed Spanish looking girl of about 18 years of age.

Yes, unlikely as it may seem, this obnoxious, loud, and tiny red-haired maniac is husband to this luscious person of near monumental sexual appeal. Now, you might have some doubt in the bedchamber of your mind about her level of satisfaction herewith. She is really a good girl, though, perhaps, somewhat dim in matrimonial practices. And, you can just forget the housework. It doesn't exist.

The second female person to come out, shading eyes against the bright sunlight suddenly baking her face is very attractive but only slightly younger than St. Patrick. It is the incredible Jezebel Lee and besides a darling saffron shift, she is wearing a set of elaborate gold earrings of an ancient Celtic design.

"I apologize to you for the interruption, gentlemen and ladies. Mr. Hurly has suffered a dizzy spell and fainted before the door as we now see here."

All the while he is looking at the gentlemen his peripheral vision or whatever it is is taking in the ladies as well. Suddenly the bell rings and the lights flash on.

"Jezebel Lee!"

"Donal! Is it you?"

The few years since her tryst with Donal has not dulled her wit. She tosses out a disclaimer most handily.

"I now have the honour of being Mrs. Niblett Grimes, Master Donal."

She turns her red hair toward the others.

"Gentlemen and Meg, this is a very old friend of mine from his Dublin days. Donal MacCarthy of Kerry. Donal, this is Georgie Carewe and this, dear, is Charlie Mountjoy. He's in the army, you know."

Wow again! What else can happen? Donal is quick to bow to the tall and handsome commander of Her Majesty's Irish

Army.

Hearing the name of Donal MacCarthy quite honestly makes Mountjoy quite alert and apprehensive and curious.

"Have you come to join us too, MacCarthy? Many of your clansmen have. What are your interests? I am informed that you no longer serve in Earl James Southern Army."

"I no longer trust O'Neill's motives. He speaks of Catholic Ireland, but any man who would deny me my title and hand it to that conniving Florence MacCarthy must be doubted."

Randall Hurly is not going to be denied the stage. He bursts forward between the legs of many standing there to address his wife.

"Come with me, Meg, We're leaving."

Donal puts a hand on Hurly's head and turns him around. He has a need to do a bit of confirming of his theories.

"I've been taken by your earings, Mrs. Grimes. May I ask where you obtained them? Kate would love them, I know!"

"They are from Meg, here. David McWilliam Burke over there gave them to her for a kindness she did him. She felt they didn't suit her, being so dangly, so she gave them to me. Some would say they are old-fashioned, but I like them. Whatcha think?"

Jezebel gives her head a shake and twist to show them off. Donal is gasping and finding it hard to swallow. She is wearing a fortune of ancient gold in her ears.

"They are very nice, Mrs. Grimes. Stunning."

From the open doorway there appears a spectre. It is the incomparable and incomprehensible Florence! How he got there, only the others know. He is still adjusting his breeches and oozing confidence and looking down his nice nose.

"You are as quick to pass a compliment as you are an insult, Donal MacCarthy."

"Well, well," states Donal calmly. "Look who we have here."

"Strange, isn't it Donal, how our paths keep crossing?"

"I now see no need for introduction," says Carewe.

"Oh, I know your guest very well. Very well indeed. Let me see if I have this right, gentlemen. Florence MacCarthy, recent of the Tower of London on suspicion of treason and a plot against the Queen and now the confident of the Great O'Neill.

236

Just a fortnight ago he was O'Neill's guest and pledged his army of 2,000 to him in return for my title of Mor."

"You are mad, Nonthus, you bastard!" shouts Florence.

"Not so mad as you if you think you can any longer collude with O'Neill."

"So this is why you were delayed in your return here, Florence. More of a diversion to meet with the enemy, I'd say," says Carewe.

"This is preposterous. How can you believe him, one of England's most dangerous antagonists and murderers, over me?"

"Governor Carewe, sir. You know me to have ignored O'Neill's summons of all chiefs to Holy Cross. My brother and I have remained loyal throughout the burnings and the attacks," says David.

"Yes, David Barry, you have been loyal to the Crown. What say you in this?"

"I believe what Donal says, Governor Carewe. He has talked about nothing else since we left to come here."

"If the Queen excused the charges against him, what are we to believe?" asks the calculating Mountjoy.

"Believe this, Lord Mountjoy. As I left London there was a quiet rumour that Florence was also in league with that popinjay Sir William Stanley and Captain Jacques de Franceschi in a plot to assassinate the Queen."

"A silly story to alienate me from those in Court who I sought to use for information in aide of Munster!"

"Very clever, Florence. Then why did you not use the information for Ireland's sake instead of your own? Why were you suddenly pursued by Bostock and Flowers? Something is badly amiss here! We lack certain elements of truth," says Carewe.

"We must make absolutely certain that Florence is made comfortable until these accusations can be confirmed or put aside once and for all," says Mountjoy.

He calls to Burke.

"Kindly escort Lord MacCarthy to my headquarters. Better for all if he is safe and at ease."

Burke moves swiftly to Florence's side. Florence is livid but remains calm. He has a few parting words for Donal.

"I'll make you pay for this, Nonthus!"

"Don't waste your breath on threats. You may find you have little left to spare, you counterfeit Englishman."

"This is absolutely ridiculous! I am sent by our Queen to settle Munster and because I have gone to O'Neill to assess his strengths and report to you two gentlemen I am branded a traitor?"

"Ah, but that is why you are going away with my man Burke, here. We too, must assess the situation. Your soldiers and horse will stay with us. I shall be along in a day or so. Take him to Cork, Burke."

"May I have a word with Burke before he does so, Governor Carewe? It is a matter of some importance."

"You may, but make it quick. Florence. You are to make yourself ready."

Donal takes the frightened Burke along the mill race to the edge of the mill.

"Well, then, Burke. Have you decided to tell me where the gold is hidden?"

"I cannot, sir. My father would kill me if I did."

"I will kill you if you don't."

Unbeknownst to either Donal or Burke, Randall Hurly has tucked himself in behind them and is listening and nodding his noggin quite comfortably. He cannot, however, contain himself.

"It occurs to me, gentlemen, that there is plenty of killing to be done for everyone. No need to do it to each other, I'd have to say."

Donal turns, searching for the source of this voice.

"What nonsense is this?"

"No nonsense, Donal MacCarthy. Send Burke back to take Florence out of here. I need to talk to you."

Donal looks intently at Randall and something clicks. Slowly he speaks.

"Do as Randall suggests, Burke."

"Remember, sir. I've told you nothing. I will do as you say and take Lord MacCarthy to Cork."

Randall is drawing crosses in the dirt with the toe of his little boot, waiting for Burke to get out of earshot.

"What is this, Randall? Go ahead and surprise me. Tell

238

me what you know, please."

Randall takes a peek from under his hair.

"I know where the gold is."

"How would you know that?"

"I put it where it is."

"You hid the gold?"

Donal is staying serious but feels that perhaps he might swat this fellow alongside his wispy red head.

"Yes. I'm the one who hid it for William Burke."

"Could you retrieve it then, Randall Hurly?"

"Of course I can, Donal and for you I will, but it must be done secretly. If the Burke's find out..."

"How can we be assured of secrecy in this turmoil?"

"When this hopeless battle for Kinsale starts everyone will be too preoccupied to notice us come here."

"I certainly agree with you about that. It is going to be complete bedlam. We'd best get back to Mountjoy and see what they know about O'Neill and the Spanish, then say our goodbyes."

"They'll tell you nothing about either, what with Florence tossing in the surprise of the whole campaign and upsetting their own plans."

Randall is right. When they return to say goodbye, Carewe advises Donal that he would like a private word with him.

Now wot?

The what is that Carewe has chosen a course of action which will involve Donal to a rather high degree and with some complication.

"I have made a decision," he says to Donal. "Would you walk with me for a brief moment?"

"Of course, sir."

They begin their stroll back toward the old mill, hands clasped behind their backs like a couple of old priests in the parish cemetery.

"You have saved us from great problems with Florence. You may have known that we were aware of his transgressions, but your sight of him in O'Neill's camp enables us to take strong action which will ultimately weaken O'Neill and his armies considerably."

239

"You were already suspicious of him?"

"Oh, yes, we were. It came about through his wife, Lady Ellen. She has been helping us as well. He put his advancement above his children and she rebelled. He really is, as you say, 'a counterfeit Englishman,' isn't he?"

"He is and I cannot say I am surprised by Ellen having to turn against him. In a way I'm very glad she has come to her good senses. What will be done with her and Florence?"

"I have the notion that Florence should be sent back to the Tower. Lady Ellen will very likely, be given some of her old land and a house. She will be comfortable, but not so comfortable as you."

"I don't understand. What does that mean?"

"I shall recommend to the Queen that you should have Castle Lough, all of the old ploughlands of Clancar's and a few other baubles. The title of Mor will be restored to you, I am certain of that."

"I am most grateful. How can I repay you?"

"There is always something a warlord can do for his Governor."

"That being?"

"My place in Mallow has grown quite short of good cattle. Too much raiding and so forth. Not enough time on my part to make it right."

"As good as done. Would you take 5,000 of Donal O'Sullivan's black ones? He withheld the White Rod from me and owes me at least that much in back rents."

"So I understand. Yes, I'd say 5,000 black mountain cattle would do nicely to restock my herd."

Chapter Twenty Three

The Battle of Kinsale

*"Next day Mounjoy turned his guns with
their muzzles away from Kinsale. Slow
Tyrone was now at hand. The siege of
Kinsale was done. In Spain, doubtless,
no one remembers him, but the genius
of Irish history absorbs affectionately
the whole story of his heroic defense
of Kinsale against great odds. Spaniard
as he was, Don Juan de Aquila is now
one of the notables of Irish hisotry."*
        O'Sullivan's Irish History

The bitter winter cold is setting in and the armies of
O'Neill, O'Donnell, and Tyrell are marching at speed from the
north. Some are crossing the Lee River and making for Kinsale.
Some are coming down the Glaslyn River where they will join
with the Spanish invaders and break the encircling army of
Mountjoy. All are weary and disgruntled. The conditions are
deplorable, it being the worst winter in a century, and there is
great need for haste.

There would be no such need for speed had the Spanish
landed where they were supposed to, that is to say in Dublin
Bay or at Galway. But, no, Florence, using his cousin Don
Dermutio Carty in the Spanish Court and the Vatican, caused
them to change their plans and land at Kinsale, to occupy the
town and put ashore the artillery in Castle Park and disburse
the troops around the ramparts. By the time those great warriors of the north, O'Neill, O'Donnell, and Tyrell, are arriving at
Colcorran above the city, they are cold, hungry and exhausted.
But, no more so than the English forces who are now cut off and
are going to be pinched between the Spanish and the Irish
armies. The bitter cold and the snow is blowing through the
hillside camps of all the adversaries.

Inside the sheeted tent the Irish leaders are having a go,
arguing fiercely on the strategy to be employed and where

O'Neill, still in charge, is trying to exert his authority upon a sea of frayed nerves.

"We will not have a frontal attack. That is out of the question. Our men are completely worn out and our supply trains are caught in the snow and rain. They will not be here for two days."

The hotspur, O'Donnell, forever impatient with life as well as meeting his maker, thinks other.

"We cannot wait, Hugh! We must hit them before they completely smash the Spaniard, D'Aguila!"

"What have we to hit him with, O'Donnell?" asks Tyrell. "The chief says we must wait, so we will wait."

"We have enough men to overrun all the positions if we strike now. We must, by Jesu, do it immediately."

O'Neill's boot is tapping nervously under the boards as he maintains his patience.

"I've just said there will be no attack. We will march to the west and try to relieve D'Aguila. You, O'Donnell, will act as rear guard and swing your army by broad front to the south behind us. We will meet at Millwater Ford. There is no other sensible way!"

O'Donnell is seething at the lack of regard for his determination to get on with an attack.

"Christ's wounds, sir. We must take some action. This delay takes us nowhere!" he roars and stomps out of the tent.

The next night, far out on the dark and distant edges of the picket lines, one of O'Neill's patrols is stopping to build a fire and warm itself.

This is stupid soldiering at its worst.

Anyhow, their counterpart, the English foot patrol of Mountjoy's, knows that this is not star-light, star-bright. That is a fire down there by the river and it sure as hell isn't ours. Let us go and look at these furry visitors. One cannot rule out that they might have been thinking maybe these people have a few biscuits and some hot meat there upon that fire, but their main purpose, or so they always say, is to kill them, then see about something different to eat than horsehocks.

This is just too easy, so they won't kill them. Not yet, anyhow. They will take their carelessly stacked weapons and ask a few questions, maybe even find out who they are and how

242

many of them there are in the camps upon the hills. Surprised, they find only four men at the fire and they soon have them at sword point with fusils added for emphasis.

"Stay right where you are and don't even move your eyes!"

"Martin, I told you we shouldn't light a fire!"

"Martin, you should have listened to him," says the leader of the English patrol.

"And, I told you we must be stealthy. Stealth," I said, "will keep us safe."

"Just be quiet. You damned Irish are always blathering about something. Where is the main body of your advance group and where is the rear guard?"

"You cannot think we would tell you, do you?"

"See this flask of brandy? It is yours if you tell us where O'Donnell is camped. And, we will kill you if you don't tell us."

"You'll let us go if we tell you O'Donnell is just beyond that hill watching for us to return?"

"Of course we'll let you go. You can leave the instant you tell us how many men he has with him. We'll have to keep your weapons, of course, but you can leave."

"We'll just take the flask. O'Donnell is three miles north and west near Ballintuber and he has 3,500 men and horse."

"Good. That's just about where we had them pegged. Kill them, Burns."

So, the lads never got a taste of the whisky, but to the east sits the traitorous Irish general, Brien MacHugh Oge MacMahon, who is in the intriguing process of obtaining another bottle of "Aquavitae", otherwise brandy, from Carewe. George is delighted to supply him with the lovely potion, but only in accordance with a set of high-priced ground rules.

"You will supply me with the information of the planned attack in return for the drink."

"Of course, my Lord, of course!" Which the rotten blighter does, complete with his hand drawn map, which isn't pretty, but it is exact. "And many thanks. If you have any more brandy I can tell you the Spanish have another 700 men under Pedro de Soto coming in from Castlehaven where they landed due to the extraordinary weather conditions which seem always to accompany their ships."

"Fair enough, I'd have to say. I'm sending Captain Roger Harvey down there to greet them and perhaps clean up a few O'Driscolls under the authority of fire and sword. Put your lip over this Jerez I'm passing to you."

Another message was passed back to Carewe from MacMahon.

"Did you know the Spanish have Dunboy on the Beara Peninsula? Cam O'Sullivan gave it to them just last week. Could you spare another thimbleful?"

The reply this time came from Mountjoy.

"Greetings. Yes, we knew about Dunboy. See if you can talk Cam into defending from the land. We'll take him from the sea. Sorry, but this is absolutely your last bottle from us as we are down to eating the crates in which the brandy came. Best wishes for the holidays." Mountjoy, Lord Deputy.

That was the whole of it, with brandy being put into play as the life-shortening role for the troops of the Irish and the Spanish.

At about this time, Donal, Cormac and Pat Spleen are returning from their successful raid with some of the cattle promised to Carewe. They are coming up the mountains in the west with their drovers and dogs working hard to keep the cattle together as it is a ponderous and dusty way, the rains and snow of Kinsale not reaching them at this point. As they draw to Drinagh, Donal catches a glimpse of a familiar rider coming fast toward them. It is brother Frank, for God's sake! And, he looks like he has been in a frightful fight and come out of it bruised, bloodied and badly caked with foreign substances.

"Frank! Over here! Where are you off to so fast?" shouts Donal.

"We're off to see the wizard, Donal. Actually, she's a witch, but don't mention that to her. She is going to turn some wood into gold and I would do with a bit of that, I can tell you! Her name is Berry Dhóne and what we will do is get some of the gold from her since you don't seem to have any."

"But, Frank. You cannot get gold from a witch!"

"Really, Donal? Well, maybe she can tell me how to get rich. I want to get rich and somebody around here ought to be able to tell me how."

244

Cormac is edging away, not wishing to become directly involved in this scene. Donal knows he will get nowhere with his brother if he doesn't change the subject.

"Where have you been, Frank? You look a terrible mess, you know?"

"I've been quite busy, actually, Donal. I've just killed Diarmuid Moal, Florence's brother."

"You've what?" asks Donal increduously. He then repeats, "What!"

"It's your ears, isn't it, Donal? They just haven't been quite right since that James Desmond smacked you alongside your head with his broadsword up at Cork in '80. I don't think he should have done that just because you told him how to fight a battle, you being already fifteen. It did make a proper loud smack when he hit you. A regular percussion of noise, it was. Did he hurt you? You layed there quite still for a period."

"Frank, try to stick to the point. You say you killed Diarmuid Moal? How? How...no, why did you do that?"

"Well, when I got to Carbery headed toward Bantry, the O'Donovans were still in rebellion and they ambushed me. They wanted to know who I was and if I might possibly be the commander they were expecting. These men were from Skibbereen way and I didn't much care for their looks. You know what I mean about the Skibbereeners? Can't look you in the eye and sort of keep their heads turned and spit through their teeth and blow their noses with two fingers, you know what I mean?"

Donal, at this point, dares not interrupt Frank and ask what in the name of the Holy Father he was doing going to Bantry and what the Skib men were up to.

"Please, Frank. Get on with how you, or why you killed Diarmuid!"

"Right. Well, I saw they had the mischief written all over them and I thought fast. I told them I was their man and my name was Finighin MacCarthy. I had to outfox them at every turn. I asked where they were going and they told me they were after the renegades who had rustled their cattle. Then they asked me what my plan was."

"You? You had a plan, Frank?"

"Yes, I did. 'What's your's?' I asked them right back and

245

they said they had just told me and the nasty looking one with the black teeth and the black hair and a turned eye got distressed and asked me again what my plan was so again I said I agreed with his. You can see by that that I was miles ahead of that lot. 'Let's do the raid,' I said."

"Well done, Frank. Then what?"

"The black one said, 'That is some brain you got on you, Finighin or whatever your name is.' which I thought was a very nice thing for him to say."

"So, how did you happen to kill Florence's favorite brother?"

"Well, then we went ariding up to Broad Strand and hid in the woods. I told O'Donovan to run and tell his Chief Donal Y Pypy we might need some help as there seemed to be an awful lot of men there playing with his cows. The very next morning it was very foggy and I had drunk too much mead the night before. You ever get that way, Donal, where they just don't seem to be able to make it fast enough?"

"Much like our father, I'd say."

"Oh, yes. Where was I? Oh, yes. As the rustlers started up out of the strand we attack them and what with my head being on the hurt and it being foggy I just layed about me with my sword, striking a few O'Donovans and a few rustlers in near equal measure when out of the fog your ghost came riding. You had on your grey cloak and you were riding a grey stallion, or was it a mare. I always get those two mixed up."

"We all do, Frank. Go on."

"I fell down on my knees and started praying because I thought it was you coming from the dead, but you kept riding at me and coming at me with your axe raised. I closed my eyes and started the Caonian for the dead Chiefs and you know I can't sing for sour owl shit and this upset the horse you were on and it started rearing at the mournful sound I was giving out with and then your ghost fell off on top of me. It was then my quick mind decided for me that it wasn't you at all, at all, but someone who looked like you."

"Slow it down, Frank. Easy. Easy."

"Thank you. This man made me very angry for looking like you and not being you. He had dropped his axe in the crash and was groping for it but that was no good to him as I

246

had it in my hands and then I buried it in that usurper's head. Then Donal Y Pypy appeard out of the fog and mist."

"You mean Y Pypy got there in the fog and all, too?" asks Cormac.

"Yes, of course, Cormac. Then he said, 'My God, Frank, you have murdered Diarmuid Moal! Get out before you are torn limb from limb! Ride out of here and find your brother and tell him Moal is dead.' I tried to tell him I didn't murder him, I just killed him, but he sort of rolled his green eyes and threw me back on my horse and told me to head for Killarney before a Moal man in return got his axe stuck in my head, of all the things to say to a great warrior like me!"

"Mary and Joseph! That's it, for certain!" says Donal.

"He looked like you, Donal. I swear he did!"

Donal and Cormac are staring at each other, hoping this is a bad dream. Realizing that it isn't, they must now get on their way as fast as possible and into the protection of Cork.

"Where to now, chief?" asks Cormac. Do we have to take Frank with us wherever it is we're going?"

"We must forget going to Kinsale. It's Cork City, Cormac. Cork City for you, Frank, Donogh and Thady Phale. You must take the animals to Carewe in Cork by the shortest route. I will meet you there. Now I must return to O'Donovan's Mill and find Randall Hurly!"

The northern chief, O'Donnell, is moving his men southward toward the Millwater Ford and his scouts sight the English forces at dawn. His eyes narrow and the ancient Celtic blood rushes to his head. He is, by God, O'Neill or no O'Neill, going to attack them and get his pound of flesh. He quietly orders his lieutenant, Magnus, to prepare the flanking formation.

Magnus is doing the best he can with the tired horse and foot soldiers who are struggling to get into formation. Ahead, the English forces are moving relentlessly forward. The light artillery is in place, facing the Irish.

O'Donnell now orders the columns forward, horse to front, foot to rear. There is little enthusiasm except on the faith-crazed face of their leader.

"Sound the pipes to battle!"

"In the name of the Holy Father....."

His voice is being drowned out by the noise of the pipes, of the men, and roar of cannonry fired at the Irish.

"We shall win this battle for our faith...."

The thunder of guns from below, the cannon balls tear into the frontal movement of O'Donnell's men, slaughtering them and the final wail of the piper signals their death.

The English troops at O'Donovan's Mill have moved to the higher ground to the north and east and are hurrying their columns to catch out the armies of O'Neill andTyrell.

Donal arrives at the deserted millsite and finds Randall Hurly waiting inside the house Mountjoy and Carewe had used the week before. They show each other their pleasure at being reunited in common cause.

"You have made it, Donal. I knew you would."

"Randall, you wouldn't believe what I've just been through in getting here!"

"I think I would, but how do you feel about getting out the gold?"

"I would be most pleased, friend Randall!"

"Then let us go about it."

Donal and Randall Hurly are now walking along a high, snow-covered bank over the stream. Randall has already started explaining things.

"Can you see that there is a bit of a cave below us?"

"I can, Randall. Am I getting the right feeling?"

"I'd say you are, Donal. That little cave called Pol Cat is where we put the gold that Burke brought."

"It would sink out of sight in the tidal wash from Oysterhaven Bay!"

"We weren't that stupid, Donal. There is a fine limestone ledge where the wildcats have a den. It's high and dry. Hang me over the side here and I'll just have a peek."

Donal is looking sideways and rather skeptically at Randall, but then goes about turning him upside down and by his ankles he hangs him over the edge. Randall is quite happy in this position, dum-de-dumming to himself. Donal continues to lower him below the level of the top of the nearly hidden cave. There is the scream of a startled wildcat and Donal nearly launches Randall in surprise.

"Mary and Joseph! What was that?"

"Just the old cat that lays there all the time. She's gone out now. She is very much afraid of warriors like me!"

"So am I, Randall Hurly, so am I! Can you see anything in there?"

"Oh, yes, Donal. In the sunlight reflecting off the water I can just make out the chests the McWilliam Burkes left. It's there all right."

Donal is starting to shake a bit in the excitement.

"Bring me up, please, Donal"

Donal, in his enthusiasm to do so, tosses Randall into the air and catches him. He hugs him and puts him down. A few silver icicles are dislodged from the tree which Randall has struck in his brief flight and are falling around them in a pretty winter spectacle.

O'Neill and Tyrell are now marching toward Kinsale from the north by Ballyregan Ford when they see O'Donnell's men being killed by the English in the hills to the West. The O'Donnells are being hit hard and being forced down the river. O'Neill stands on a hillock and watches as the disaster reveals itself amidst the sounds of battle and the horrendous cries issued forth as the English continue to advance and destroy all before them.

"He's done it. The fool has done it! Get your men and swing them by four columns to try to save him!"

Tyrell sees it differently.

"Begging your pardon, sir. It is already hopeless."

"Do as I say!"

Which is to say, go get yourself and your followers killed while trying to rescue a cause that is lost, lost, lost.

Randall is taking Donal on an exaulted stroll along the millstream.

"Randall, I don't know what to make of you! With all that gold there you took none, but yet you tell me? I cannot believe it."

"Do it again, Donal, please."

"Do what again?"

"Throw me way up into the air. It was great fun!"

This is a good way to celebrate. Pitch a little fellow high up in the air. That's it. Donal quickly does as bid and repeats several times to the gleeful shouts of the hurled. Disturbed, the

249

beautiful icicles from the overhanging trees sparkle downward. Now he sets him down and tousels his bright red hair with a laugh of his own.

"You didn't answer me, Randall. Why didn't you take the gold?"

"Donal, if I have to explain that to you, maybe I should keep the gold. But, no, it is yours. It was always meant to be yours. As you were once told, I believe.

Randall looks up at Donal while saying this and winks a meaningful wink.

"However, should you, out of your good nature decide to help me and my wife Meg, according to legend and tradition, then I'd be compelled by custom to take it. How does that suit you?"

"To the boots, Randall. To the boots! You shall have a share!"

"There is, I have happened to notice, a small chest among the others."

"Shall we say it is your chest?"

"That would suit me to my boots, too. Thank you."

On the hillsides above Kinsale the armies of O'Neill and Tyrell are being closed upon by two battle groups of Mountjoy's. The Irish battalions of the three commanders stand their ground but are soon being overwhelmed. Though out-numbered, the English forces are in their own element in the massive movement. It is no contest and the slaughter of wounded begins. O'Neill roars to one of his horse commanders.

"Tell Tyrell to pull back and form behind me. We must retreat to the river and north!"

The killing continues and there is no bother with prison-ers. Only the war horses of the Irish are collected and led away. The red blood of the Irish mingles with the snow and makes a ruby river of slush running down the hillsides.

As more of the English forces puff their way up the steep hills they fall upon the depleted armies in front of them with their swords and go about their trade of hacking them to death. It is a scene of total disaster.

O'Neill again speaks to his aide-de-camp.

"It's no use. Those who can must get away."

Struggling, only a pitifully small number of survivors are able to follow. Those at distance in the east try to escape, but cannot. O'Neill and Tyrell retreat along the road to Innishannon and Bandon.

The butchering of the lost Irish troops continues for three hours.

Below, in Kinsale City, the telescopes of the Spanish watch in horror, and volunteers come to their commanders to foray against the English to draw off Mounjoy. They are refused with religious clucks by D'Aguila's priests.

"Make peace with the English," they advise, "there is no other way to see Catalan again."

Which is true.

Chapter Twenty Four

Florence in the Tower of London; Donal and Kate's Happy Ending

"Florence, (in the Tower of London) prefered the miserable lot of continued imprisonment, to the denuding of himself and his children of the last remnants of his property."
                          Daniel MaCarthy Glas

Down below at Donovan's Mill, inside the ring of battle, three carts pulled by bullocks are being loaded with treasure. Pat Spleen is responding to Donal's call and is helping heave the heavy casks onto an already overloaded wagon. They now stand back while Hurly and his wee men finish the loading of the two other carts. With whoops of delight, they disappear down the lane. Pat Spleen, ever the wary Scot, asks Donal about Randall.

"Can he make it out of the valley and past the English? I can't see how."

"Oh, I can see how, all right. And he is going to deliver every sou to Castle Lough in record time."

"But he's such a little shite!"

"Yes," says Donal wistfully, "Isn't he?"

He makes a half turn and then is back to Pat.

"I left too quickly to learn what happened with Florence. And, with David Barry as well."

"Florence is on his way to the Tower. That much is certain. David Barry? God only knows, but I strongly suspect that he, too, is on his way to London for the full pardon from the Crown he thinks he deserves."

Away to the Court where Queen Elizabeth, Lady Ap Huw, and a few other favourites are looking at a few new dresses recently arrived from the continent. The mood is a happy one in light of the news of what is happening in Ireland. You'd certainly think that the Queen of this most powerful nation on earth has more important things to do, but no.

"And so, ladies, I am celebrating a great victory for our beloved Empire. I shall have new dresses made in commemoration."

"Then Florence MacCarthy's treachery with the Spanish has been thwarted?"

"We cannot be certain that seeing O'Neill was a treasonous act, Lady Ap Huw. It was the Spanish and the lords of the North who were thwarted and have been vanquished forever."

"And thus Florence is a hero!"

"He's nothing of the sort. Truth be known, it was Donal MacCarthy who sussed him out for Mountjoy and Carewe. He's been returned to the Tower under my protection once again."

"Then he is alone and remains misunderstood?"

"Only for the moment is he alone. Lady Ellen is on her way to be at his side. She serves us usefully. A court will likely be held over him. There will be long delays and much sympathy for him and his family."

She pauses and puts the bait before the Welsh courtier, Lady Ap Huw.

"Will no one rid me of this Irish blight?"

"He has asked for Lady Ellen and not me, has he?"

"So it would appear, yes. He is as duplicitous in his bed chamber as he is in his dealings with England."

Silence follows as the wheels grind slowly.

"Is he not, my dear?" she asks Lady Ap Huw.

"Yes, your Majesty, he is."

Another silent salient is established.

Lady Ap Huw is truly fuming by now. She stirs from her seat beside the Queen and rises.

"I see. Your Majesty, would you excuse me from this company? There is a bit of something which I must attend to."

"Of course, Lady Ap Huw. One must do what one must do."

In the City of Cork, Donal, Frank, and Cormac have now rejoined and are standing in a proper row in Governor Carewe's room in Cork Castle and Carewe seems mightily pleased to see these renegades.

"Welcome you here, MacCarthys. I must say I am surprised and pleased that you are here and not camped outside

254

the walls of the city intending to do me harm."

"We are pleased to be here and hope our gift of black cattle was well received. They are a scrawny lot, but Donal O'Sullivan has fallen upon hard times."

"Yes, indeed he has with more such to follow. As to the cattle, they'll do very nicely. A month for them on the hills of Mallow and we're laughing."

"That being the case, we beg to take our leave of you. There is much yet to be done in our country."

"Before you go, there is something that may interest you somewhat. A group of our lads intercepted a messenger from the Vatican. It seems he was carrying a papal bull for you."

"I cannot imagine...."

"Nor could we. I have taken the liberty to read it. The Church has finally recognized the marriage of your father and Eílis Cremin. It seems you are the legal heir and Ellen is not!"

Frank is apparently quite excited by this news, though why, God only knows. He asks:

"What about me and Cormac. If he is legal, then we must be something, too!"

Carewe is most agreeable on this day.

"That is correct, Frank MacCarthy. You are something!"

"That's good enough, isn't it, Frank? Governor Carewe says you are something."

Donal looks at his faithful and loyal brothers with great fondness on his smiling face.

"Let us all go home."

"You will guard and care for Cormac and Frank, won't you Donal? There will be no repercussions from this government for their past sins."

"That is most gracious of you, my Lord George. Frank especially becomes nervous under threat of bodily damage."

"I can feature that easily enough. Be well and be on your way!"

Away in London town, Florence is in the Tower. No doubt about it. He is already making himself at home and writing his usual two or three letters a day complaining about how unjust the system is and how he should be back in Ireland counting his gueeves and collecting his poundage hogs from his tenants. He is still waiting for Ellen to arrive, though he has suspicions about her personal fidelity and loyalty to him.

But wait! There is a knock on his door and the Keeper stands outside his apartment.

"What is it?"

"You have two visitors from Ireland, my Lord Florence."

"Really? And, who might they be?"

"They are David Barry and his nephew, William."

"Hardly my first choice, but ask them in, please."

The last time Florence and David Barry met face to face was at O'Donovan's Mill before the Battle of Kinsale. One would certainly think that David is up to something. But he has a lackey with him who carries a full crate of wine. What can this be about?

"Well, David, what a pleasant surprise. What brings you to London and by what honour do I owe a visit?"

"The honour is mine, Lord Florence. William and I were invited to London to receive forgiveness of the misunderstood debt you were to collect from me."

He more or less pushes his nephew to the fore.

"William, this is Florence MacCarthy Reagh, recent of Carbury and husband to Lady Ellen."

"My Lord, a privilege to know you!"

"Yes, I suppose it is. Thank you."

"We've brought you a small gift to help you pass the time in better comfort."

"It is but a crate of wine from Spain, sir," says William.

"It is uncommonly civil of you, David. A gift from you to me! Yes, most uncommon, but thank you very much!"

"You are most welcome, Florence. I hope it goes down well."

"Rest assured it will, David and William. Well, well, well. Is there anything I can offer you?"

"Not a thing, Florence, but thanks for asking. We're in a bit of a dash, being scheduled to take leave on the evening tide and hours of shopping yet to do on Saville Row."

William is anxious to make his impression lasting.

"A pleasure to have met you, My Lord. Uncle Davie has promised to buy me black leather buskins!"

"Devastating, I'm sure!"

"Ah, these young lads, Florence! Nonetheless, we must

256

be off. Goodbye, then."

"Safe journey to you both."

The two visitors go to the door to leave and Florence is already inspecting the wine. As David and William are walking hurridly down the hall to exit, Lady Ap Huw steps from the shadows and joins them.

"That went rather well, David. Now we must hurry out and away before he drinks any of the wine."

"What was the name of the potion you put into the wine and will he not see some have been uncorked?"

"It is called belladonna, my dear. Belladonna for deep, deep sleep. Marvelous stuff. Cures all ills, don't you know? And, there is nothing uncommon about the corks. All Spanish wine, in my opinion, looks corked."

She pulls the hood of her cloak over her head and slides through the doorway with a final remark.

"My greetings to your handsome friend, Donal MacCarthy Mor, should you be so fortunate as to see him once again!"

"We shall see him, I'm certain of that. I will be pleased to pass your greetings to him, my Lady!"

In a moment they have parted and disappeared once more.

Standing on the battlements of Castle Lough in a driving winter's rain is Donal, waiting the return of Pat Spleen with news of the leaders from the North and the fate of the Sugaun Earl, Fitzthomas Fitzgerald. A soaked, lone figure in drenched cape on a struggling and tired horse is making his way along the shoreline of Lough Leane. Donal knows the news is grim, but must hear it for himself. Spleen enters the castle through the east gate, dismounts and joins Donal on the rampart.

"You've made good time in such a filthy set of weeks. Welcome home."

"Thank you , Donal. If I might say it was the most heart-breaking journey I have ever had to make. The tales of the scenes of the past battle have not yet left my head."

"I feared as much and I'm afraid of what you are here to tell me. How bad was it?"

"The worst defeat ever. O'Neill and all the others have been beaten to a bloody pulp."

"Did any of the officers and men escape?"

"Only the barest few, but there will be no saftey for the leaders. Their lands will be attained and they must somehow leave Ireland for Spain or France."

"They never got it right, did they?"

"No, they got absolutely nothing right. I'd have to say there are more answers needed, but there is no one left to give them other than those who are fleeing."

"To think that I might have joined them had it not been for Frank's escapades. I'd surely be dead if I had gone there."

"You can be certain of that, Donal."

They make their way down the mural staircase toward the great hall.

What has happened to Sugaun?"

"He was captured with only a few loyal men. They were pardoned but the Earl Desmond was sent to stay in the Tower."

In the Tower? In company with Florence. How ironic."

"There is a bit of better news, but only in a way."

"What is it, Pat? We could use a bit of something not so dreadful."

"Nicholas Browne is coming back to Molahiffe. He cannot seem to stay away, can he?"

"Nicholas Browne again at Molahiffe! I will have to have it rebuilt. It was pounded into the ground. It's the least I can do."

"I don't suppose you have any desire to claim it from him, have you? If you do, I will leave you."

"No, Pat. Never. I give you my word that the only thing I wanted from that place was the gold we got. You have no need to leave here, ever. You have a share of the treasure coming to you."

"Ach, what would a common gallowglass be needing treasure for?"

"A certain scullery maid here would help you rid yourself of it. Deny that and you are a false man!"

"I can't deny it, Donal. Remember, I once said the word of a scullery maid is often the most reliable."

"You did, indeed, Pat. There is other good news as well, Pat."

"What could that be, Donal. Kate is not expecting again,

258

is she?"

"Not quite yet, Pat Spleen, but the promise is there. No, my news is that you could be surprised by a little fellow jumping out at you to challenge your intentions!"

"You can't mean Randall Hurly?"

"I can and do. That fierce warrior has assumed the duties of surveyor of all those who appear to have evil purpose about the castle. He and Meggin are well established in quarters above the murder hole!"

"Christ! I shall never be safe from such a fearsome foe!" He smiles warmly at Donal at the thought of Randall, but especially of Meg.

Donal turns on the staircase and laughs, knowing full well what Pat has in mind.

"Now, will you join my family and me in a warm drink and dry yourself by the fire before you go to find your young and very pretty scullery maid?"

"I will, Donal, but only for a moment. Coleen has a splendid way of ridding me of the saddle weariness and stiffness of the joints."

"I'm sure she has. Fair enough, but I insist that you two have a share in the reward of our own good fortune and persistence."

They arrive in the great hall to find Kate with their new baby, Donal Oge. Fortunately for Pat, Randall Hurly is nowhere to be seen. Kate is sitting by the roaring fire in comfortable surroundings, to be sure. Comfortable is perhaps, not the correct word. Opulent? Not quite, but more than comfortable and she is wearing some very precious jewelry of an antique design. And, a very expensive green velvet dress that didn't come off the rack anywhere in Kerry. Oh, she is so gorgeous! Still a lovely young girl despite her thousand worries and recent pregnancy, etc.

A young girl, small and seemingly frail, tends the baby at the same time as they play with a small wolfhound puppy. Donal goes to kiss his wife and Pat greets Kate and strokes the puppy's shaggy head.

"A far cry from past horrors, Donal. You look properly at home."

"Well, Pat, I say we should count ourselves lucky we

259

were not there at Kinsale, though Lord knows we tried hard enough to get our work done and get there."

"Yes, Donal, one might almost think that someone watches over you!"

Kate looks seriously at Pat.

"That is certainly so, Pat. Whenever Donal was away I got the feeling that someone protected him."

"In my life I have been blessed with the powerful friendship of others. You, Pat, and even Nicholas Browne have had a strong role in keeping me safe. I have always been protected by some power and it should not seem strange then that we appear so blessed. Friendship is everything, or so I think. Will you take a cup in friendship and gratitude?"

"I will, of course. It has been a long road from the Cork gaol together some twenty years ago."

Donal goes to the young girl with the baby, Donal Oge.

"Let me take my son while you get us all a warm drink. Will you fetch that for us?"

"Certainly, my Lord. It is always my pleasure to serve you," says the wee girl.

The girl turns and rises to do as asked. As she does so we can recognize the lovely, mystical smile and her devotion to Donal.

It is Ethné.

THE END

Glossary

An Drimuin - Mountain. In the case of the MacCarthy chief, he was so named because of his great size.

Bailey - Castle wall or outer defensive wall

Banshee - Otherworld woman who is heard to cry when death is near. The cry is said to be similar to that of a keening woman.

Bauran - An Irish drum.

Bonnacht - A professional Scottish soldier.

Brehon Law - Ancient Irish law.

Bullock - An oxen.

Crubeans - Ham shanks.

Eowu - A sheep.

Fusil - Early muzzle loaded blunderbuss.

Gallgoidel - Descendants of the Viking-Irish or "foreign Irish."

Gallowglass - The armed retainers of a chief.

Garrane - Horse or pony.

Iuschabau - Poitín; a powerful distilled drink.

Kerne - Lightly armed foot soldiers.

Leinte - A light linen shirt or tunic.

Lanabh - Lamb.

Senachel - A trusted aide, captain or lieutenant.

Sept - Extended family group within a larger tribal grouping, e.g. the Reaghs were a sept of the MacCarthys.

Skein - Short dagger.

Sugaun - Straw; a rope with a left hand twist.

Tanaiste - Heir to the title who acted as lieutenant to the chief.

Trews - Trousers.

Tuatha Dé Daanan - Tribes of the god Danu, who settled in Ireland.

Relationships in the life of Donal Nonthus

Donal "anDrimuin" MacCarthy Mor, chief of Clancarthy

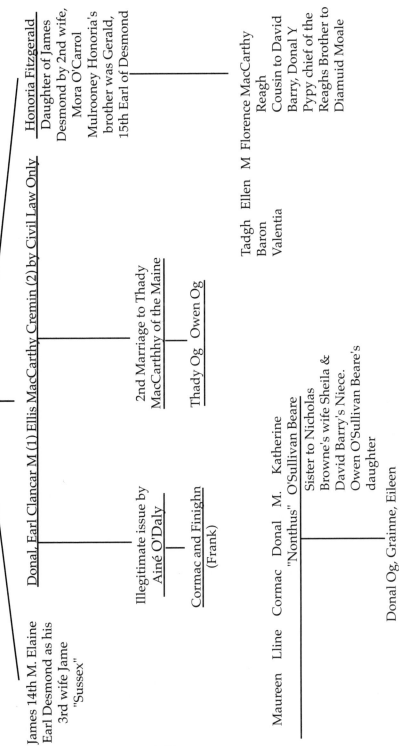

James 14th M. Elaine
Earl Desmond as his
3rd wife Jame
"Sussex"

Donal, Earl Clancar M (1) Ellis MacCarthy Cremin (2) by Civil Law Only

Honoria Fitzgerald
Daughter of James
Desmond by 2nd wife,
Mora O'Carrol
Mulrooney Honoria's
brother was Gerald,
15th Earl of Desmond

Illegitimate issue by
Ainé O'Daly

2nd Marriage to Thady
MacCarthy of the Maine

Tadgh Ellen M Florence MacCarthy
                   Reagh
Baron
Valentia

Cousin to David
Barry, Donal Y
Pypy chief of the
Reaghs Brother to
Diamuid Moale

Cormac and Finighn
(Frank)

Thady Og Owen Og

Maureen Lline Cormac Donal M. Katherine
                        "Nonthus" O'Sullivan Beare

Sister to Nicholas
Browne's wife Sheila &
David Barry's Niece.
Owen O'Sullivan Beare's
daughter

Donal Og, Grainne, Eileen

Browne of Molahiffe

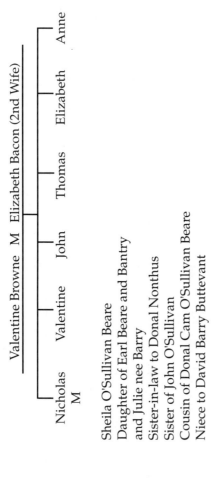

Valentine Browne M Elizabeth Bacon (2nd Wife)

Nicholas   Valentine   John   Thomas   Elizabeth   Anne
M

Sheila O'Sullivan Beare
Daughter of Earl Beare and Bantry
and Julie nee Barry
Sister-in-law to Donal Nonthus
Sister of John O'Sullivan
Cousin of Donal Cam O'Sullivan Beare
Niece to David Barry Buttevant